MURDER AT
THE VICTORIA AND ALBERT MUSEUM

By Jim Eldridge

MUSEUM MYSTERIES SERIES

Murder at the Fitzwilliam

Murder at the British Museum

Murder at the Ashmolean

Murder at the Manchester Museum

Murder at the Natural History Museum

Murder at Madame Tussauds

Murder at the National Gallery

Murder at the Victoria and Albert Museum

HOTEL MYSTERIES SERIES

Murder at the Ritz

Murder at the Savoy

Murder at Claridge's

LONDON UNDERGROUND STATION MYSTERIES SERIES

Murder at Aldwych Station

a&b

MURDER AT THE VICTORIA AND ALBERT MUSEUM

JIM ELDRIDGE

Allison & Busby Limited
11 Wardour Mews
London W1F 8AN
allisonandbusby.com

First published in Great Britain by Allison & Busby in 2022.

A CIP catalogue record for this book is available from the British Library.

First Edition

ISBN: 978-0-7490-2821-3

Typeset in 11.5/16.5 pt Adobe Garamond Pro by Allison & Busby Ltd.

Printed and bound by
CPI Group (UK) Ltd, Croydon, CR0 4YY

For Lynne, for always

CHAPTER ONE

London 1899

The tendrils of thick, pea-souper fog snaked through the London night, fog so thick that the lights from the gas lamps in the streets were rendered useless, just blobs of pale luminous green obscured by the thick, curling, crawling smog. Anyone in the streets, and there were very few people about, had scarves tied around their noses and mouths to stop the acrid stench of burnt coal and coke being drawn down into their lungs. As it was, it stung their eyes, acid tears running down making furrows in the grime the fog brought to their faces.

No one ventured out into this fog unless their business was of vital importance. The hansom cabs were tied up, their horses stabled, because no horse could find its way in this dense murk. The prostitutes were off the streets. The beat coppers had retreated to their police stations. Even the cats had stayed indoors. Only the rats could be heard, scuttling through the rubbish in the backstreets, scavenging for food.

The exception was by the massive marquee in Kensington that hid the yet to be dug foundations for the new Victoria and Albert Museum. Inside, the body of a man was laid to rest on the cobbled ground. A respectable-looking man. Expensive shoes. A Savile Row tailored suit. The only thing that marred the image was the gash where his throat had been cut from ear to ear.

The fog crept under the marquee and lapped at the man's dead body like green waves at the seashore. Then slowly engulfed him.

CHAPTER TWO

Daniel Wilson sat in the small, decorative balcony of their two-storey house overlooking Primrose Hill in north London. There was just enough space for two chairs either side of a small table, at which he and his wife, Abigail, would sit when the weather was fine and gaze out over the space of grass, trees and wildflowers that reached from their back gate to Prince Albert Road. Across that road was London Zoo with its menagerie of rare and exotic animals, and beyond that the vast open space that was Regent's Park. He was glad that the thick fog that had plagued London for the last two days had finally lifted so that he could savour the magnificence of the view.

Daniel still marvelled at the fact that he, a workhouse boy from Camden Town who'd entered the world of menial work at the age of twelve and who'd spent most of his thirty-eight years living in the north London slum, was now here, in what was for him one of the most desirable parts of London. The success that he and his wife had experienced as the Museum Detectives, as the press called them, had given them the financial freedom to be able to take a long-term rent on this three-bedroomed detached house, which had electric lighting and a gas stove in the kitchen. It was a far cry from the house where he'd previously lived, and into which Abigail had moved to join him after they'd first met in Cambridge five years ago. Their previous house had been a two-up two-down terrace, with a scullery at the back and a lean-to outhouse in the backyard for the toilet. All the cooking had been done on a solid fuelled iron range in the kitchen next to the scullery. Washing had been done in the basin in the scullery, using hot water heated in kettles on the coal-fired range. Baths, which before they'd taken once a week, had been in a tin bath, brought into the kitchen from the hook where it had hung just outside the back door to the yard. It was half-filled with a mixture of hot water heated in saucepans on the range, and cold water from a tap in the scullery, carried through in a bucket. The same bucket had been used after bathing to empty the tin bath. Daniel and Abigail had shared the same bath water, taking turns to go first: one week it would be Abigail, the next Daniel, and so on. Unless both of them had had an unfortunate accident, like falling over into a pile of horse manure in the road, in which case it necessitated filling the bath twice. Now, they had a bathroom indoors, with hot water available from the tank above the boiler. They also had an indoor toilet, which meant no more trips out to the outhouse in the depths of winter holding a candle or an oil lamp. No more having to listen to the scuttling of rats and mice in the backyard.

We should have done this years ago, he thought.

The change had come the previous year, after Abigail returned from leading an archaeological expedition to the pyramids in Egypt, funded by Arthur Conan Doyle. Abigail, who had gained a Classics degree at Girton College at Cambridge University, had already established a reputation as a highly esteemed archaeologist for her excavations and researches in Egypt before she met Daniel when he'd been hired to investigate a murder at the Fitzwilliam Museum in Cambridge. At that time, Daniel had not long established himself as a private investigator after many years serving as a detective at Scotland Yard. His most notable work had been as part of Inspector Abberline's squad investigating the Jack the Ripper murders. Although that case had resulted in no convictions, it had cemented Daniel's reputation as Abberline's sergeant, and a brilliant and dogged detective. Unfortunately, the hierarchy of the Metropolitan Police, and especially at Scotland Yard, valued sticking to orders from on high above detection brilliance. That had led to Abberline resigning from the force, with Daniel following shortly after.

Abigail's return from Egypt the previous summer had led to them both realising that this relationship was one that was for ever. And so, after years of deliberating and putting things off, they'd married, and the former Abigail Fenton became Mrs Abigail Wilson, although when giving lectures and talks on archaeology, she was still billed as Abigail Fenton.

'It's important you keep your own name,' Daniel had insisted. 'You've spent your career building the reputation of Abigail Fenton, not Abigail Wilson.'

With marriage had come the move. Daniel had always been the reluctant one, his house in Camden Town, small and lacking all amenities, had been the one secure place in his life. Abigail never complained about it, even though she'd come from a far more comfortable background in Cambridge. It was Daniel who said: 'We're both nearly forty. We don't want to be lugging a tin bath around as we get older, and have to put up with going out into the dark whenever we need to use the toilet.' And so they'd moved. Not far, just a mile or so, but the social distance between Primrose Hill and Camden Town was enormous. And the glory of sitting on this balcony, as he was now, and looking out over the acres of fresh greenery from his own house filled Daniel with a happiness that was almost overwhelming.

'Enjoying the view?'

Abigail stepped through the French doors of their bedroom to join him, settling herself down on the other chair.

'I am,' said Daniel. 'And I was just thinking, we should have done this years ago.'

'We're doing it now, and that's what counts,' said Abigail. She held a single sheet of paper, along with the envelope from which she'd taken it, in her hand. 'A uniformed messenger has just delivered this.'

Daniel frowned. 'I didn't hear the bell ring.'

'I was in the living room and saw him approaching,' said Abigail. 'As he looked official, I opened the door.' She held the piece of paper out towards him. 'It's from Buckingham Palace. Someone called Sir Anthony Thurrington, personal secretary to the Queen.'

Daniel looked at her stunned, then turned his attention to the letter, which bore the words Buckingham Palace at its letterhead.

'You'll see he says we are invited to a private audience

with Her Majesty Queen Victoria this afternoon at 2 p.m. at Buckingham Palace. He adds it is a matter of the utmost urgency.'

'I'm not sure if we can make it,' said Daniel doubtfully. 'It's very short notice. I was intending to clean the windows this afternoon.'

Abigail stared at him. 'What!'

He grinned at her. 'I was joking, obviously.' But then he looked serious as he added: 'But there is a point to be made here. These people who think they are so important that they can just summon people to drop everything and come running at their whim.'

'She is important! She's the Queen, for God's sake! How much more important can anyone be?'

'Yes, but it's a point.'

'You used to do it when you were at Scotland Yard,' accused Abigail. 'You summoned people to attend.'

'That was on official business.'

'And what do you think this is?'

'It says a private audience.'

'You think she's inviting us to the palace for tea and cakes and social chit-chat?' demanded Abigail, outraged.

'All right, there's no need to get upset.'

'There's every need to get upset. This is the Queen. Empress of half the world, and you're quibbling over whether to go and see her at her summons.'

'I'm not quibbling.'

'Yes, you are.' She frowned. 'What could she want with us?'

'Perhaps she wants to congratulate you on your expedition last year to Egypt. The first to be led by a British woman.'

Abigail shook her head. 'If it was that, this Sir Anthony wouldn't have added this is an urgent matter. What's happened to the royal family recently that might concern us?'

'The Queen formally laid the foundation stone for the new Victoria and Albert Museum last month,' mused Daniel.

'How does that affect us?'

'I have no idea. I'm just digging up things that have been in the newspapers lately. A few days ago there was a suggestion of a scandal involving the Prince of Wales in one of the gutter press rags.'

'What sort of scandal?'

'I didn't read it properly. I just saw it in the newsagent's shop when I was picking up a copy of *The Times*. Knowing what they say about the prince, it could be some woman he's supposed to be having an affair with, or something to do with his gambling.'

'I can hardly see that the Queen would want to talk to us about anything like that,' said Abigail.

'True,' Daniel agreed. Suddenly a thought struck him and he reached and picked up that morning's *Times*, which he'd put on the table. 'Wait! I saw something in this morning's paper. I haven't read the story properly, but the words Victoria and Albert were in there.'

'What was it about?'

Daniel turned over the pages of the newspaper, then said triumphantly: 'I think this might be it. "The dead body of a man was discovered yesterday morning at the site of the new Victoria and Albert Museum which is currently under construction. The dead man has been identified as one Andrew Page, a curator of the South Kensington Museum."'

'That's got to be it,' said Abigail.

CHAPTER THREE

The hansom cab dropped Daniel and Abigail at the imposing East Wing of the palace, then turned and made its way across the courtyard towards the Mall, leaving Daniel and Abigail to approach the two soldiers on duty in sentry boxes either side of the entrance.

The soldiers, standing rigidly to attention, their rifles held firmly, butts on the ground, gave them barely a glance before resuming their fixed gaze directly ahead.

'What do we do?' asked Daniel. 'Is there a bell we ring?'

A well-dressed man in his early sixties appeared from the palace entrance and came down the steps towards them.

'Mr and Mrs Wilson, I presume?' he asked.

'Yes,' said Daniel.'

'I am Sir Anthony Thurrington, one of the Queen's advisers. Thank you for coming, and for being punctual.'

He held out his hand to them and they each shook it.

Thurrington was a short man, thin, expensively attired in a long dark frock coat with a white carnation in the buttonhole.

He went back up the steps and into the palace, Daniel and Abigail following. Once inside he stopped and turned to look at them enquiringly as he asked: 'If you saw this morning's newspapers, I believe you may already have an idea why the Queen has summoned you.'

'The body of the man found at the site of the new Victoria and Albert Museum?' asked Abigail.

'Exactly so,' said Thurrington. 'She has heard of your reputation for solving murders committed in the nation's most prestigious museums and wishes you to investigate.'

'I assume the police are already engaged on the case,' said Daniel.

'They are,' said Thurrington. 'A Chief Superintendent Armstrong is the officer in charge.'

'And he has been advised of our involvement?'

Thurrington hesitated, then said, 'Not directly. I believe Her Majesty wished to talk to you first. Have you met the Queen, or been to Buckingham Palace, before?'

'No,' they replied.

'Just a few words about the protocol before I take you to the throne room, which is where she'll see you. The Queen will be seated during your audience with her. She is eighty years old and rather frail, but her mind is still vitally alert. You are to remain standing. When you arrive in front of her, you, Mr Wilson, will bow. There is no need for a deep bow, a head and shoulders will suffice. You, Mrs Wilson, will curtsey. Again, there is no need for an over-ostentatious curtsey, a discreet bob will be all that is required.

'Do not offer to shake her hand. If she wishes to shake hands, she will proffer hers. You will refer to the Queen as "Your Majesty" the first time she speaks to you, and thereafter as "ma'am"; pronounced as in "jam", not as in "farm".' He looked at them enquiringly. 'Do you have any questions before I take you through?'

'None, but I'm sure we will have some afterwards. Especially finding out as much as we can about Mr Page, the man who was killed.'

'That's no problem. I will escort you out after the audience with Her Majesty, and we can talk details then.' He hesitated for a moment, then said in low and confidential tones: 'I must alert you to the fact you will undoubtedly be aware of a smell of damp here at the palace. This is because Her Majesty spends very little time here. You must be aware that after her beloved Albert died nearly forty years ago, she became somewhat of a recluse, electing to stay at Windsor, Balmoral, or her residence on the Isle of Wight, Osborne House. For many years after Prince Albert's death, Buckingham Palace was abandoned, and it was only after some gentle persuasion that she returned to occasionally to take residence here. She could not, and still cannot to a great extent, abide being here with the memories of happy times with her late husband.

'She is only here at the moment because she decided to journey to the site of the new museum from Buckingham Palace as it was nearer than her other residences. She had stated her intention to return to the Isle of Wight before this appalling incident. Now, she wants to stay here until the mystery of this dreadful occurrence is solved. So I can only urge you to discover who the culprits are as swiftly as possible. As I said, the Queen is frail and the damp in this building does not aid her health. Now, if you're ready, please follow me.'

He led the way along a series of wide, long corridors, the high ceilings and supporting columns decorated with gold-painted mouldings. Every wall was covered with large paintings, some portraits, some landscapes. But despite the aura of wealth and grandeur, they both caught the pervading smell of damp as they walked.

Finally, Thurrington stopped beside a pair of tall, dark wood double doors, on either side of which stood a footman wearing an ornate costume adorned with frills of lace around the knees and carrying decorated wooden staves. Thurrington murmured something to the footmen, and they knocked at the door with their staves. The door opened and Thurrington walked through, followed by Daniel and Abigail, passing two more footmen into the throne room.

Having been told that this was a 'private audience', both Daniel and Abigail were stunned to be presented with the sight of the Queen sitting on an ornate gold throne on a raised platform, surrounded by what looked to be a crowd of about twenty people. Most of the men and women standing behind the throne and to either side of the Queen seemed to be servants, with possibly some royal advisers, notably the elderly men, some bearded or moustachioed, who wore dark formal suits and sombre expressions. The two of the group who caught the eye of both Daniel and Abigail were a short man of Asian appearance, wearing ornately decorated Indian clothes, who stood to one side of the throne, and a stately looking woman in her mid-forties standing on the other side.

'That's Princess Beatrice,' Abigail whispered to Daniel as they neared the platform, accompanied by Sir Anthony Thurrington. 'The Queen's youngest daughter and her constant companion.'

'And the man in the Indian costume?'

'No idea,' said Abigail.

They reached the raised platform and Thurrington stepped forward.

'Mr and Mrs Wilson, Your Majesty,' he said.

Daniel made his discreet bow, as instructed and Abigail lowered herself into a curtsey, before straightening up.

Thurrington had told them that the Queen was frail, but she didn't look it. She was dressed in a long black dress, trimmed with a collar of white lace, which encased her stout figure. On her head she wore a lace cap barely covering her grey hair, which had been pulled back. Her face looked pale and strained, but there was a strength to her which showed in the firmness of her jaw and the steely light in her eyes as she studied them. Physically frail, perhaps, but most definitely not in an emotional sense. This was a strong determined woman, very much in charge.

'You are the couple who I believe are known as The Museum Detectives?'

'We are, Your Majesty.'

'No doubt you have heard of the outrage that has been perpetrated at the site of the new museum dedicated to my late and dearly beloved Albert, the Victoria and Albert Museum in Kensington. The dead body of a man has been found there. Apparently murdered.'

'So we understand, Your Majesty.'

'I cannot have this!' Although she kept her voice level, there was no mistaking her anger, her indignation. 'This museum is to be a testament to my dear Albert, to laud his achievements and make his name known for generations to come. This appalling murder desecrates his name and everything he stands for. I will not have it! You will find out who committed this heinous crime and bring them to justice. It is the only way to clean this taint from the museum.'

'Yes, ma'am,' said Daniel.

Victoria turned to Abigail and asked: 'Mrs Wilson, you are a detective as well?'

'I am, ma'am.'

'I was informed you were an archaeologist. That you'd recently led an expedition to the pyramids.'

'That is correct, ma'am.'

'The first by a British woman.'

Abigail was about to tell her that actually there were other British women who'd carried out archaeological excavations in Egypt before her, but then reasoned that none of them could be said to have *led* an expedition. That, coupled with the thought that correcting the Queen in front of the whole royal entourage was not necessarily a wise move. Instead, she nodded and said: 'Yes, ma'am, I'm honoured to say.'

'I hope you and your husband are as successful in solving this case as you were in Egypt,' said the Queen. 'You will keep me informed of progress through Sir Anthony Thurrington.'

'Yes, ma'am,' said Abigail, and once more bobbed into a curtsey while Daniel added his own 'Yes, ma'am' and gave a small bow, before they both followed Thurrington back towards the double doors, past the footmen, and into the long corridor.

'If you come to my office, I'll appraise you of the situation, and give you a list of any contacts you need for your investigation,' said Thurrington.

As they walked along the corridor, Abigail commented, 'This is the first time we've been asked to investigate a murder at a museum that hasn't even been built yet.'

'That's not strictly true,' said Sir Anthony. 'To be exact, the Victoria and Albert Museum will be the final and concluding phase of a museum that has been developed at the site over the last forty years.'

'You mean the South Kensington Museum,' said Abigail.

'Yes, but in fact its roots can be traced even further back to the Great Exhibition of 1851, which was Prince Albert's concept. You remember it, I'm sure.'

'Neither of us were even born then.'

'Yes, but you know *of* it.'

'Hyde Park,' said Daniel. 'The vast building made of glass, known as the Crystal Palace.'

'Vast, indeed,' nodded Thurrington. 'Nearly nineteen hundred feet long by five hundred feet wide, built of a cast iron frame and filled with massive glass windows. Even the ceiling was made of glass. Most of the glass was made in Birmingham in order to showcase the importance of the Midlands in glass production.'

'Yes, we've seen it,' said Daniel. 'It was moved and re-erected in Sydenham a couple of years after the Exhibition and the area was renamed Crystal Palace.'

'Ah, but you never saw it in its glory as the home of the Great Exhibition,' enthused Thurrington. 'Magnificent! It was called The Great Exhibition of the Works of Industry of All Nations, and that's exactly what it was. The building's vastness meant that it was able to house trees of all kinds. Statues were everywhere. Working examples of industrial machinery. People could watch the entire process of cotton production, from spinning to the finished cloth, for example.

'The huge Trophy Telescope with a focal length of 16 feet towered over the people who came to admire it. The gems and diamonds on show included the world's largest known diamond, the Koh-i-Noor, along with the Daria-i-Noor, one of the rarest pink diamonds in the world. There were arts and crafts from all over the world. The New Zealand exhibits were all made from natural resources made by the Maori. The exhibition was the perfect combination of old handcrafts and modern machinery.'

By now their journey through the maze of twisting and turning corridors and passages had brought them to a door marked 'Sir Anthony Thurrington'. Thurrington pushed it open and ushered them into his office. The room was quite spartan when compared with the opulence of the throne room and the high-ceilinged corridors: a large desk and three chairs. The walls were lined with shelves filled from ceiling to floor with papers and books. Thurrington gestured for them to sit before taking his seat behind the desk.

'Getting back to what I said about the Victoria and Albert Museum stemming from the Great Exhibition: Prince Albert's idea was to make the exhibition permanent, and on a grand scale. His ambition was to create a museum of design that would inspire others and lead to this country being one of the foremost in the world when it came to combining the arts with the sciences. The first stage came with the opening of the South Kensington Museum, in 1857, the existing buildings that you referred to. The first of those buildings was opened by Queen Victoria and

Prince Albert. It was also known as the Museum of Works of Art, and it included a Department of Science. It also housed the National Art Training School, which became the Royal College of Art.

'The following year new galleries were added, including some displaying pictures from the National Gallery. The building also included a Female Art School. As you know, in December 1861, tragically, Prince Albert died. But the work continued in his name. In 1860 he'd already started to have a roof built over the open court, creating new galleries, and this work continued after his death, and was finished in 1862. This roofing created two new huge display areas, the North and South Courts.

'In 1863 residential buildings for senior staff were built, along with more galleries.

'In 1865 a huge gallery was built to display Raphael's full-size tapestries for the Sistine Chapel, which were loaned from the Royal Collection. In that same year a new grand central entrance was built. Between 1867 and 1873 the Science Schools were added. Then, between 1879 and 1883 the National Art Library was built.

'Finally, in 1891, proposals were invited to unify the whole range of buildings as one museum. The chosen design was that by Aston Webb, the architect. This would have new galleries, a new entrance, and a new public face along Cromwell Road and Exhibition Road. The whole building would house the art and science collections. And now, with the laying of the foundation stone by Her Majesty, construction can at last begin. I assume you will be visiting the site where the body was discovered.'

'Indeed,' said Daniel.

'I will send you a letter of authority to give you unfettered access to the site, and to wherever else you need to visit, and anyone you feel it is necessary to talk to.'

'Anyone?' queried Abigail.

'Anyone,' confirmed Thurrington firmly. 'The Queen is determined that this case be solved, and urgently.'

'If you could let us have details of the murdered man to begin with,' said Daniel.

Thurrington nodded and took a sheet of paper from his desk, which he passed to them.

'I had anticipated that. This is Andrew Page's private address. His wife's name is there as well, Mrs Gretchen Page.'

'Gretchen?' queried Abigail.

'She's German,' explained Thurrington. 'I've also given you the name of his immediate colleagues at the museum, and his solicitor in case you need to enquire into his private business.'

'Thank you,' said Daniel, putting the sheet of paper into his pocket.

Thurrington took a card from his desk drawer and wrote a few words on it.

'As an interim measure until my official letter arrives, this card, signed by me and on the authority of the Queen, gives you permission to go anywhere and interview anyone.'

'Thank you,' said Daniel, and he added the card to his pocket.

Thurrington looked at them pointedly as he said: 'One thing I would add. Because of protocol and convention, we prefer it that nothing that is said between yourselves and the Queen is passed on to other parties.'

'The press?' enquired Daniel.

'Exactly,' said Thurrington.

'So the fact that Her Majesty mentioned Abigail's expedition to Egypt…?' queried Daniel.

'That would be acceptable,' said Thurrington. 'It's praise for a British subject and gives no information about Her Majesty.'

'By the way,' asked Abigail, 'who was that Indian man who was with Her Majesty? She seemed very reliant on him.'

'Oh, she is. That's The Munshi.'

'What's a Munshi?'

'It means secretary or teacher in Urdu. His name is Abdul Karim and he came to work as a waiter at the palace in 1887, but Her Majesty was so impressed by him that a year later he was appointed her private secretary. As well as acting as her secretary and her clerk, he's also teaching the Queen Urdu.'

'She's learning Urdu at her age?'

'She feels it's something she needs to do as Empress of India.'

'That is very advanced thinking for her,' said Abigail.

'It is,' agreed Thurrington. He gave a sly half-smile. 'Not that all the family would agree with you.'

'Oh?'

'I'd better give you advance warning because undoubtedly you'll encounter them sooner or later, as Her Majesty has given you the authority to carry out your investigation among members of the royal family. Certain of her family don't approve of the Munshi. And they include her eldest son and heir to the throne, Prince Albert Edward.

'To give you an example, in 1889 the Prince of Wales hosted an entertainment for the Queen at his home in Sandringham. When Karim found he'd been allocated a seat with the servants rather than the gentry, he retired to his room feeling he'd been insulted. When the Queen learnt of this she remonstrated with her eldest son and told him that he should have been seated among the household. The following year the Queen attended the Braemar Games, accompanied by Karim. Her son, Prince Arthur, approached the Queen's Private Secretary, Sir Henry Ponsonby, to express his outrage at this Indian being allowed to mingle with the gentry. Sir Henry informed him that Karim was there by order of the Queen and advised him to take the matter up with his mother.'

'And did he?'

'No. The problem is that the Queen has a very high opinion of the Munshi, as he has of himself. Meanwhile, her family have a very low opinion of him. Very low indeed.'

CHAPTER FOUR

Daniel and Abigail walked away from Buckingham Palace and headed to Trafalgar Square.

'Where to first?' asked Daniel, studying the details he'd been given for Andrew Page. 'The widow?'

'I suggest the scene of the crime,' said Abigail. 'Or, at least, where the body was dumped. He may not necessarily have been killed there.'

'In that case, we'll take a cab,' said Daniel.

'I can remember when you said you liked to walk everywhere,' smiled Abigail.

'Ah, but that was when I was an urchin from the slums. Now I'm living in middle-class comfort in Primrose Hill. Also, we're on a mission from none other than Her Majesty the Queen, which means costs will be reimbursed.'

As always, there was a line of horse-drawn hansom cabs waiting for passengers at Trafalgar Square, and they commandeered one to take them to the South Kensington Museum. As they journeyed, Daniel tapped his pocket.

'I'm glad Sir Anthony gave us that card of authority,' he said. 'I remember seeing pictures in the newspaper about the Queen laying the foundation stone for the new museum, and it was done in this enormous marquee, almost as big as parts of Buckingham Palace, so I expect there'll be officials on duty there who'll otherwise send us away with a flea in our ear.'

'Yes, I saw that,' nodded Abigail. 'A marquee so big it housed the Queen in her open landau drawn by four horses, along with sundry servants, and what looked to me like hundreds of courtiers and officials. And it could hardly be said that she laid the foundation stone. There it was, standing about four feet high next to her coach, held up by chains to a ten-feet-high hoist.'

'But she was there and saw it lifted into place,' countered Daniel. 'I expect in royal terms that counts as laying a foundation stone. After all, she's almost eighty. You surely didn't expect her to lift it herself and slide it into place, then pick up a spade and start shovelling cement.'

Abigail laughed. 'What a wonderful image! It would have increased her popularity among the general public.'

'It would also have finished her off,' said Daniel. He gave a sly smile. 'I'm surprised the Prince of Wales didn't suggest to her that she do it.'

'Daniel, that's a wicked thing to say!' said Abigail.

'Well, he has been waiting a long time to be king,' said Daniel. 'He's nearly sixty. He surely must be wondering if he'll ever get on the throne, and if so, how long he'll be on it.'

The hansom cab dropped them at the corner of Cromwell

Road and Exhibition Road. The enormous marquee of striped material was still there, enclosing the building plot that would bring together all the existing buildings and galleries and unite them into this new museum. They approached the entrance to the marquee and found a man sitting on a stool just inside it.

'Private property,' the man said, getting to his feet as they were about to enter. 'No admission.'

Daniel took the card that Sir Anthony Thurrington had given him from his pocket and held it out to the man.

'We're here on official business on the orders of the Queen,' he told him. 'Her Majesty has asked us to investigate the murder of the dead man who was found here yesterday, Mr Andrew Page.'

The man read the card, then immediately stood almost to attention as he handed it back to Daniel.

'This is an honour, sir, madam,' he said. 'And I'd be most grateful when you report back to Her Majesty if you'd mention my name and tell her I was very helpful. I'm Stephen Ward. I was the one who found him, you know.'

'In that case, Mr Ward, your information will be invaluable and we will certainly make sure Her Majesty knows how vital your assistance has been. We are Mr and Mrs Wilson. Would you show us where you found the body, and in what circumstances?'

'Certainly.'

With that, Ward led them to where the foundation stone had been put in place and now stood up prominently from the ground.

'It was here, right by the foundation stone. How it is, the place is closed up during the night, and I'm the first one on duty in the morning. At one o'clock my relief, Billy Carter, comes on and takes over, and he locks up at six o'clock.'

'How do you lock a marquee?' asked Abigail, curious.

'There's a bar that goes across the entrance with a padlock on it. Me and Billy are the ones with the keys, so he locks it at night and I unlock it in the morning.' He shook his head ruefully as he added: 'Of course, it only keeps out carriages and such. If anyone wanted to get in at night, they could slide under the canvas. That's what the police think must have happened.

'Anyway, I came in and saw this bloke lying by the foundation stone. At first, I thought he was a drunk who'd sneaked in the tent to sleep it off, but when I shook him, I saw his throat had been cut.'

'Was there much blood?' asked Daniel.

'No. If there had been I'd have spotted it before I touched the body. So somebody must have killed him somewhere else, then brought the body here. There was blood on his shirt over his heart, so he must have been stabbed as well. Why would they do that?'

'That's what we're hoping to find out,' said Daniel.

'It's sacrilege, that's what it is. To dump a dead body at the same spot where the Queen laid this stone. I was here on duty when she did it, so I saw it all, the whole occasion from where my post was, just outside the tent. I was on guard to make sure that only the right people came in.' He pointed at the foundation stone indignantly. 'It's special, that is.'

They looked at the words carved in capitals in the stone:

THIS STONE WAS LAID BY HER MAJESTY QUEEN VICTORIA, EMPRESS OF INDIA, ON THE 17TH DAY OF

MAY 1899 IN THE 62ND YEAR OF HER REIGN, FOR THE COMPLETION OF THE SOUTH KENSINGTON MUSEUM INAUGURATED BY HIS ROYAL HIGHNESS THE PRINCE CONSORT AND HENCEFORTH TO BE KNOWN AS THE VICTORIA AND ALBERT MUSEUM.

'That's more special because of what's under it,' the man continued. 'A casket made of beaten copper decorated with gold, with a Royal Crown on top, was buried beneath the foundation stone so it'll be there for ever. I saw it myself before they put it in place. Inside the casket is a letter to the Queen by the Duke of Devonshire with a history of the museum and all the different things that are inside it. Like I say, it's very special.'

Daniel looked around at the vast area inside the marquee. 'Apart from the foundation stone having been put here, no work seems to have actually started on the building,' he commented.

'Well, it's really only the new entrance that's going to go up, along with some new galleries and such. The new facade, is what they call it. And there's things to be sorted out first before work proper begins, like how the new rooms and galleries are going to be linked up with the older ones.'

'You said the police came?'

'They did. I hailed a passing bobby. There's usually one around here, what with all the museums and such being here and got to be protected. The bobby took a look, then went off and came back with a detective from Scotland Yard.'

'Did you catch the detective's name?'

'He was an Inspector Feather. He asked a lot of questions. Then he went into the building and asked for someone senior to come out and take a look. It was one of the secretaries who came out, poor woman, and she looked at the dead man and said "Oh my God! It's Mr Page!" I thought she was going to faint, but she didn't, fair play to her. She stood her ground, even though you could see she was all shook up. The detective took her back into the museum. Then he came back to talk to me more.'

'Do you know the secretary's name?'

Ward shook his head. 'No. But you'll soon find out if you go into the museum. They'll know.

'The detective then asked me about finding the body, and he asked for Billy's address. He wanted to talk to him to make sure he'd locked the padlock properly the night before, and if he'd seen anyone suspicious before he locked up. Billy told me all about it when he came in today at lunchtime so we could change shifts.'

Abigail looked around the marquee, puzzled.

'But you're here this afternoon, not Billy?' she said.

Ward looked a bit awkward.

'The truth is, Billy's a bit of a sensitive soul. He took a look at the stone when he arrived for his shift yesterday and said he couldn't cope with being where a murder had been done. He's afraid of ghosts. So, after we'd talked and he'd told me what the detective had asked him about, he said he had to go home. He said he needed time to recover.'

'How much time?'

'Well, I'm hoping not long. He asked me if I'd do his afternoon shift yesterday, and then do another double shift today. If he don't turn up tomorrow, I'm gonna have to see the boss and ask them to get someone else in for the afternoons. I don't mind doing a double shift two days on the trot, the extra money is always useful, but I need my own time.'

'Had Billy seen anyone suspicious?' asked Daniel.

'No. Nothing. But then, he was quite shaken up when he was here.'

'Had you seen Mr Page before?' asked Abigail.

'He seemed familiar, so it's possible I might have, ma'am. But not that I can recall. There's been lots of people passing in and out of here ever since the marquee went up, most of 'em to do with the new museum.'

'Do you know where they took the body?' asked Daniel.

'No. They just put it in a van and went off with it.'

They thanked Mr Ward and left the marquee.

'We need to talk to the secretary who identified Page,' said Abigail.

'Yes,' agreed Daniel. He took out his watch. 'But it's coming up to five o'clock. The office will be closing soon, if it isn't closed already, and we need time to talk to her properly, and also to his colleagues on the list that Thurrington gave us. I suggest we return tomorrow morning.'

'A cab again?' asked Abigail.

'How about a walk?' asked Daniel. 'It will clear our heads.'

'My head doesn't need clearing,' said Abigail. 'But, if yours does, I'm happy to walk with you.'

As they walked, they discussed what they'd learnt so far about the murder.

'He was killed somewhere else and his body dumped there, right by the foundation stone with that inscription,' said Abigail.

'So it's intended as a message of some sort, aimed either at the Queen, or the late Prince Albert, or the museum itself. But which?' asked Daniel. 'The fact that it was a curator who died at the museum suggests the message is aimed at the museum. But why? And why now? The South Kensington Museum has been there for nearly forty years.'

'Lately there's been some publicity given to those who believe that museums in the Western world that display items from poorer nations are guilty of theft, and that the items should be returned to their original countries,' said Abigail. 'There's been quite a lot about Egyptian artefacts in museums in England.'

'I thought all the items in our museums had been bought and paid for.'

'Usually, yes. But, if you remember, what we found on our first investigation in Cambridge is that not all of the money paid gets back to the people who should have got it.'

'Wherever there's money being paid out, there are always unscrupulous people who want a bigger share,' said Daniel.

'Do you think that's what's happened here? There's been some financial chicanery and maybe Andrew Page was involved? And this is revenge?'

'I don't know. I'm sure it'll be a possibility we have to look into. Or maybe it's nothing to do with that, maybe Andrew Page was killed because of someone he'd angered in some other way.' He sighed. 'I think this is going to be a difficult one to unravel.'

'Why? We've only just started. And we have unfettered access to everyone.'

'Yes, but with the Queen herself involved, I can see that changing. I bet there are lots of vested interests at stake, most of which we don't know about.'

CHAPTER FIVE

When they arrived home they were surprised to find their old friend, Joe Dalton, a reporter with the *Daily Telegraph* waiting for them.

'Joe!' Daniel greeted him cheerfully. 'This is a surprise! Have you been waiting long?'

'Ten minutes or so.'

'What brings you here?'

Dalton smiled. 'I thought that would have been obvious to the museum detectives.'

Abigail gave a mock shudder, then asked: 'You've heard?'

'All Fleet Street has heard. We had a press release from Buckingham Palace telling us that Mr and Mrs Wilson have been asked by Her Majesty Queen Victoria to investigate the recent appalling murder of Mr Andrew Page, whose body was discovered at the site of the proposed Victoria and Albert Museum. So, naturally, I've come for a comment from you.'

Daniel shook his head. 'I'm afraid it'll have to be "no comment" at this stage, Joe, until we receive official confirmation of our appointment. At the moment, all we've got is a card of authority. We don't want to jump the gun and then find out Her Majesty has changed her mind.'

'But we can offer you a cup of coffee and an off-the-record chat,' said Abigail.

'That way we can pick your brains.'

Abigail led the way into the house and stopped. She picked up a buff envelope that was lying on the doormat.

'It's got Buckingham Palace stamped on it,' she said, examining the envelope. 'So either this is to authorise us, or it's to say Her Majesty has changed her mind.'

They went through to the kitchen, Abigail opening the envelope as they walked.

'It's our authority,' she announced. 'We are officially on the case.'

'Excellent,' said Daniel, filling the kettle and putting it on the gas stove.

'So now can you give me a comment?' asked Dalton, sitting down at the table.

'To be honest, we know very little at this stage. Andrew Page was a curator for the Victoria and Albert Museum and his body was discovered by a security guard inside the large marquee outside the entrance. His throat had been cut and the lack of blood at the site suggests he was killed somewhere else and his body dumped there.'

'We know that already,' said Dalton, slightly impatiently. 'What have you got? What did Her Majesty say to you when you saw her?'

'She ordered us to find out who had committed the murder,' said Abigail.

'Is that it?' asked Dalton, disappointed.

'She also talked to Abigail about the expedition she led to the pyramids last year,' said Daniel.

'What did she say about it?'

'She was complimentary.'

Dalton gave a muted sigh. 'It's not much,' he complained.

'We've only been commissioned to look into the murder a couple of hours ago,' said Abigail. 'We need to look into things before we can start commenting on the case.'

'And even then, we can't really report on how it's going in case it puts the investigation at risk,' said Daniel. 'You know that, Joe.'

'Yes, I suppose so,' said Dalton. 'But I can say you were invited to the palace to meet the Queen, who asked you to look into the murder?'

'Yes,' said Daniel. 'As the palace have already told the press that, I don't think that's breaking any confidences.'

'What was she wearing?' asked Dalton, his pencil poised over his open notebook.

'Are you writing the fashion column now?' asked Abigail with a smile.

'Our readers like this kind of detail,' said Dalton.

'She was dressed the same way she's been dressed for the past forty years. In black.'

'Who else was there when you met her?' asked Dalton.

'Ah, now that would be breaking confidences,' said Daniel. 'I'm afraid we've been warned off talking about our audience by some senior people at the palace.'

'I'm guessing that would be Sir Anthony Thurrington,' said Dalton. 'He's the Queen's watchdog.'

'Why don't you talk to him?' asked Abigail. 'He'd be able to give you what you want.'

Dalton shook his head. 'He only gives out what *he* wants us to know, which is usually nothing.' He sighed. 'All we've got is a dead man.'

'We know the dead man's name,' said Daniel. 'Andrew Page. That's a start. Often we don't even have that. What do you know about him?'

'Nothing,' said Dalton. 'I've never come across him or heard anything about him. But then, I'm about news.' He looked thoughtful. 'Perhaps I'll talk to Adrian Hegley. He's the *Telegraph* arts correspondent. He must have known him. The trouble is he's a terrible gossip, so much of what he says we can't print.'

'Why?'

'Because his stories are usually scurrilous and full of innuendo.'

'That doesn't stop some papers printing them.'

'The gutter press, possibly, but not *The Telegraph*. We are respectable.'

'He still sounds like the person we need to talk to,' said Daniel. 'We have to start somewhere, and a gossip is usually a good place to begin. Even if it's unreliable, there is often a grain of truth in there somewhere, and at this moment we know hardly anything about Andrew Page. Is he usually at the office?'

'Not Hegley,' said Dalton. 'He spends most of his time swanning around town with his arty friends, picking up stories. I do know that tomorrow afternoon he's going to be at the

Lyceum, interviewing Henry Irving. I believe you have more than a nodding acquaintance with Irving's manager, Bram Stoker. I'm sure he'd be happy to let you wait for Hegley until the interview with Sir Henry is over.'

CHAPTER SIX

Detective Inspector John Feather was full of gloom as he entered Scotland Yard to begin his day. He'd passed various news-stands on his journey to work and seen the headlines on some of the tabloids: 'Queen Summons Museum Detectives'. Even the broadsheets carried the story. It meant Chief Superintendent Armstrong was going to be in a foul mood all day.

This was confirmed for him when he entered his office and found Detective Sergeant Cribbens already there, sucking on his foul-smelling pipe.

'The chief was in asking for you,' said Cribbens, and gave an unhappy look at his boss.

'In a bad mood?' asked Feather.

'Very,' nodded Cribbens, and gave a heavy sigh. 'He's not happy.'

When is he ever, thought Feather as he walked along the corridor to the chief superintendent's office.

He knocked at the door, and at the bark of 'Come in!' from within he entered.

Chief Superintendent Armstrong was sitting at his desk, an open copy of *The Times* clutched so tightly that Feather thought he was going to tear the pages.

'Where have you been, Inspector?' he demanded.

'I went back to the site where the body was found at the Victoria and Albert Museum to talk to the guard on duty again, in case he remembered seeing anything.'

'Did he?'

'No.'

'How about people turning up since the body was discovered? Sometimes the criminal returns to the scene of the crime to gloat.'

Feather weighed up whether to tell him that Daniel and Abigail had visited the site the previous afternoon. The guard on duty had told him proudly they'd had a card of authority 'from the Queen'. He decided not to mention it, it would only inflame the chief superintendent's anger even more.

'He didn't say,' said Feather.

But Armstrong wasn't listening to him, his attention had gone back to *The Times*, which he thrust at Feather.

'Have you seen this, Inspector?' he demanded. 'Victoria and Albert Museum Murder. The Queen Calls in the Museum Detectives.'

'Yes, sir,' said Feather. 'It's in most of the papers.'

'How did this happen?' demanded Armstrong, outraged. 'The body was only found the day before yesterday. We're not magicians able to produce a murderer with a wave of a wand. What on earth prompted Her Majesty to do this?'

'She's apparently very upset about the body being dumped there because she feels it taints the memory of the late Prince Albert.'

'For God's sake, he's been dead nearly forty years!' said Armstrong. 'How much longer is she going to go on about him in this way? It's not about him, it's about a murder.'

'She feels the fact that the body was left there, and as it's someone who worked for the Victoria and Albert Museum who was murdered, that it's an attack on his memory.'

'But why didn't this Sir Anthony Thurrington get in touch with us before bringing in Wilson and Fenton?'

'It's Wilson and Wilson now, sir. They're married.'

'My point remains the same. Has this Sir Anthony got in touch with us? Have we spoken to him?'

'No, sir.'

'Why not? We could have pre-empted this.'

'With respect, sir, our contacts have been with the dead man's employers, the museum, not with Her Majesty.'

Armstrong scowled and threw the newspaper to one side.

'We have to recover this situation. Our reputation is at stake. *We* are Her Majesty's police force, not the bloody Wilsons.'

'Yes, sir.'

'So what's happening about it? What indications are there?'

'Well, it looks like he was stabbed through the heart first, then afterwards his throat was cut.'

'I know that, I mean: why was he killed?'

'We don't know yet, sir.'

'Have you spoken to his wife? I assume he was married.'

'Yes, sir. I saw Mrs Page yesterday.'

'Has she got any idea who'd want to kill her husband?'

'No, sir.'

'What sort of woman is she?'

'As I understand it, she's German.'

'German?'

'Yes. She met Andrew Page when he was in Germany as part of a tour of the Continent acquiring objects for the new museum.'

'I thought this new museum was about British products?'

'According to the people I spoke to at the museum, it was inspired by the Great Exhibition of 1851, which – if you recall – was entitled The Works of All Nations.'

'Happily married?' asked Armstrong.

'She didn't suggest there was anything wrong in the marriage,' said Feather.

'No, she's hardly likely to,' grunted Armstrong. 'Makes her a suspect. How often have we found the people closest to a victim are often the murderer?'

'Quite often, sir,' said Feather.

'*Very* often,' Armstrong corrected him. 'Poke around, Inspector. See if there is anyone else involved in that marriage. Either with him or with her.'

'Yes, sir.'

'And look into his work colleagues. Jealousy. Rivalry. That sort of thing. You'd be surprised what some people will do to get promotion.'

'Yes, sir.'

'And keep in touch with the Wilsons. We've found that useful before, finding out what they're up to, who they suspect. They like you. They'll talk to you. We have to do everything to beat them to the outcome of this case. I'm not going to have

Scotland Yard come second best to a pair of amateurs.'

'In fairness, Chief Superintendent, they have been doing it for a long time now. Their first case together, at the Fitzwilliam, was nearly six years ago.'

'Well, we've been in this business a lot longer than that, and we're going to be the ones who claim the credit for solving this one, regardless of whoever Her Majesty deems to bring in.' He looked grim. 'Go and see them, Inspector. Find out what they know. Do it today.'

Daniel and Abigail were putting on their coats prior to making for the V&A to talk to Herbert Tweed, Andrew Page's immediate boss, and also the secretary who'd identified him, when the doorbell rang. Their visitor was John Feather.

'You're going out?' he asked.

'A good detective always spots the evidence,' smiled Abigail. She removed her coat and hung it back on the coat hook on the hall. Daniel did the same.

'You're sure you don't mind?' asked Feather.

'You're always welcome,' said Abigail.

He followed them through to the living room and they settled themselves on the comfortable chairs.

'I've been sent by the chief. He wants to find out what you know about this murder at the Victoria and Albert Museum,' Feather told them.

Daniel grinned. 'Let me guess, he's annoyed at the fact that we've been called in?'

'Annoyed is an understatement,' chuckled Feather.

'Your visit is actually very opportune,' Abigail said. 'We'd like to know what you've picked up so far about this murder.

We understand you were first on the crime scene.'

'After the guard and the constable,' said Feather.

'The dead man was killed elsewhere and his body dumped at the museum?' asked Daniel.

'That's how it looked to me,' said Feather. 'You've been to the site?'

'Yes, and we spoke to Mr Ward, the guard who found him.'

'Have you spoken to Page's colleagues at the museum?'

'No, that's where we were heading just now,' said Abigail. 'The site is all we've looked at so far.'

'So you haven't met Mrs Page yet?' asked Feather.

'We thought we'd go and see her later today,' said Daniel. 'Have you talked to her?'

'I have,' said Feather.

'And?'

Feather frowned. 'Let's just say she didn't come across as the grieving widow.'

'Perhaps she's in shock,' said Abigail. 'Different people react to grief in different ways.'

'True,' admitted Feather. 'Also, she's German.'

'German?'

'Apparently she met Page when he was in Germany looking at things for the museum.'

'How long ago?' asked Daniel.

'I didn't ask,' Feather admitted. 'I got the impression they'd been married for a while.'

'How old was Page?'

'Late thirties. His wife's about the same.' He looked at them, curious. 'Changing the subject, what was it like meeting the Queen?' he asked. He took a copy of the *Daily Telegraph* from his pocket and showed them the page where they were mentioned.

'She's a very impressive woman,' said Daniel. 'Very determined to get to the bottom of this.'

'What's Armstrong's attitude towards us?' asked Abigail. 'Annoyed, obviously, but is he barring us from Scotland Yard as he's done before when his nose has been put out of joint?'

'The opposite,' said Feather. 'He's desperate to solve this before you do, which is why he's sent me to call on you and find out what you know.'

'At the moment, nothing that isn't already common knowledge,' said Daniel. 'Does this mean that we might be able to work together. Share information?'

'At least unofficially,' said Feather.

'Well, at the moment we've got nothing you don't know already,' said Daniel. 'But rest assured, if we pick up anything, we'll let you know about it. What have you got that isn't already in the papers?'

'Not a great deal,' admitted Feather. 'They've reported that Page's throat was cut, but they don't seem to have mentioned that he was stabbed through the heart first.'

'So, the killer making absolutely sure he was dead?' suggested Daniel. 'Have you spoken to his colleagues at the museum?'

'Some of them,' said Feather. 'The secretary who identified him wasn't there when I called, she'd gone home suffering from shock. I spoke to Page's boss, a man called Herbert Tweed. He had no idea why anyone would wish to harm Page. He said he was a man liked by everyone.'

'Except for at least one person,' commented Abigail.

'What was the name of the secretary who identified the

body?' asked Daniel.

Feather took his notebook from his pocket and checked. 'Miss Amelia Hart,' he told them. 'But, like I say, she wasn't there.'

'Perhaps she will be when we call,' said Daniel. 'We'll catch up with you after we've been to the Victoria and Albert, and also talked to Mrs Page, and compare notes.'

'We're also going to see the arts correspondent of the *Telegraph* at the Lyceum. We're hoping to pick up some gossip about Mr Page.'

'Gossip is what I could do with,' said Feather. 'At the moment, everyone's being very nice about the dead man.'

Herbert Tweed, the chief curator at the Victoria and Albert, was in his fifties, a large man in every sense, over six feet tall and with an ample stomach barely contained by his ornately decorated waistcoat and jacket.

'Terrible tragedy,' he said.

'You've no idea why anyone would want to kill him?' asked Daniel.

'None,' said Tweed.

'What exactly were his duties here?' asked Abigail.

'We have six curators here at this moment, each with his own particular area of expertise,' explained Tweed. 'Mr Page was involved with technology, especially in the production of ceramics. His remit was to travel and find examples of industrialised pottery factories that were new to us in Britain, so we could compare British methods with those of other countries.'

'So he travelled all over the world?' asked Abigail.

'No, just Europe,' said Tweed. 'For farther-flung countries, Africa, the United States, Asia, Australia, we depend on local people letting us know of new developments. Anything that we feel merits a closer inspection, we send one of our senior analysts out to investigate. The same goes for arts and crafts. For example, at this moment one of our historians, Jeremy Purbright, is in America studying Native American art.' He smiled at Abigail. 'There will always be work for you here, Mrs Wilson, should you ever decide to be involved in our Asian and African projects. With your experience of Egypt.' He shook his head in admiration. 'The first British woman to lead an archaeological expedition to the pyramids. The sun temple at Abu Ghurob, wasn't it?'

'It was,' nodded Abigail. 'And thank you for those kind words, Mr Tweed, but I feel quite settled at the moment working with Mr Wilson on our investigations. How often did Mr Page travel to Europe?'

Tweed looked thoughtful. 'His last visit was four months ago. He spent three weeks looking at industrial areas in Germany.'

'Did he find anything of interest?'

'Not interesting enough to merit inclusion. We already had quite a bit from Germany from Mr Page's previous excursions there.'

'What did you know about Mr Page's private life?' asked Daniel.

'His private life?'

'Yes. Away from work.'

'Well … nothing,' said Tweed, somewhat nonplussed. 'I know he was married, but we never socialised with one another. In fact, I don't believe Page socialised outside of work with anyone from the museum. He was very much work-orientated.'

'Would it be possible to talk to the secretary who identified him when his body was discovered?' asked Abigail. 'We understand her name is Miss Amelia Hart.'

'Yes, of course. I sent her home after the body was discovered, thinking it would have been distressing for her, but she came back to work this morning and took up her duties again and performed them with the same efficiency as ever. A remarkable young woman. I wish all our employees had her resilience.'

He led them from his office to an outer office in which four women sat at desks. On each desk was a strange-looking machine, on which the women were striking a series of keys rapidly. A sheet of paper poked out of the top of each machine, and as the women pulled a handle to one side of the machine after striking the keys, the paper moved upwards.

Daniel gazed at the machines, fascinated and intrigued.

'What are those machines?' he asked. 'I've never seen the like of them before.'

'Those are typewriters,' said Tweed with a proud smile. 'We use them for producing letters, and also for copies of important documents which were previously produced by handwriting. Actually, the typewriter has been around for a number of years, but they've been going through various changes in their design. The ones we use here are made by Remington, an American company. Most typewriters are made in America. We're currently looking at the new one made by an American company called Underwood. Each change in design makes it easier to use.' He smiled. 'Mark my words, within a few short years, most companies and organisations in this country will be using these to produce letters and documents.'

'So the museum is ahead of the game.'

'We've always been ahead of the game in the museum's previous incarnations, and now as the Victoria and Albert. Remember, it all stemmed from the Great Exhibition, which was about technological innovation as well as arts and crafts. The typewriter is just one example.' He raised his voice to call: 'Miss Hart, please!'

One of the women stopped typing and turned to look at Mr Tweed, and seeing him standing with two strangers to the office, she rose from her chair and joined them, looking at Daniel and Abigail warily.

'Miss Hart, these are Mr and Mrs Wilson. They've been commissioned by Her Majesty the Queen to look into the unfortunate incident.'

'Mr Page,' she said quietly.

'Just so. They need to talk to you.' He turned to Daniel and Abigail. 'You may use my office.'

'Thank you,' said Daniel.

'But only if you feel up to it,' Abigail said to the young woman. 'We don't want to cause you further distress by dredging up the memory of what you saw.'

'That's all right,' said Hart. 'If it helps to find the person who did it, I'll answer any questions. And it is a sort of royal command, isn't it.'

'I'll remain here until you've finished,' Tweed said.

Daniel, Abigail and Amelia Hart walked through to Mr Tweed's office, where they each sat. Amelia Hart was in her twenties, smart, attractive, and seemed very composed. Daniel had already decided to let Abigail do the questioning, to put the young woman at her ease.

'What can you remember of what happened?' asked Abigail.

'Mr Tweed said there'd been some kind of accident in the marquee, and he asked me if I'd go and see if I recognised the man who'd been injured.'

'Injured?' queried Abigail. 'Not killed?'

'Injured,' nodded Hart firmly.

'So you were unprepared for what you saw?'

'Not really. When I reached the marquee, the guard told me there was a dead man inside. He wanted to know if I knew who he was.'

'Were you reluctant to go in at that point?'

'No. I knew it was my duty, however unpleasant the sight might be. I went in and the man took me to where the body was beside the foundation stone. I recognised him straight away as Mr Page.'

'You worked with Mr Page?'

'We secretaries type up whatever we're required to do if it's been authorised by Mr Tweed or any other senior staff. I'd typed letters and reports for Mr Page.'

'What sort of person was Mr Page?'

Her features softened and Abigail thought there was a hint of tears in her eyes as she said, still composed: 'He was a lovely man. A gentleman. Kind. When his work took him away to other countries, he always brought something special back for we secretaries.'

'The security guard said you left the marquee.'

'Yes, I came back here and told Mr Tweed that the … the dead man was Mr Page. The guard had told me he'd sent for the police.'

'And you took the rest of the day off.'

'Only because Mr Tweed insisted. I was ready to continue.'

'Did Mr Page have any enemies that you know of?' asked Daniel.

'Oh no!' said Hart. 'He was very popular. He was a kind and gentle man.'

'So there was no one at the museum who may not have been keen on him.'

'When you say "keen"?' queried Hart, puzzled.

'It's very rare for someone to be universally liked,' said Daniel gently. He gave a rueful smile. 'I can think of a few people who aren't very fond of me, even though I've never done them any harm. There's usually someone who feels annoyed or upset over some slight or other, even if it's just imagined.'

She hesitated again, then said, awkwardly: 'Well, there's possibly Mr Oakley.'

'Mr Oakley?'

'Gideon Oakley. He's another of the curators. I got the impression he was jealous of Mr Page.'

'Why?'

'I don't know. It was just things he said. Well, muttered under his breath when he saw Mr Page.' Hastily she added: 'Not that I'm suggesting he could have had anything to do with the terrible thing that happened. It's just that, he's the only one I can think of who may not have been particularly fond of Mr Page.'

'We understand,' smiled Abigail. 'Where might we find Mr Oakley? Just to talk to him, see if he knows anyone who might have wished harm to Mr Page?'

'He has a desk in the offices. All the curators do. But usually he's to be found in the Fine Arts section of the museum. He's the curator for pottery and ceramics.'

'Thank you,' said Abigail. 'Out of curiosity, did you know Mr Page socially, outside of work?'

Hart looked at her as if she'd made an indecent suggestion.

'Certainly not,' she said. 'I am a secretary. Mr Page is an executive.'

CHAPTER SEVEN

The ceramics section of the Fine Arts displays at the South Kensington Museum, soon to be generally known as the Victoria and Albert, was dedicated to all kinds of pottery, from delicate porcelain and beautifully decorated ceramics, to examples of early earthenware from medieval times, all kept in glass cases. There were also examples of early Egyptian and Roman pottery, which Abigail recognised.

'This is an astounding collection,' she said. 'Full compliments have to be paid to Mr Oakley if assembling these is his work.'

'I heard my name,' said a voice close by.

From behind a glass display case appeared a tall, thin man, his scalp showing through his sparse hair covering, and with a thin straggling beard. With his dark formal clothes and his intense and slightly unnerving gaze from his deep-set eyes, he resembled a funeral director more than a museum curator.

'Mr Oakley,' said Daniel. He proffered his hand. 'Allow us

to introduce ourselves. We are Daniel and Abigail Wilson and we've been asked to look into the death of Mr Page.'

Oakley regarded them quizzically, then, with some reluctance, took Daniel's hand and briefly shook it.

'Yes,' he said. 'I saw it in the newspapers. How can I help you?'

'How well did you know Mr Page?'

'I wouldn't say I knew him at all,' he said.

'It has been suggested to us that you didn't like him,' said Daniel politely and with a look of apology.

'Gossip,' snapped Oakley. But then he added: 'However, in truth, I didn't like him. I will not pretend. I am not a hypocrite. I will not weep pretend crocodile tears over someone I had no respect for. Someone I believe was a criminal.'

They studied Oakley, surprised at the vehemence of his tone as he made the allegation.

'What sort of criminal, Mr Oakley?' asked Abigail. 'What sort of illegality do you think he was involved in?'

'I don't know,' admitted Oakley, and the frustration of not knowing showed in his face, in his whole manner. 'But I have my suspicions.'

'It would help us greatly if you would share those suspicions with us,' said Daniel.

'Very well. Do you know anything about ceramics?'

'Not really,' said Daniel. 'Although my wife, as an Egyptologist, is an acknowledged expert on Egyptian and Roman pottery.'

Oakley nodded. 'Yes, I'm familiar with Miss Fenton's – or, forgive me, Mrs Wilson's reputation. I've read some of your pieces in magazines, Mrs Wilson. Very impressive.'

'Thank you, Mr Oakley,' returned Abigail. 'I was just offering my praise on the collection you've assembled to my husband. You have an excellent and discerning eye.'

'Thank you,' nodded Oakley. Then, bitterly, he added: 'It's a pity the museum authorities don't share your opinion. Or, rather, the person responsible for the curators.'

'I don't understand,' said Abigail, puzzled. She gestured at the glass cases that surrounded them. 'The range here is truly breathtaking. There are pieces here similar to some of the pieces I discovered when I was excavating inside the pyramids, and the way they have been cleaned so meticulously, but at the same time with such care, means you have some of the very best examples of pottery of the kingdoms in the world. The same is true of the Roman pieces you have. And then we come to the beauty of the ancient Chinese pieces, and the modern porcelain. It is truly a collection to be proud of, and I would have thought the museum would have been only too keen to give you carte blanche to expand the collection.'

'That was my hope, too,' said Oakley. 'I was born and raised in Stoke-on-Trent, the pottery capital of this country. I was brought up with the feeling of clay beneath my fingers. I know everything there is to know about pottery: earthenware, chinaware, stoneware, you name it I have lived with it. And not just English pottery. You've commented on the Egyptian and Roman pieces, and from the Orient. I have studied ceramics of many countries, including Germany. Meissen porcelain, obviously but also Bartmann jug-making, the pottery of Höhr-Grenzhausen and Ransbach-Baumbach areas of Westerworldkreis. Yet when I suggested that I add the pottery of Germany to my curating area, I was refused. Instead, they gave the post to Andrew Page!'

'I can understand your feelings of resentment,' said Abigail, 'but I'm not sure where the criminality comes into it?'

'The way he got the position,' said Oakley.

'Are you saying he doesn't really know much about German pottery?' she asked.

'No, no. He has a certain knowledge, admitted. But it's not a patch on mine!' He looked at them with deep intensity as he said: 'He can only have got the post by underhand methods.'

'What underhand methods?'

'Blackmail,' said Oakley through gritted teeth.

'Blackmail?' echoed Abigail. She looked at Daniel, uncomprehending. 'Who of?'

'It has to be Raphael Wilton. He's the Senior Director of Acquisitions. He's the one who appoints curators to their different areas.'

'But what makes you think that Mr Page was blackmailing this Mr Wilton?'

'It has to be. It's the only answer. And I've seen them together, whispering, with Mr Wilton looking worried. Page had something on Wilton and he used it to exert pressure in order to get the German post. There's obviously something going on there. Page must have found a way to coin money hand over fist in Germany. And I don't think that Wilton is the only one. Have you seen Page's house?'

'No.'

'A mansion in one of the most expensive areas of London. Where does he get the money from? As a curator he only earns the same as I do, and I can't afford anything a quarter as grand as that. Not even a quarter! Far, far less!'

They were interrupted by the arrival of one of the attendants.

'Excuse me, Mr Oakley, a gentleman has arrived who says he has an appointment with you. A Mr Webley.'

'Ah, yes. I've been expecting him.' He turned to Daniel and Abigail. 'Please excuse me. I was here waiting for him. He has some pots made by the monks of Glastonbury Abbey in the Middle Ages to show me.'

'Of course,' said Daniel. 'Thank you for your time.'

As they watched Oakley walk away, Daniel muttered: 'That was very interesting. If Page was blackmailing this Mr Wilton, then he could well have been blackmailing other people. And blackmailers often end up dead.'

'*If* he was,' pointed out Abigail. 'It could well be just an accusation by a bitter and jealous man who's been passed over in favour of someone else. There could well be a very valid reason why Page got the German connection instead of Oakley. We need to talk to this Mr Wilton.'

Daniel looked at his watch. 'But not today,' he said. 'We have an appointment with a gossip from whom we'll hopefully learn more about Mr Page.'

Albert Edward, the Prince of Wales, glowered at his private secretary, Michael Shanks, and showed him the newspaper.

'Have you seen this?'

'Yes, Your Majesty.'

'Did you see that Mama's given this pair carte blanche to poke around wherever they want in order to find out who killed that busybody Page? It's unimaginable to have this pair of guttersnipes poking around in one's private life.'

'I'm sure it won't come to that, sir.'

'Oh it will, mark my words.' He threw the newspaper down angrily. 'Mama's got this obsession with giving common people the right to poke around in our family's business that they shouldn't have. That John Brown fellow was bad enough, but then we had that Indian wallah.'

'Abdul Karim.'

'Absolutely disgraceful! And now we have these two!'

'Mrs Wilson was formerly known as Abigail Fenton, Your Majesty, before her marriage to Mr Wilson. She has a Classics degree from Cambridge University and is an internationally esteemed archaeologist. Her work at the Egyptian pyramids—'

'Forget the bloody pyramids, Shanks! The other half of this duo, Daniel Wilson...'

'A former detective inspector at Scotland Yard.'

'And before that? A workhouse boy! For God's sake. Where does Mama find these dreadful people?'

When Daniel and Abigail arrived at the Lyceum, they found Bram Stoker, the theatre's manager, in the lobby checking that the posters promoting the forthcoming productions were displayed properly.

'Good afternoon, Mr Stoker,' said Daniel.

Stoker's face lit up at the sight of them.

'Good afternoon, Mr Wilson. Good afternoon, Miss Fenton.' He smiled. 'Or, more correctly, Mrs Wilson. I saw in the papers that you'd married. I meant to send a card of congratulations, but…' He sighed and waved a hand to indicate the theatre. 'Things kept getting in the way.'

'Fenton or Wilson is fine,' said Abigail. 'Although, as we

know one another, perhaps you wouldn't object to calling me Abigail?'

'Abigail it is!' beamed Stoker. 'Abigail and Daniel. And in return, please call me Bram. What can I do for you?'

'We understand Adrian Hegley, the arts correspondent from *The Telegraph*, is here interviewing Sir Henry.'

'One of a crowd of journalists,' said Stoker. 'Sir Henry is holding what he terms a "conference with the press" about his plans for the next season. He's talking to them on the stage.'

'Ah,' said Abigail. 'His natural habitat.'

'Exactly,' smiled Stoker. 'Do you know Hegley?'

'No,' said Daniel.

'You can't fail to miss him. Flamboyant is the word for him. A human peacock. Today he's wearing a coat of many colours, most of them garish, adorned with a fur collar. If he tries to escape with the herd, I'll bring him back.'

'Thank you,' said Abigail. 'And we must congratulate you on the success of *Dracula*. It really is one of the most talked about novels. Deservedly so. I enjoyed it enormously.' She gave a roguish smile as she added: 'I may be wrong, but I thought I detected a certain similarity between the count and Sir Henry, both in your description and some of his mannerisms?'

Stoker laughed. 'Fortunately, Sir Henry has not yet taken to sucking the life blood from those who surround him. Although, sometimes it feels like it.'

They were suddenly aware of men appearing from the auditorium, all talking and chuckling to one another.

'It seems the audience with Sir Henry has finished,' said Stoker. He scanned the crowd as they passed them, then called out 'Adrian! A moment!'

A small man with a mop of red hair and a large red beard, both of which seemed to have a life of their own, sprouting out from his head in all directions, left the crowd and joined them, an inquisitive look on his face. He was dressed as Stoker had described him, wearing a coat that looked to be made of patchwork, cloth squares of different colours sewn together and topped with a fur collar.

'Adrian, these are Mr and Mrs Wilson.'

'Of course! The Museum Detectives!' He held out his hand. 'This is a pleasure!'

Daniel and Abigail shook his hand, and Daniel said: 'Joe Dalton suggested you were the person we need to talk to.'

'Really? To what end, pray? Joe is a lovely man but our paths rarely cross. He is so serious. I am also serious, but in a different way to Joe. He is serious about things like politics and other such trivia. I am serious about things that really matter: the arts.'

'It's about people in the arts we wish to find out about. Or, rather, certain people. In particular, those involved with the Victoria and Albert Museum.'

'Ah, the gruesome murder!' exclaimed Hegley. He turned to Stoker. 'This would make a plot for one of your books, Bram. A dead man with his throat cut but no trace of blood. Your Count Dracula at work?'

'Thank you, Adrian, that is indeed a *novel* suggestion,' responded Stoker with a mocking smile.

'Oh, bravo! A *novel* suggestion!' He chuckled. 'Will we see more puns making an appearance in your future works?'

'Very likely, and some of them may even be deliberate,' said Stoker. 'Now, if you'll excuse me, I must attend to Sir Henry.'

With a smile of farewell to Daniel and Abigail, he headed for the auditorium.

'There goes one of the cleverest men in theatreland,' said Hegley. 'If you are to pick my brains, can I suggest we do it over coffee. There is an excellent little coffee shop in the Strand, which also does exquisite pastries.'

With that he swept out into the street.

'Coffee and pastries?' murmured Daniel doubtfully.

'The Queen is paying,' Abigail reminded him.

A short walk later they were in a small coffee shop with coffees in front of Daniel and Abigail, and coffee and a plate of assorted cream pastries in front of Hegley, which he was savouring with delight.

'We're trying to find out about the private life of Andrew Page,' explained Daniel.

'To see if he'd upset anyone badly enough that they'd want to kill him?' asked Hegley through a mouthful of pastry.

'That's one aspect to it,' affirmed Daniel. 'At the moment we know very little about him, except for the fact that he worked as a curator for the Victoria and Albert Museum, and is married to a woman called Gretchen from Germany. And that he was killed.'

'I'm guessing you want the dirt on him,' said Hegley with a lewd wink.

'If there is any,' said Daniel.

'Well, that depends on how you view his romantic entanglements.'

'Apart from his wife, you mean?'

'Have you met his wife?' asked Hegley.

'No,' Abigail admitted.

'I have doubts if there is still a romantic spark there. There may have been once, but his attentions have definitely been elsewhere of late.'

'You mean he has a mistress?'

'*Mistresses*,' smirked Hegley.

'Did his wife know?' asked Abigail.

'I don't see why not, everyone else did. One lady in particular he shared with a certain very well-known member of the royal family.' He winked. 'One might even say an heir.'

'The Prince of Wales?' asked Daniel.

'Tut-tut,' said Hegley. 'One doesn't bandy actual names about. One could end up in the Tower.'

'Would it be indiscreet to enquire the lady's name?' asked Abigail.

'Absolutely indiscreet,' said Hegley, putting on an air of shock. Then he gave the same wicked conspiratorial smile again. 'Luckily, discretion is not my middle name.' He picked up another pastry. 'Are you sure you don't want any of these? They really are exquisite.'

'No, thank you,' said Abigail. 'You were about to say the lady's name.'

'Was I really? How shocking of me.' He looked around to make sure there was no one within convenient earshot, and whispered: 'Lady Vanessa Horden. Wife of Lord Horden, the art collector.'

'Does Lord Horden know?'

'He certainly knows about his wife and the prince, who is astonishingly indiscreet, but whether he also knows about Page is a matter of speculation.'

'You said *mistresses*,' Abigail reminded him.

'Ah, now the identities of those ladies may be harder to track down. I tend to move in society circles, hence Lady Horden is known to me. But, if rumour is to be believed, Page also dallied with ladies of the lower orders. And for that you'd need someone who moves in the world of the demi-monde.'

'Can you suggest anyone worth talking to?'

'Not in that world, it's not one I inhabit. But if you really want to know, I'd suggest you talk to the household. No man has secrets from his servants.' Suddenly the expression on his face became thoughtful and he mused: 'Of course, the real mystery is how he could afford the lifestyle.'

'He lived expensively?'

'I'm guessing that presents for his amours didn't come cheap. They glittered, my dears. Necklaces. Earrings. And not paste, but the real thing.'

'Diamonds.'

Hegley smiled.

'His ladies had exquisite taste. And, of course, he had to keep his dear wife in the same manner, otherwise she would have been quite vindictive towards him. She may have even considered the dreaded D word.'

'Divorce?'

'Which wouldn't have gone down well with his employers. They're terribly old-fashioned.'

'But you say everyone knew about his mistresses.'

'It's one thing to know, even to flaunt it, providing it doesn't come to public notice through a court of law. Until then, it's deniable.' He gave his leering smile again as he added: 'A lesson our dear prince learnt when Sir Charles Mordaunt threatened to name him as co-respondent in his divorce case. In the end,

Sir Charles decided not to proceed against Prince Edward and instead named another gentleman, Viscount Cole, who had fathered a child upon Lady Mordaunt; but it was a close call for his highness.'

'So how did Page afford his lifestyle?' asked Daniel.

'That, my dears, is a mystery to me. I've never involved myself in matters of accountancy. Although I would suggest questions might have been asked about how the funding for the new museum was distributed. And if any of it was … borrowed.'

'There must have been rumours.'

'There are always rumours. It's what high society runs on. But how true those rumours might have been, you'd need to talk to someone who's studied the world of public finances.'

'Who can you suggest?'

'Well, there's the financial journalist for our own paper, the *Telegraph*, Henry Grimson. But the real experts are to be found at the *Financial Times*. They keep a very careful eye on all financial dealings.'

'And are any of them particularly involved in finances for museums?'

'There's a man called Magnus Evans. I believe he's very knowledgeable on that subject. I have to admit, I don't really know him personally, only by reputation. I understand he's quite a severe character. Not very sociable, which is why our paths don't really cross.'

CHAPTER EIGHT

'What an odious man,' said Abigail as they walked along the Strand after leaving the coffee shop, where Hegley remained to sample more pastries and coffee.

'Part of being a detective,' said Daniel. 'It's all about information.'

'This isn't information, it's gossip and rumour.'

'Which often contains information, if you can sift through it.' He looked thoughtful. 'According to Hegley, Mr Page and the prince shared the favours of the same lady. Could there be a motive for his death there?'

'Unlikely, I would have thought,' said Abigail. 'If every man who became involved with one of the prince's female conquests was murdered as a result of the situation, London would be strewn with corpses.' She thought about it, then suggested: 'We could always talk to the prince about his relationship with Lady Hordern, and ask if he knew about her relationship with Andrew Page.'

'Difficult,' said Daniel. 'This is the heir to the throne, and he has a notoriously short temper when it comes to people enquiring into his private life.'

'Yes, but we have a royal command from his mother,' Abigail pointed out. 'And I've generally found that bullying types invariably concede when Mummy is giving the orders.'

'True,' agreed Daniel. 'But can I suggest we keep that one up our sleeve for the moment. The idea of Andrew Page being murdered and his body dumped so openly in such a site as the new museum workings just because he shared a mistress with the prince seems to be stretching it a bit.'

'But it's possible.'

'Anything's possible,' said Daniel. 'But as we've now heard two impressions of Mrs Page, one from John Feather and the other from Mr Hegley, I think it's about time we called on the widow and talked to her ourselves.'

Andrew Page had lived in Belgrave Square. Daniel and Abigail exchanged curious looks as they approached the front of the towering three-storey white brick house, with marble columns either side of the black oak front door.

'I can see why both Hegley and Oakley mentioned the money. This looks a very expensive house in a very expensive part of town. It's starting to make Oakley's allegations of blackmail look feasible.'

'Possibly Mrs Page is the money,' suggested Abigail.

'A German heiress?' asked Daniel.

'It's a possibility,' said Abigail. 'Or it might all be on borrowed money.'

'Even on borrowed money, it would cost a lot to keep up the interest payments.'

Daniel rang the bell, which was answered by a tall portly man with luxuriant side whiskers. He was dressed in a striped waistcoat and a high-collared crisp white shirt.

'Mr and Mrs Wilson would like to talk to Mrs Page,' said Daniel. 'We are here at the command of Her Royal Majesty, Queen Victoria.'

If the butler was impressed by this, he didn't show it. Instead, he told them: 'If you will please wait here, I will see if the mistress is available.'

He then shut the door.

'No invite for us to wait inside,' commented Daniel. 'Obviously the idea of a royal command from the Queen doesn't impress him.'

'If his mistress is German, perhaps we should have said we're here on Kaiser Wilhelm's instructions,' said Abigail.

The door opened and the man in the striped waistcoat looked out at them.

'The mistress will see you,' he announced. 'If you will follow me.'

The interior of the house was as luxurious as the exterior, the walls adorned with paintings, some portraits and some landscapes. They followed the butler towards the rear of the house where he led them to a large conservatory, where a small forest filled the large glass room.

A tall, elegant woman in her thirties was standing expectantly. Next to her stood a tall, bearded man in his forties who regarded Daniel and Abigail suspiciously.

'Mrs Page,' said Daniel. 'Our apologies for disturbing you

at this time, and please accept our condolences on the loss of your husband. I am Daniel Wilson and this is my wife, Abigail. We have been tasked by Her Majesty, Queen Victoria, with finding out who killed your husband.' He produced the letter Sir Anthony Thurrington had sent them and proffered it to her. 'This letter is our credentials to say we are working with the authority of the palace.'

She took the letter from him, scanned it, then passed it to the man who read it with more attention before returning it to Daniel.

'This is my brother, Heinrich Kurtz,' she said. 'He's here in England on business.'

Daniel and Abigail both nodded in greeting to Kurtz, with Abigail asking: 'Have you come to England from Germany, Mr Kurtz?'

Kurtz hesitated momentarily, then said: 'From South Africa.'

'My brother is a mining engineer,' said Mrs Page. 'He works there. How may I help you?'

'As we've explained, we are looking into your husband's death. Can you think of anyone who might wish him harm?'

She shook her head. 'No, Andrew was very popular. There is no one I can think of who would wish him harm.'

'Has he been troubled lately? Anything worrying him?'

'No.'

Daniel and Abigail exchanged careful looks. The quiet monosyllabic answers and the woman's great composure did not suggest a grieving widow. There were no hints of tears having been shed recently; but often people didn't react with open grief on the death of a loved one; that happened after the initial shock had worn off.

Daniel turned to Kurtz. 'What about you, Mr Kurtz? Did you know your brother-in-law well?'

'No,' said Kurtz. 'I rarely come to England.'

Abigail took over, asking the widow: 'Had your husband said anything in the last few days to suggest he was in fear of his life?'

'No,' she said. 'He was as normal.'

'How about the other people at work? Or people he had been negotiating with for the purchase of objects for the museum? Had he expressed any awkwardness in any of his business dealings in recent times?'

'No,' she said again. 'There was no discontent or disagreements.'

Abigail looked questioningly towards Daniel, who nodded and said: 'Thank you for your time, Mrs Page. Mr Kurtz. We'll leave you now, but if anything occurs to you, we'd be grateful if you would contact us.' He produced a small visiting card with their address on it, which he handed to Mrs Page.

When they were once again outside in the street, Daniel said ruefully: 'Well, that was a non-event.'

'We could hardly start pressuring the grief-stricken widow,' pointed out Abigail.

'Did she seem grief-stricken to you?'

'No,' admitted Abigail.

When they got home it was to find an envelope waiting for them on their doormat.

'Buckingham Palace again?' asked Daniel as Abigail picked it up and opened it.

Abigail passed the single sheet of paper to him.

'Not unless Her Majesty has started sending threatening letters,' she said.

Daniel looked at it. The page bore four words in block capitals that said: 'STAY OUT OF IT'. At the bottom was a crude drawing of a knife with blood dripping from the blade.

CHAPTER NINE

Chief Superintendent Armstrong scowled as he read yet another newspaper's report of the murder at the Victoria and Albert Museum, which extolled the expertise of the so-called Museum Detectives, Daniel and Abigail Wilson.

No mention of the expertise of Scotland Yard, he growled to himself.

A knock at his door led to him putting the newspaper in the drawer of his desk; he didn't fancy anyone coming in and commenting on the newspaper's take on the situation.

'Come!' he called.

The door opened and the tall, austere figure of Commander Evan Haggard, Deputy Head of Special Branch entered. He was thin and hollow-cheeked enough to be described as cadaverous. He shut the door and seated himself opposite Armstrong. His expression, normally grim, seemed even grimmer today.

'This murder at the Victoria and Albert Museum,' he said,

his eyes beneath his bushy eyebrows boring into the chief superintendent's face.

'Yes, Commander,' said Armstrong. 'We are actively pursuing lines of enquiry. I've instructed one of our men, Inspector Feather, to take charge of the investigation.'

'Her Majesty has brought in these Museum Detectives, the Wilsons,' said Haggard in an accusing tone.

'Yes, sir,' said Armstrong, and his tone took on one of indignation. 'And completely unnecessarily, in my view.'

'That may be, but that's the reality of the situation. Very unfortunate.'

'Very unfortunate,' agreed Armstrong.

'They're loose cannons. Especially Wilson. The last time he was involved in a case where we had an interest, in Oxford, it resulted in one of our men getting shot dead. We're not happy about him having carte blanche to poke his nose around in this case.'

'I share your view, but unfortunately they seem to have been given this carte blanche by the Queen herself.'

'Yes. Bad advice from people too afraid to stand up to her. Something needs to be done to stop them.'

'You're going to see the Queen?' asked Armstrong.

Haggard stared at him, shocked at this suggestion.

'Absolutely not! I am a loyal servant of Her Majesty. It's not my place to question her decisions.'

It's going to be mine, thought Armstrong, his heart sinking. *They're going to load the responsibility of stopping the Wilsons on my shoulders and ruin my career.*

'No,' continued Haggard, 'we have to do this without involving Her Majesty. I will have a firm word with Mr and

Mrs Wilson and put them straight about which areas of this case are off limits to them. But policy dictates that I cannot put anything in writing to them. So, I need you to write to them and invite them to a meeting here. When they arrive, I'd appreciate it if you will bring them to my office.'

Armstrong felt a wave of relief surge over him as he heard these words. He was off the hook. Or was he?

'I have to warn you, Commander,' he said cautiously, 'that Wilson is a tricky customer. A maverick. A rebel. From my experience of the man, he does not take easily to being warned off, even by officials.'

'He *will* be warned off,' said Haggard firmly. 'Unless he fancies spending the rest of his days in prison.'

'I very much doubt if even the threat of prison will put a stop to his activities,' warned Armstrong.

'Possibly a threat to imprison his wife?' mused Haggard.

Armstrong gave a rueful sigh.

'His wife is as bad as he is. Possibly even worse.'

'Then we shall have to see what happens,' said Haggard. 'But I shall make them very aware that there are certain things about this case that threaten the security of this nation, and as Deputy Head of Special Branch, I cannot allow them to be jeopardised.' He glowered at the chief superintendent. 'Your man, Feather?'

'The very best, Commander.'

'I understand he is a close friend of the Wilsons.'

Armstrong looked uncomfortable. 'I'm not sure if he could be described as a *close* friend.'

'That's how it's been reported to me,' snapped Haggard. 'I'm worried that he might be tempted to pass information on to them.'

'With respect, sir, I'm intending for the opposite result. I've encouraged him to be in contact with them in order that we can find out what they know, so that we can act on it.'

Haggard looked doubtful. 'A dangerous course of action, in my opinion, Chief Superintendent. As you yourself said, they are tricky and devious. But you think you know best. Let's hope your confidence has not been misplaced.'

The offices of the *Financial Times* seemed to belong to an earlier era than many of their sister newspapers. When Daniel and Abigail entered the reception area, they were reminded of a finance house, such as one of the major banks, rather than the usual hustle and bustle that seemed to go with most of the national press.

They approached the reception desk and asked if it was possible to see Mr Magnus Evans.

'Mr Evans does not see people without an appointment,' they were told in frosty dismissive tones by the superior-looking woman behind the reception desk.

Daniel took the letter from Sir Anthony Thurrington from his pocket and passed it to her.

'We are here on instructions from Her Majesty the Queen,' he said.

The woman read the letter and her expression changed to one of bewilderment as, for a moment, she lost her composure. Then she recovered herself and forced a smile at them.

'If you'll wait here, I'll see if Mr Evans is available,' she said.

She rose to her feet, still holding the letter, and was about to walk off when Daniel stopped her, holding out his hand.

'The letter, please,' he said politely. 'We will show it to Mr

Evans if and when we see him.'

She handed the letter back, then disappeared through a pair of double doors.

'That gave me so much pleasure,' smiled Daniel. 'Putting people in their place who believe they are superior to we mere mortals who do not normally inhabit these grand surroundings.'

'You're a rebel at heart, Daniel,' said Abigail. 'I'm surprised you're not out in the street rabble-rousing with the communists.'

'I believe in law and order too strongly. And justice. But justice for all.'

The woman returned.

'Mr Evans will see you,' she said, 'If you will follow me.'

She led them through the double doors and along a short corridor to a small office. Magnus Evans was a short, shrewd-eyed, grey-haired man in his sixties who rose to his feet as they entered.

'Thank you, Mrs Ponsonby,' he said; and the woman left, pulling the door shut behind her. Evans gestured for them to take the two chairs opposite his desk. 'Mr and Mrs Wilson,' he said. 'Mrs Ponsonby has advised me of the communication you carry with you. I'd be grateful if you would allow me to peruse it myself.'

Daniel handed him the letter, which he read, then returned it with a chuckle.

'An order from Her Majesty herself. This is a first for me.'

'And a first for us,' said Daniel. 'She has commissioned us to look into the murder of Mr Andrew Page.'

'Ah yes, at the site of the new Victoria and Albert Museum,' said Evans. 'I read about it in the newspapers. We, ourselves, did not cover it. Our readers prefer to read about finance and speculation. So, bearing that in mind, how can I help you?'

'We're interested in finding out about the financial arrangements for the Victoria and Albert Museum. The funding. Where it comes from and how it's administered.'

'Why?' asked Evans.

'In case it may be connected with Mr Page's murder.'

'You think there might be a financial motive for his death?'

'We don't know. At the moment, we're exploring every avenue. A suggestion of financial skulduggery has been made to us, either involving Mr Page, or in which someone involved in any financial chicanery may have felt it necessary to silence him.'

'It sounds to me like the ravings of someone with a highly developed sense of the imagination. The plot for a cheap novel.'

'True, but there have been instances of financial irregularities that have resulted in murder,' said Daniel. 'I spent many years as a detective at Scotland Yard working with Inspector Abberline and came across many such cases.'

Evans frowned. 'Yes, there have been instances of such things,' he agreed reluctantly. 'What do you know about the funding of museums?'

'The majority of the museums we've been commissioned by to investigate crimes on their premises are funded privately, the money administered by a Board of Trustees,' said Abigail. 'When I was hired by the Fitzwilliam at Cambridge to curate their Egyptology exhibition, for example, my salary was authorised by the Board and administered by Sir William Mackenzie. Similarly with the Ashmolean in Oxford and Madame Tussauds. However, two have been funded by government money.'

'*Public* money,' Evans corrected her. 'Collected by the

government from we, the public, in the form of taxation.'

'Public money,' agreed Abigail, 'administered by Parliament. As was the case with the British Museum, who employed us, and the National Gallery. Although even there, the extension of the National Gallery, the National Gallery of British Art, was privately funded by Sir Henry Tate, the sugar magnate.'

'To an extent,' said Evans. 'Parliament was required to pay for the site.'

'A former prison,' put in Daniel. 'Which meant that Parliament already owned the site.'

A slight smile appeared on Evans's face. 'True. Let us say that Parliament donated the site.' Then he added as a compliment. 'I can see you have been doing your background work.' He jabbed a finger towards Daniel's jacket, and the letter inside it. 'But you have a letter of authority from the Queen that gives you carte blanche to make any enquiries of anyone at all. Why don't you ask these questions about funding and finances of the Victoria and Albert Museum themselves? Why come to me?'

'We will,' said Daniel. 'But I learnt one important thing during my years as a Scotland Yard detective: that if you ask any individual or organisation about their own financial arrangements, you will get an answer slanted to what they wish to tell you; not all there is to be known. Before we talk to them, we'd appreciate learning from you how the Victoria and Albert's finances operate.'

Evans thought it over, then nodded in agreement.

'Their day-to-day finances are much the same as the museums you described: a Board of Trustees administering funds either from private sources or from the public purse. In the case of the

Victoria and Albert Museum, the problem has been getting the approval of those public funds from Parliament. I'm sure you know how long the whole development has taken.'

'Yes, Sir Anthony Thurrington told us of its history. Almost fifty years in the making, we understand.'

'And still not finished,' said Evans. 'Although, hopefully, this last phase will complete it, although I have seen estimates of ten years for this final section to be completed.'

'Why so long?' asked Abigail.

'Unfortunately, at each stage of its development, Parliament as the main source of funding has found other calls on its purse. The Crimean War, for example, was very costly and the bills for that were still being paid long after the conflict had ended. Proposals for this last phase of the project – the new galleries and the new facade, which will link the whole complex – were invited from architects in 1891 and the work given to Aston Webb, but it was another seven years before Parliament was able to allocate funds from its surplus for the development. Capital projects funded by the state move at a notoriously slow place, as opposed to those funded by private capital. Private investors want a speedy return on their money. With public investment, on the other hand, who knows which party will be in power when a project reaches completion? No politician wants an opponent taking the credit for a decision that they made, perhaps ten years previously.'

'Am I right in thinking that a private investor sees the money as his, and therefore keeps a close eye on it. While, whether it's called "public money" or "state funding", money put up by the state is spent over a longer period of time, and in that time, with different political parties taking over the reins of government, there may not be such a close eye kept on how it's spent?' asked Abigail.

'You are very wise, Mrs Wilson,' said Evans.

'So there is greater potential for fraudulent activity?'

'Indeed. I'd say that was a fair summing up. Some contractors are aware that there may not be the closest scrutiny of their costs when it comes to building, or refurbishment, especially on very large projects. And the Victoria and Albert Museum is a *very* large project.'

They decided to catch a series of buses home; the first to Euston Station, the second onward to Primrose Hill. As always, their preference was for the upper deck. Daniel, in particular, loved to observe the city from the top deck of a bus.

'So, fraud or blackmail are possible motives,' said Daniel, once they'd settled themselves into a seat at the front, his favourite location, despite it being right behind the horse and therefore in a direct line from its flatulence.

'But which way?' asked Abigail, fanning away a sudden burst of equine fumes. 'Page being involved in a fraud against the museum? If so, surely the museum would simply have him arrested.'

'Unless it was a case of thieves falling out,' said Daniel. 'Or, the alternative is that he discovered a fraud happening and was killed to silence him.'

'We still haven't looked properly into his private life,' said Abigail. 'All these mistresses he's supposed to have had. That's an area for jealousy and rage.'

'Yes,' mused Daniel. 'And, if Hegley is to be believed, that'll mean a lot of uncomfortable nosing about with a range of women from all classes.'

They discussed their options for the rest of the journey, but by the time they arrived home they both agreed that they'd barely begun to scratch the surface of the case. A letter was waiting for them when they arrived home.

'Be careful,' cautioned Daniel. 'If it's another threatening letter we might be able to get fingerprints off the envelope.'

'Any fingerprints will be the postman's,' said Abigail. 'Any useful ones will be on what's inside.'

She looked at the envelope. 'This one's addressed properly. The threatening one didn't even have our names on the envelope.'

She opened the envelope, looked cautiously in, then took out the sheet of paper inside.

'It's a letter from Chief Superintendent Armstrong.'

'What's he writing to us for?' asked Daniel, surprised.

'He's inviting us to meet him at Scotland Yard at our earliest convenience. He says he'll be available all of this afternoon, and all day tomorrow.'

'What's the tone of it?' asked Daniel.

'Polite and formal,' said Abigail.

'You sure it's from Armstrong?'

'It's signed by him,' said Abigail, showing him the letter.

'That means nothing,' said Daniel. He looked at the letter suspiciously. 'The only time he gives the appearance of being nice to us is when he wants something. What's he after?'

CHAPTER TEN

Rather than call on Chief Superintendent Armstrong at Scotland Yard for their first visit the following morning, instead they opted to make for the Victoria and Albert to make the acquaintance of Raphael Wilton, the Senior Director of Acquisitions.

'He might not see us,' said Daniel. 'Especially if, as Oakley suggests, Page was blackmailing him.'

'So long as we have that letter from Buckingham Palace, I can't see him refusing,' said Abigail.

When they arrived at the museum, they were informed by Raphael Wilton's secretary that Mr Wilton was very busy with many meetings scheduled, and it was unlikely he would be able to see them today. At which point Daniel produced the letter from Thurrington and handed it to her.

'Perhaps you'd show him this letter from Buckingham Palace giving us the authority of Her Majesty to conduct our enquiries and see if he can squeeze us in between his other meetings,' he said with a polite smile. 'If that proves impossible, we shall have to report back to Her Majesty that we were unable to see him. Her Majesty has told us personally that she is most keen to ensure we have every co-operation in this matter.'

The secretary took the letter and disappeared.

'I love us having that letter!' exulted Daniel. 'It gives us a feeling of power I've never known before.'

'Be careful about getting too carried away with that feeling,' cautioned Abigail. 'Remember, pride comes before a fall.'

'But not in this case, I fancy,' murmured Daniel as Wilton's secretary returned.

She handed the letter back to Daniel and said, 'Mr Wilton will see you now.'

'Thank you,' said Daniel.

Raphael Wilton was a man in his late fifties, elegantly turned out, complete with a flower in his buttonhole. He looked at Daniel and Abigail warily as he waved them to the two chairs opposite his desk.

'I saw the letter,' he said. 'How may I help you?'

'How well did you know Andrew Page?'

There was a moment's hesitation, a look of concern in his eyes, before he said: 'I knew him the same as I do most of my curators. As an employee.'

'Not socially?'

'No.'

The shortness of his answers and his whole body language, shifting slightly in his chair, made both Daniel and Abigail aware how uncomfortable Raphael Wilton felt about this meeting.

'We understand that you made the appointment of Mr Page to explore the ceramics industry in Germany.'

'I'm not sure if I did,' said Wilton.

'Is there someone else who appoints the curators to their different areas?' asked Abigail.

Wilton hesitated, then said: 'It's usually my decision, but I ensure I take advice from others.'

'From Mr Tweed?' asked Daniel.

'Sometimes from Mr Tweed,' acknowledged Wilton, although again they felt a reluctance on his part to answer.

'The reason we ask is because we're looking for the reason why Mr Page was killed,' said Daniel. 'So far, nothing seems to surface. The only point of dissension seems to be with Mr Gideon Oakley, who seems to feel some resentment that Mr Page was appointed to curate the ceramics contacts in Germany when Mr Oakley does appear to have the best qualifications to deal with the ceramics industry. Or, anything to do with pottery.'

'We've seen the ceramics collection that Mr Oakley has assembled, and I must say it's one of the best I've ever seen anywhere in the world,' added Abigail.

'Yes, that's true,' conceded Wilton. 'Mr Oakley definitely has a great knowledge of pottery in all its forms.'

'But you chose to give the German post to Mr Page,' said Abigail. 'We're curious as to the reason why.'

Wilton hesitated, then said: 'I assume you've met Mr Oakley.'

'We have,' said Daniel.

Wilton paused again, longer this time as he weighed up how to answer their question. Finally, he said: 'Perhaps Mr Oakley does have a slightly better knowledge of ceramics than poor Page did, but knowledge isn't everything. Sometimes it can be irritating. What's more important is being able to communicate with people, put them at ease. Page was very good at that. Sociable. Mr Oakley can be a bit – how can I put it – overeager to impart his knowledge. It can come across as a superior attitude, which puts people off. Especially when the people one is dealing with are experts in their field.

'Secondly, Mr Page's area of speciality is in engineering and technology, and we were interested in the ceramics *industry*, the processes by which pottery is produced on an industrial scale, not the artisan aspects. Mr Oakley's expertise was in the art of pottery. Mr Page's was in industrial technology.'

'I still get the impression Mr Page was selected because he had a more winning personality than Mr Oakley,' smiled Abigail.

Once more, Wilton shifted uncomfortably in his chair.

'Mr Page was very successful at making useful contacts and keeping them,' he said. 'Now, if there's nothing else, I do have another appointment. But if you have any further questions, don't hesitate to contact my secretary and we'll make an appointment where I'll be able to give you more time.'

As Abigail and Daniel left the building, Abigail said: 'Wilton's got a point. Oakley is definitely overbearing and pushy. Not what's needed in someone negotiating terms of trade.'

'True, but Wilton was hiding something. Didn't you get that feeling?'

'Very much,' agreed Abigail. 'So, blackmail is still a possibility.'

When Daniel and Abigail arrived at Scotland Yard and

asked to see Chief Superintendent Armstrong, they showed the sergeant at reception the letter requesting them to call and expected to be taken to Armstrong's office. Instead, they were surprised to see the chief superintendent himself appearing down the wide marble staircase towards them.

'Good,' he grunted. 'You're here.'

'We are,' said Daniel.

'There's someone who wants to talk to you.'

'Oh? Who?'

'You'll find out when you meet him.'

Daniel and Abigail exchanged puzzled looks, then followed Armstrong towards the stairs that led down to the basement.

'What's down here?' muttered Abigail.

'The cells,' said Daniel.

Abigail frowned. 'He's going to lock us up?'

'Also, the conveniences. And, at the end of the corridor, Special Branch.'

Abigail looked concerned.

'Special Branch? They're the people who arrested you and beat you up in Oxford.'

'No, they arrested me, but after someone else had beaten me up,' Daniel corrected her.

'But what do they want with us?'

'Somehow I have a feeling it's to do with the murder. Whenever there's something that involves the royal family, Special Branch are there looming dangerously in the background.'

They made their way through a maze of corridors that twisted and turned, before Armstrong stopped at a door that had no identifying name outside it. He knocked, and at the summons 'Enter!', opened it.

'Mr and Mrs Wilson are here, Commander.'

'Commander?' whispered Abigail.

'Top brass,' Daniel whispered back.

'Please come in!'

Daniel and Abigail walked in and found a thin-faced man in a dark suit and high starched collar sitting at a desk. He waved at two chairs facing his desk.

'Commander Haggard, Deputy Head of Special Branch,' Daniel whispered as they walked to the chairs and sat down.

'Thank you, Chief Superintendent,' said Haggard.

'Thank you, sir,' said Armstrong, and left, closing the door after him.

'Thank you for coming, Mr and Mrs Wilson,' said Haggard. 'I wish to speak to you about this investigation you are carrying out into the murder of Andrew Page.'

'At the command of Her Majesty, the Queen,' said Daniel.

'Of course,' nodded Haggard. He didn't appear impressed. 'What have you discovered so far?'

'At the moment our investigation is at an early stage,' said Daniel. 'We know little more than the police are already aware of.'

'I've been informed that you visited the late Mr Page's widow,' said Haggard.

'That is correct,' confirmed Daniel.

'What did you talk to her about?'

'About her husband. As I'm sure you're aware, in order to find out why someone has been murdered it's vital to discover as much as you can about the victim in case a possible motive presents itself.'

'And did it, from what Mrs Page told you?'

'To be honest, Mrs Page wasn't very forthcoming,' said Abigail. 'We got the impression that they may not have been the very close couple she insisted they were.'

'What gave you that impression? Something she said?'

'More the way she said it. Her manner was aloof.'

'Possibly because she was in mourning for her late husband?'

'Possibly. We decided to leave deeper questioning till later.'

'I understand her brother was with her when you called. Heinrich Kurtz.'

'Yes,' said Abigail.

'You have been watching them?' asked Daniel.

Haggard ignored the question.

'What did Mr Kurtz say to you?'

'Very little,' said Abigail. 'He said hello to us, and that was about it. Mostly he stood there in silence and watched his sister as we talked to her.'

'He offered no reasons for Mr Page's death?'

'No. As we said, apart from a brief hello, I don't think he said anything. We did wonder if his command of English stopped him making conversation. He is German, we assume.'

'He is, and I can assure you his command of English is as good as yours or mine.'

'Then perhaps it might be worth our while to pay another call. We understand he's staying in England for a while.'

'Did he tell you that?'

'No. Mrs Page said that he was in England on business.'

'Did she say what business he was in?'

'She said he was a mining engineer working in South Africa.'

'Did they say which part of South Africa?'

'No.'

'The Transvaal.'

'So, you know him?' said Daniel.

'We know of him,' said Haggard. 'And, to answer your question, no, we don't think it a good idea for you to call on him again.'

'Why not?'

'Let us say he's a person of interest to us and you poking around asking him questions might make him decide to leave the country.'

'You're watching him,' said Daniel. 'Keeping him under observation. May we ask why?'

'You may ask, but we cannot say more because national security is at stake. All I will say is that we do not wish you to have any further conversations with Heinrich Kurtz.'

'And if he's there when we visit Mrs Page again, as we feel we need to, to talk about her husband?'

'We'd prefer if that didn't happen,' said Haggard.

'Perhaps you'd like to explain to the Queen when we tell her that we have been prevented from talking to Mrs Page. We are acting on her command,' said Abigail.

Haggard scowled, then frowned.

'You may talk to Mrs Page. We understand the police will be doing that as well. But we say to you the same as we've said to them: keep your questions and any other conversation solely to the topic of her husband. You are not to quiz Mr Kurtz.'

'Even if we feel he is connected to Mr Page's death?'

'He isn't,' said Haggard quickly.

Too quickly, thought Daniel and Abigail. They exchanged looks, then nodded.

'Very well,' said Daniel. 'We shall leave Mr Kurtz out of

things.' Then he enquired pointedly: 'But if we feel he might be connected in some way because of things he says to us, unsolicited?'

'Then you come and report that to us,' said Haggard. 'You are not to investigate Heinrich Kurtz.'

'Even though we have a royal command which gives us access to whosoever we wish to talk to?' asked Daniel.

'If we feel it necessary, the prime minister shall convey our wishes on this matter to Her Majesty,' said Haggard.

Later, as Daniel and Abigail walked up the stairs from the basement to the reception area, Abigail said: 'So, we've been warned off. No digging into Heinrich Kurtz. What do you propose we do?'

'We dig,' said Daniel. 'But discreetly, aware that Special Branch will be watching our every move, as well as every move that Mr Kurtz makes.'

'And what will they do if they catch us?' asked Abigail.

Daniel gave a shrug, then said, 'I suppose they could kill us.'

'Would they do that?'

'They're Special Branch,' said Daniel. 'Of course they would.'

When they reached the reception area, Daniel headed for the reception desk.

'Where are you going?' asked Abigail.

'I thought we'd see if John Feather was in. If so, we'll appraise him of Commander Haggard's interest.'

'Surely he will have already been told.'

'Not necessarily,' said Daniel.

John Feather was in, and after a message had been sent up to him, he came down the stairs to join them.

'Well, well, to what do I owe this pleasure?' he asked with a welcoming smile.

'You didn't know we'd been summoned?' asked Abigail.

'No.' He looked puzzled. 'Who by?'

'Initially, by the chief superintendent; but it turned out there was someone else who wished to see us.'

'Who?'

Daniel looked around the reception area, then said: 'It might be easier if we carried on this conversation elsewhere.'

'My office?'

'There's a risk that Armstrong might pop in if he hears we're seeing you. What about Freddy's?'

Abigail looked doubtful at the suggestion of the coffee shop that was well known for being frequented by officers from Scotland Yard. 'You don't think that's just as risky? A lot more ears to eavesdrop?'

'No, it'll be fine,' said Feather. 'It's always too noisy for people to listen in. Sometimes I can hardly hear myself.'

They headed across the road to Freddy's coffee shop. As always it was full of policemen, cab drivers, and various other locals. It was also very noisy. They ordered three coffees and found a table at the back.

'The beauty of this is that the chief superintendent's encouraged me to talk to you,' grinned Feather. 'So any reports of us getting together here will meet with his approval. So, who wanted to see you?'

'Commander Haggard,' said Daniel.

'Special Branch,' said Feather, impressed. 'You must have upset something, or someone.'

They related the substance of their meeting with Haggard, and the fact they'd been warned off from talking to Heinrich Kurtz.

'Was her brother there when you talked to Mrs Page?' asked Abigail.

'No,' said Feather. 'But even if he had been I doubt if I'd have been warned off like that. Whatever I find goes to Armstrong, so he'd pass it back to Haggard. The powers-that-be have no control over whatever you discover.'

'But we haven't discovered anything about Kurtz,' said Abigail.

'The fact that you've been warned off from looking into him suggests Special Branch know something about him.'

'But what? And is it connected to Page's murder?'

'It must be, otherwise why warn you off?' Feather frowned. 'I suppose I could always go back to see Mrs Page and hope her brother's there, and I could let you know what I find. I assume he's staying with his sister while he's in England.'

'We don't know, we didn't ask,' admitted Daniel. 'It might be worth finding out. But we don't want you putting yourself at risk over Kurtz. You still have a career at Scotland Yard to think about.'

'Don't worry, I won't go blundering in asking awkward questions about South Africa. I'll be bland. See what I can tease out without being obvious.' He looked at them inquisitively. 'Haggard mentioned the Transvaal?'

'Yes.'

'That's Boer territory.'

'Yes,' said Daniel. 'It came up when we were looking into a murder at the Ashmolean in Oxford.'

'Well, I'll see what I can find without frightening Special Branch,' said Feather. He gave a rueful sigh. 'To be honest, I was wondering where to go next with this case. So far, I've got nothing to indicate who might have wanted Page dead.'

Daniel and Abigail exchanged quizzical looks, then, when Daniel nodded, Abigail said: 'We've got a possible motive that we're looking into.'

They then told Feather what they'd picked up from Magnus Evans, and the allegations of blackmail.

'It may come to nothing, but – like you – at the moment we're clutching at straws and hoping that one of them might lead to something.'

'Have you talked to Billy Carter?' asked Feather. 'The other guard at the Victoria and Albert marquee.'

'No,' said Daniel. 'We understand from Ward, the guard we saw, that he took time off from work after the body was discovered.'

'He's afraid of ghosts,' added Abigail.

'I thought I'd call on him, see if he saw anything or anyone suspicious before he locked up for the evening,' said Feather. He finished his coffee. 'Well, so far we don't seem to be any further forward, but there are avenues to explore, which is one thing. A word of caution, though. Be careful of upsetting Special Branch.'

'Oh, we will,' Daniel assured him.

'There's another thing,' said Abigail. She reached into her bag and took out the threatening letter and passed it to Feather. 'This was pushed through our letter box.'

Feather studied it, then put it back in the envelope.

'You must be doing something right,' he said.

'Unless it's someone who saw us mentioned in the papers,' said Abigail.

'Yes, you may be right. What are you going to do about it?' asked Feather. 'Ask for police protection?'

Daniel chuckled. 'If Special Branch start following us, we'll have all the protection we need. No, we wondered if you could take it to your friendly scientist, Dr Snow, and he could check it for fingerprints.'

It had only been fairly recently that Scotland Yard had taken on board the idea of using fingerprints to identify possible criminals. At first there had been resistance from the commissioner and some senior officers, including Chief Superintendent Armstrong, who dismissed it as a foreign fantasy and a waste of time and money. The science of fingerprints had initially been developed in South America before spreading to North America and parts of Europe, before being looked at in England, albeit with great suspicion. However, as more and more cases showed the importance of fingerprints in bringing criminals to justice, there had begun to be a grudging acceptance that fingerprints really were an important tool in the fight against crime.

'Leave it to me,' said Feather, putting the envelope in his pocket. 'I'll give it to Robert Snow and let you know what he says.'

CHAPTER ELEVEN

Over breakfast the following morning, Daniel and Abigail discussed their next move.

'This business of us being warned off by Special Branch raises the issue of why?' said Daniel.

'Because there's a possible tie-up between the murder of Andrew Page and his brother-in-law, Heinrich Kurtz,' said Abigail before spooning porridge into her mouth.

'Exactly,' nodded Daniel. 'Is Kurtz the murderer, or perhaps behind the murder?'

'It's going to be difficult for us to find the answer if Special Branch are watching us,' pointed out Abigail. 'We can't question Kurtz, and the only person who knows him is his sister. And we can hardly ask her about him. If he's guilty she's going to cover up for him, especially if she's involved in some kind of conspiracy.'

'I've just thought of someone who might be able to help

us,' said Daniel. 'His name's Simeon Benton. He's quite high ranking at the Foreign Office. He might know about Kurtz. Kurtz is a foreign alien, after all.'

'Why would this Simeon Benton help us? And if Special Branch start asking him questions about why we were talking to him, we'd soon have them on our backs.'

'I met Simeon when I was working with Fred Abberline at Scotland Yard and we were investigating a murder. Special Branch were involved in that one as well, and they'd pulled in Simeon's brother, Randolph, on suspicion of being an accomplice to Irish terrorists, who they thought were behind the murder. As it turned out, Abberline and I uncovered the real murderer, who was nothing to do with terrorism of any sort. However, after the interrogation they put Randolph through, he died. As a result, Simeon has no love for Special Branch.'

'And you think he'll help us?'

'I'm sure of it. And nothing will get back to Special Branch.'

Inspector Feather returned to the marquee outside the site of the new Victoria and Albert Museum. As before, he found Stephen Ward sitting on a chair just inside the entrance to the marquee.

'Good morning, Mr Ward,' he said.

'Good morning, Inspector? Any news on the murder?'

'Not as such,' said Feather. 'I'm here to see if Billy Carter will be back at work today.'

'No,' said Ward. 'It seems he left the job.'

'Oh? Did he say why?'

'I never spoke to him myself. I was just told by Mr Tweed. There's apparently a new bloke starting tomorrow, so I'm doing all day today again. At least it'll be the last day of that. Still, I can't complain. The extra money's been useful.'

'Do you have an address for Billy Carter?'

'No, sorry. I think, like me, he lives over Paddington way, but I'm not sure where. They'll have his address in the office.'

'Thank you,' said Feather.

Simeon Benton was in his early forties, an elegant man, tall and muscular, his fashionably thick pomaded hair brushed back to show a strong face, square jaw, bushy eyebrows, and a flattened nose from his time playing rugby at Cambridge University. It was their former studentship at Cambridge that Benton mentioned when they met him in his office at the Foreign Office.

'Mrs Wilson,' he said, smiling as he shook her hand. 'Or, Miss Fenton, as was. I still recall the shock waves you sent through the old guard at Cambridge, you and the other young ladies of Girton. Some of the other men may have been suspicious of you women, but they all talked about them. Especially you. "The young woman who's going to make waves in Egyptology" I recall one of them telling me. He was quite envious of you.'

'It seems a long time ago,' replied Abigail. 'But very happy times.'

'And you, Mr Wilson,' said Benton turning to Daniel. 'It's a pleasure to see you again after all this time. I still feel a great sense of gratitude for what you did for poor Randolph.'

'Unfortunately, we couldn't save him,' said Daniel.

'But you exonerated him, saved his reputation from the criminal smears that were being made against him by those swines in Special Branch.'

'Actually, it's because of Special Branch that we are here today,' said Daniel.

'Oh?' said Benton, suddenly suspicious.

'If they found out we were asking you certain questions they'd slam us both in jail.'

'You're sure?'

'We were warned personally by none other than Commander Haggard.'

Benton's face darkened in anger. 'In that case, your secret is safe with me. How can I help you?'

He gestured to two comfortable leather armchairs for them to sit in, and took the third for himself.

'Do you know anything about a man called Heinrich Kurtz?' asked Daniel. 'He's a German, based now in South Africa where he works as a mining engineer.'

Benton smiled. 'I can understand why Special Branch don't want you sniffing around him.'

'It's a mystery to us, which we're hoping you'll be able to explain,' said Daniel.

'First, what's this to do with?'

'Kurtz is the brother of Mrs Gretchen Page, the widow of Andrew Page.'

'Ah, the body at the site where they're building the Victoria and Albert Museum.'

'That's the one,' said Daniel.

'And you think that Kurtz might be involved in his death?'

'I'm not sure. It's just that he was with Mrs Page when we met her, and there seemed to be a strange sort of atmosphere there. A wariness.'

'Guilt?'

'I don't know. There was just … something off.'

Benton nodded. 'What I'm about to tell you, you never heard from me.'

'Understood,' said Daniel.

'Mrs Page's brother, Heinrich, works for the Boer government of the Transvaal. Last year he was working for the German government and he came to London as part of a German government mission for unofficial talks with the British government in an attempt to forge an Anglo–German alliance. They met with Joseph Chamberlain, the Foreign Secretary.' Benton gave Daniel a rueful look. 'Apparently the talks did not go well.'

'I'm surprised,' said Daniel. 'I would have thought that as Germany's Kaiser Wilhelm is Queen Victoria's grandson there would have been a family basis for some kind of friendly alliance.'

'Yes and no. Although Wilhelm claims he is passionately fond of his grandmother, there is ample evidence to suggest his fond feelings do not extend to the rest of the British side of his family, nor to Britain as a nation. Do you know about the Jameson Raid and the Kruger telegram?'

'No,' said Daniel.

'Strange, I thought everyone knew about the Jameson Raid, even if they were unaware of the Kruger telegram. In 1884, gold was discovered in the Transvaal, a Boer republic in South Africa. It made Transvaal the richest nation in southern Africa. The problem for the Boers was that they were basically an agricultural people without the wherewithal to develop the gold fields. As a result, they imported immigrants from Britain to work them. These English-speaking immigrants were known as Uitlanders. In 1895 there was a plot by Cecil Rhodes, the prime minister of the British Cape Colony in South Africa, and a gold magnate, to take control of the Transvaal. A party of six hundred armed men, mainly Rhodesian and British South Africa policemen, under the leadership of Leander Starr Jameson, who was the administrator in Rhodesia of the British South Africa Company of which Rhodes was chairman, came across the border from Bechuanaland aiming to take Johannesburg by force. The hope was that this invasion would result in an uprising in support of the invaders by the British Uitlanders, and the Transvaal would fall into British hands.

'However, it seems that someone had tipped off the Transvaal authorities, because Boer commandos intercepted them before they reached Johannesburg. Sixty-five of the invaders were killed and wounded, and the rest surrendered.

'When news about the failed raid reached Germany, Kaiser Wilhelm sent the president of the Transvaal, Paulus Kruger, a telegram congratulating him on repelling the Jameson raid. He went further when he approved sending a naval cruiser to the area and putting a landing party of 50 German marines ashore to go to Pretoria to protect the Germans there from further attacks by the British. He also wrote to Tsar Nicholas of Russia proposing they form a military union against Great Britain.'

'Tsar Nicholas is another of Queen Victoria's grandsons,' pointed out Daniel.

'Indeed, but although Wilhelm professes to have nothing but admiration for the Queen, he has never been fond of his Uncle Bertie, the heir to the British throne, whom he called an old peacock.'

'Why the enmity?' asked Daniel.

'Wilhelm feels that his uncle doesn't give him the respect of being Emperor of Germany, but just treats him as a common-or-garden nephew. This rankles with Wilhelm because, in his eyes, Prince Albert Edward is just an heir to the throne, not a monarch like himself.'

'That's not much of a reason for him to take such an anti-British stance,' commented Daniel.

'It is when you talk to people who've met the Kaiser. They describe him as having an erratic personality. Unstable. He falls into deep depressions and then suddenly comes out of it and starts swaggering and raging, throwing his weight around. That's what led to the break-up with his chancellor, Bismarck. In the end, Bismarck couldn't cope with Wilhelm's erratic behaviour and resigned. Or was forced to resign.

'It's said that Wilhelm is particularly jealous of Britain's navy. He wants to build a German navy that would be superior to the British.'

'It sounds as if he's planning for a war,' said Daniel.

Benton nodded. 'Yes, there are many who take that view. There are rumours that he's already arming the Boers because he believes there's another war coming in South Africa between the British and the Boers, and he is placing Germany emphatically on the side of the Boers.'

CHAPTER TWELVE

After they left the Foreign Office, Daniel and Abigail walked along the Embankment until they found a vacant seat where they could sit and look at the Thames, and talk about what they'd learnt from Simeon Benton.

'Gretchen Page's brother is working with the Boers,' said Daniel. 'There's already talk of a new Boer War. Say her brother has got some sort of spy set-up, or even saboteurs, to undermine Britain's war efforts? And Page found out about it.'

'The Boers would feel the need to silence him,' said Abigail.

'The Boers, or the Germans,' said Daniel. 'This is getting very complicated.' He looked thoughtful. 'And there's still the business of Page's wealth. How could a curator afford the kind of lifestyle he was living? We keep coming back to either blackmail or some sort of fraud.'

'There's one person who might know,' said Abigail.

'His solicitor,' said Daniel.

'Exactly,' said Abigail. 'Do you think we ought to share what we learnt about the Boers with John Feather?'

'I'm not sure,' said Daniel. 'I suppose we ought to, but he'd have to tell Chief Superintendent Armstrong, and he in turn would feed it back to Haggard, which would bring Special Branch down upon us, and possibly on Simeon.' He gave a weary sigh, then said: 'Let's talk to Page's solicitor first and see what he has to say; then we'll decide what to tell John.'

John Feather knocked at the door of the small terraced house in a backstreet behind Paddington Station, the address he'd been given by the Victoria and Albert Museum. It was opened by a small wizened and untidy man in his fifties who looked out at him suspiciously.

'Inspector Feather from Scotland Yard,' said Feather, holding out his warrant card for the man's inspection. 'Are you Mr Billy Carter?'

The man nodded.

'May I come in?'

'What's it about?' asked Carter.

'The recent murder at the Victoria and Albert Museum. I believe you were a guard there until yesterday.'

'I was,' said Carter. Reluctantly, he stood to one side and said: 'You'd best come in. Don't want the neighbours talking.'

Feather stepped into a small living room that came straight off the street. It was cramped and furnished with shabby old chairs and a rickety table, which was supported by a brick under one leg.

'Lucky you called today,' said Carter. 'I start my new job tonight as a nightwatchman, so tomorrow morning I'll be in bed.'

'What prompted you to leave the museum?' asked Feather. 'Mr Ward suggested that you didn't like being where a dead body had been left.'

'Yeh, well, there might be something in that.'

The shifty way he said it caused Feather to ask: 'But there might be something else?'

Carter hesitated, then said: 'If you must know, I wondered about Wardy.'

'Wardy? Mr Ward?'

'Yes.'

'What did you wonder about him?'

Carter hesitated, obviously uncomfortable, then said: 'I wondered if he'd had anything to do with it.'

'With killing Mr Page?'

'Maybe.'

'Why would Mr Ward want to kill Mr Page?'

'Because of his daughter.'

'Mr Ward's daughter?'

'Yes.'

Feather looked at Carter with a puzzled expression.

'Mr Carter, I think you'd better start at the beginning. What did Mr Page have to do with Mr Ward's daughter?'

'Well, he romanced her.'

'Romanced her? You mean, he seduced her?'

'I don't know if it went that far. All I know is he used to take Mary – that's Wardy's daughter – out for a while. And then suddenly he stopped doing it. She was heartbroken. Wardy was livid. Swore he'd have his revenge.'

'He said that to you?'

'No, not to me. To be honest, me and Wardy never talked

much about anything. We just handed over when we changed shifts. No, I heard this from a bloke called Dixie who was a drinking pal of Wardy's. He's on his own and he used to call in to the marquee when I was on my afternoon shift for company.'

'He came to see you rather than Wardy for company?'

'Only now and then. Anyway, it seems that Mr Page was around when Wardy's daughter called to see him one day. By all accounts, he was taken with her, and she was certainly taken with him. He invited her to have tea with him, and then lunch, and then sometimes they'd go for a walk in the park or by the river.'

'I assume that Ward knew that Page was married?'

'Yes, but Mary told him that he was getting a divorce, and when he was a free man, she was sure they had a future together.'

'Didn't Ward have his suspicions?' asked Feather. 'After all, he'd surely seen enough to make him wary of promises like that made to a young girl.'

'Well, he was dubious at first, but then he started to believe it. According to Dixie, that is. Like I say, he never said anything about it to me.'

'And you never said anything about it to him after Dixie had told you?'

'It wasn't my place. And Wardy's got a bit of a temper, and if I'd mentioned it, he might have taken offence and belted me one.'

'He's hit people before?'

'Not often. When someone's upset him.'

'So, you thought that Ward had killed Page in revenge for letting his daughter down.'

'It occurred to me, yes. And if he had, I didn't want to be

around. If Dixie told him that he'd told me about Page and Mary, he might start thinking that I might open my mouth about it. And he might decide to do me.'

'So you left because you were scared of what he might do to you? Nothing to do with ghosts?'

'Well, there's that as well. But mostly it was not wanting to be around Wardy.'

CHAPTER THRTEEN

Andrew Page's solicitor had been William Handsworth. Handsworth sat at his desk and reread the letter from Sir Anthony Thurrington before passing it back to Daniel.

'Usually, I would have to use client confidentiality to avoid answering questions about my client, even from the police, but an order from Her Majesty the Queen, plus the fact that my client is deceased, means I feel free to answer your questions.' He gave a light smile as he added: 'Also, because I fear my refusal might well end up with me in the Tower. I know beheading is no longer in use when one denies a monarch's order, but it does not do to upset the palace.'

'Thank you, Mr Handsworth,' said Daniel. 'Our main questions are about his financial affairs. We noticed that for someone on a curator's salary, he seemed to live quite an expensive lifestyle. His house, for one thing. A very large property in a very expensive area of London.'

'That I can answer without needing to look in the records,' said Handsworth. 'Mr Page was fortunate in that some three years ago a great-aunt of his died. She was a very wealthy woman and Mr Page was her only heir. Consequently, he inherited the house in Belgrave Square from her. He also inherited a share portfolio worth a great deal of money.'

'When you say a great deal?' queried Abigail.

'In the region of a quarter of a million pounds.'

Daniel and Abigail stared at him, stunned by this news.

'You did say a quarter of a million?' said Daniel.

'That was the value three years ago, when he inherited them. I believe they will have risen in value since then.'

'My God,' said Daniel, still awed as they left the solicitor's offices and stepped out into the street. 'A quarter of a million! *And* that huge house!' He groaned. 'Life isn't fair. Why didn't I have a great-aunt who left me rich?'

'Because you were an orphan and your family were extremely poor,' said Abigail. 'I think we can safely rule out financial gain on Andrew Page's part behind his death.'

'But not the possibility that he discovered someone else had their hand in the museum's till,' pointed out Daniel. 'Also, a quarter of a million pounds makes a very strong motive for murder.'

'His wife, you mean?'

'Who is now a very rich widow.' He looked at his watch. 'We're not far from Scotland Yard. Shall we see if John Feather's in?'

'You've decided to tell him what Simeon Benton told us?'

'If I can do it without creating trouble for us with Special

Branch. But at least we can tell him the financial news. A quarter of a million! Ye gods!'

They arrived outside Scotland Yard's main entrance just as Inspector Feather was climbing the stairs to it.

'John!' Daniel hailed him. 'This is very timely.'

'Have you been summoned again?' asked Feather.

'No, we were coming to see you, and here you are.'

Feather hesitated. 'Actually, I was planning to come to see you later.'

'Oh?'

'Some interesting information has come up.' He looked apprehensively towards the reception area. 'I was just about to go and see the chief superintendent with it, but before I do, I'd rather share it with you and get your opinion.'

'Freddy's?' suggested Daniel.

'I've had a lot of coffee today. Let's take a walk and find a bench.'

They walked to where there was a small area of public garden railinged off from the street. A few people were sitting in the square, taking the air, and Daniel, Abigail and Feather managed to find an empty bench.

'I've just come from Paddington,' Feather told them. 'I saw Billy Carter, the other guard who was on duty at the marquee the day Page's body was discovered.' He then told them what Carter had told him, about Page romancing Stephen Ward's young daughter; and possibly being responsible for the murder.

'I'm not saying that Ward did it, but what Carter told me has raised questions I think he ought to be asked.'

'Angry father kills the man who disgraced his daughter, then dumps the body in the marquee and claims he found it there?' said Abigail.

'That sums it up, but there are other questions we need the answers to if that's what happened. How did Ward move the body? What help did he have?'

'You think he had help?'

'As far as I know he doesn't own a cart, and I can't believe the body was transported to the site in a hansom cab. Unless the driver of the cab was an accomplice.'

'Perhaps Ward lured Page to the site and killed him there, and then cleared up the blood?' suggested Daniel.

'It's possible,' said Feather. 'In which case the site will need to be examined with a fine toothcomb to find any traces of blood. Because, if that's what happened, they'll be there. You know how arterial blood sprays when a throat is cut. It's possible the killer scattered the gravel to cover up any blood, but if it's there we'll find it. I think I have to mount a search of the site before I question Ward.'

'The concern is that if you mount a search of the site and Ward is guilty, he might decide to make a run for it before you question him,' cautioned Daniel.

'The other concern is that if I start a search of the site, I'll need to tell the chief superintendent why I'm using such a large squad of men for it, and once he hears about Ward's anger at Page over his daughter, he'll insist we arrest Ward,' said Feather. 'He's desperate to get a quick result on this.'

'You may be arresting an innocent man,' warned Abigail. 'Just because you find traces of blood elsewhere at the site, it doesn't mean that Ward was the murderer. Someone else could have lured Page to the site, killed him; then dragged the body to the foundation stone.'

'True,' said Feather. 'But who?'

'Someone who knew of Ward's anger at Page and used it, knowing that we'd find out about it once we started digging.'

Feather groaned. 'This is making my head ache,' he admitted. 'By the way, I had a report from Dr Snow on that threatening anonymous letter. The paper is the sort of cheap everyday paper that's available everywhere. Yes, there were fingerprints on it, but until the day arrives when there's a list of people and their different fingerprints, the only way to match them is if you've got someone you suspect and you take their fingerprints and see if they're the same. So, I'm afraid there's no joy there. But you said you were coming to see me. What news have you got?'

'If there was any financial chicanery happening at the museum, Page needn't have got involved. He was rich.'

'How rich?'

'He inherited shares worth a quarter of a million pounds, plus that house in Belgrave Square.'

Feather stared at them.

'A quarter of a million?'

'That's what I said,' said Daniel. 'And in that same incredulous tone of voice.'

'My God,' said Feather. Then his tone hardened as he said: 'What a motive for murder!'

'Daniel said that as well,' said Abigail. 'Also, in that same tone of voice.'

Inspector Feather's mind was in a whirl as he entered Scotland Yard, reflecting on what Daniel and Abigail had told him about Andrew Page's worth. A quarter of a million, plus the huge house in Belgravia. It was certainly a motive for murder, implicating Page's widow. But his immediate problem would be explaining to Chief Superintendent Armstrong his need for men to carry out a detailed fingertip search of the site inside the marquee at the Victoria and Albert. From his experience of the chief superintendent, he was concerned that Armstrong would immediately leap to the conclusion that Stephen Ward should be arrested and charged with the murder, especially once he'd heard the story Billy Carter had told. That was the way the chief reacted when he was under pressure from above, and there was no doubt he was under enormous pressure in this case, with the Queen herself taking an interest.

It was with a heavy heart that he knocked at the chief superintendent's door.

'Come in!' called Armstrong.

Feather entered. Armstrong was sitting at his desk studying reports and looking decidedly unhappy.

'Yes, Inspector? I hope you have some good news for me.'

'There's been a development,' said Feather. He told Armstrong what he'd heard from Billy Carter, his suspicion that Ward had killed Page somewhere inside the marquee and then dragged his body to the foundation stone. 'The thing is, it's a very large site. If it happened there, the whole area needs to be explored, looking for traces of blood. Because if it did happen, there will be blood, although it may be in the gravel. So I'll need a lot of men to go through the site very carefully, examining the ground.'

Armstrong's face lit up with delight.

'So it was him who killed Page!' he exclaimed. 'The bloke who found the body! And he found it because he put it there!'

He grinned in triumph. 'It's so often the case.'

'Not necessarily, sir. Someone else may have done it in the hope of implicating Ward.'

'Nonsense! This bloke Page seduces Ward's daughter, then leaves her in the lurch. Ward is furious. He lures Page to the site on some pretext or other and kills him. It all fits!'

'At the moment it's speculation.'

'Nine times out of ten speculation turns out to be correct,' said Armstrong firmly. 'Bring him in. Once we start questioning him, he'll crack.'

'Shouldn't we check the site for traces of blood first, sir?'

'No! Bring him in now! I'll tell the commissioner we've made an arrest, and he can tell Her Majesty. At the same time, I'll put out a press release. Case solved in record time, and we get the credit.'

'I still feel we need more to actually pin this on Ward,' said Feather, concerned.

'And we'll get it, once we've got him in here. Bring him in, Inspector. And well done.'

Daniel and Abigail sat in their kitchen compiling a list of possible motives for the murder, along with a list of possible suspects. There were politics in the form of a potential forthcoming war between Britain and the Boers, backed by the Germans, which pointed towards Heinrich Kurtz. Kurtz also headed the list, along with his sister, Gretchen, when it came to inheriting the money and the house. As Daniel had pointed out, a quarter of a million was worth committing murder for. When he'd been at Scotland Yard, murders had been committed over as little as ten pounds. The revelation from Billy Carter about Page and Mary Ward also brought up the issue of Page's romantic life. They knew that Page had shared a mistress, Lady Vanesa Horden, with the Prince of Wales, which raised the question: how many other women had he been involved with, and were any of their husbands or relatives incensed enough by it to want to kill him? And there was still the matter of the shiftiness of Raphael Wilton when they'd talked to him. There was definitely something there to be looked into.

They were interrupted in their deliberations by the arrival of a glum-looking Inspector Feather.

'What's happened?' asked Abigail when she saw his miserable expression.

'Armstrong has ordered the arrest of Stephen Ward for the murder. I wanted to tell you before you saw it in the papers tomorrow morning.'

'Armstrong's gone that far?'

'Yes. He's issued a press release, which he sent round by messenger to every paper in Fleet Street. He's going to tell the commissioner and get him to inform the Queen.'

'And we'll get removed from the case,' said Daniel ruefully. 'Case closed.'

'But it's not,' protested Abigail. 'There are various other issues at play here, any of which could be the motive for Page's murder. This business of the Boers and the Germans.'

'What business of the Boers and Germans?' asked Feather.

'We weren't going to tell you until we were sure.'

'And now you are?'

'Not really,' Abigail admitted. 'Then there's the possibility that Page had uncovered some financial skulduggery.'

'And there's a quarter of a million, plus the house for the

widow. Who, as you pointed out, is not necessarily grieving,' added Daniel.

'How sure are you of Ward's guilt?' asked Abigail.

'I'm not,' said Feather. 'I still have yet to talk to this friend of Ward's called Dixie, but Armstrong insisted we move at once.'

'Who's Dixie?' asked Daniel.

'Someone Billy Carter told me about. He's the one that Ward talked to about Page and his daughter, and apparently the one who Ward told he'd kill Page.'

'Did you check the site for traces of blood?' asked Daniel.

'No,' said Feather. 'I told Armstrong I wanted some men to do that, but he told me to do that later, after we'd arrested Ward. We're doing the search tomorrow.'

'And if you don't find any traces of blood?'

'That won't matter to Armstrong. He's dead set on us having an arrest,' sighed Feather gloomily.

CHAPTER FOURTEEN

The next morning Daniel went to the newsagents and bought a copy of every newspaper. All of them bore the same banner headline: MUSEUM KILLER CAUGHT.

The story went on to say that Stephen Ward, a security guard at the Victoria and Albert Museum, had been arrested and charged with the murder of Andrew Page, the curator whose dead body had been found at the site. The piece carried a quote from Chief Superintendent Armstrong: 'This is a triumph for honest policing. We have brought the perpetrator of this heinous crime to justice in a record time.'

Some of the papers, notably *The Times* and the *Telegraph*, went on to add that they had requested an interview with the chief superintendent, but, so far, he had not been available. Most of the papers also went on to say that they would be talking to the Museum Detectives, Daniel and Abigail Wilson, to get their opinion on the arrest.

'Which seems a good enough reason for us to get out of the house before they descend on us,' said Daniel.

'Where to? They'll be scouring the streets for us,' pointed out Abigail.

'Buckingham Palace,' said Daniel. 'We need to talk to Sir Anthony Thurrington.'

As they left the house, they saw a hansom cab at the kerb from which Joe Dalton was descending.

'Wait!' he called. 'I need your comments on this arrest.'

'And you shall have them,' Daniel assured him. 'But first we have to talk to the palace.' He gestured at the hansom. 'Perhaps you'd give us a lift there and we can talk on the way. Although, I have to warn you, Joe, much of what we say will be "no comment", until we've seen our employer.'

'You're going to see the Queen herself?' asked Joe.

'Her emissary,' said Daniel.

'Sir Anthony Thurrington?'

'The very man.'

'In that case, climb aboard.'

Dalton rattled out their destination to the cab driver. If he was impressed to be going to Buckingham Palace he didn't show it, just flicked his whip over the head of his horse and the cab moved off.

Sir Anthony Thurrington gave a winsome smile of apology as Abigail and Daniel were show into his office. On his desk were copies of the day's newspapers.

'I see an arrest has been made,' said Thurrington. 'It appears the case is solved. And by the police.'

'We have doubts about that, Sir Anthony,' said Abigail.

'Oh?'

'This man Ward had a reason for hating Andrew Page, but we wonder if he would have deliberately left the body at the site when he was aware that he would be under suspicion once the truth about Page and his daughter came out.'

'Perhaps he had no choice,' said Thurrington. 'He killed Page in a rage and was then faced with the problem of a dead body to dispose of. So he left it there.'

'That's certainly possible, but we feel it needs further investigation. It would be wrong if an innocent man was convicted and hanged because the prosecution was pushed through without a proper in-depth examination.'

'The police seem satisfied.'

'Which means they will not be investigating any further. We know Chief Superintendent Armstrong, and we know that he has a penchant for arriving at conclusions, which, although they seem to fit the superficial facts, often don't hold up when looked at in greater detail.'

'That is a serious allegation, Mr Wilson.'

'It's not intended to be, Sir Anthony. It's based on many years of close observation of the chief superintendent and his methods when we've worked on the same cases.'

'We believe he is well-meaning and honest, but he has a tendency to let his desire for a speedy result sometimes cloud his judgement,' added Abigail.

'And you think this is one of those occasions?' asked Thurrington.

'We believe it might be.'

* * *

Heinrich Kurtz threw down the newspaper he was reading with a scowl.

'It seems the police have arrested a man for Andrew's murder,' he said.

'You are not pleased?' asked his sister, Gretchen.

'I am not pleased with the way they have done things,' said Kurtz. 'The proper course of action is to inform you first, as his widow, before putting it in the pages of the newspapers.'

'Perhaps that Inspector Feather will call on me later,' said Gretchen.

'Unless it is all a ruse to lull us into a false sense of security,' said Kurtz. 'A false story, which the police will later deny.'

'The newspapers quote this Chief Superintendent Armstrong,' said Gretchen. 'He cannot go back on this.'

'I do not trust them,' said Kurtz. 'They are watching us. Their Special Branch are watching *me*.' He scowled again. 'It is becoming impossible for me to carry out my mission.' He looked pointedly at his sister. 'You will have to carry out the next assignment.'

'I cannot,' she protested. 'I am a widow in mourning.'

'In mourning?' said Kurtz sarcastically. 'For a man who cheated on you? Who whored with other women?'

'For a man who left me a great deal of money,' said Gretchen defiantly. 'Which will further our cause in a way that was not possible before. I will not do things that might arouse suspicion about me and put that money at risk. Find someone else to carry out your assignments.'

When Sir Anthony Thurrington was summoned to the Queen's private rooms, he found she was being attended by Sir James

Reid, her personal physician. Sir James accompanied Victoria everywhere she went: to Balmoral, to Osborne House on the Isle of Wight, to Windsor, and currently he was in attendance at Buckingham Palace. Every morning, Sir James examined the Queen, checking the state of her heart and lungs, her pulse, enquiring how she had slept the previous night. If she had suffered a bout of insomnia, he gave her a dose of chloral hydrate to help her sleep the following night. If her arthritis was troubling her more than usual, he gave her the sedative Trional. She was frail, but for a woman of her age she appeared to Sir James to be remarkably robust.

The Queen's Munshi, Abdul Karim, was usually present during these examinations, as he was today. At first, in the early days of his appointment, Sir James had been suspicious of the Munshi and had questioned why the man seemed to be omnipresent around the Queen. He'd felt there was something suspicious about the man, just as the Queen's older children had expressed that opinion, but as the years had passed, he'd come to accept the fact that Victoria seemed to need the support of the man. And if it sustained her, then who was he to argue with it.

He picked up his medical bag as Thurrington entered and stood, waiting to address the Queen.

'All done, Sir Anthony,' said Sir James. 'Her Majesty is all yours.'

Sir James bowed to Victoria, then left.

'Sir Anthony,' said Victoria. 'You have news?'

'Mr and Mrs Wilson have been to see me, ma'am.'

'About the arrest of this man, Ward? I saw the reports in the newspapers.'

'Yes, ma'am. It seems they have reservations.'

'About the guilt of this man?'

'Yes, ma'am.'

'They think he's innocent of the crime?'

'No, ma'am. But they are not convinced of his guilt. They feel further investigations are needed.'

'Might that be a waste of public finances?'

'They are prepared to forgo their fee if they are proved wrong in their doubts, and Mr Ward can indeed be proved to be guilty. Their concern seems to stem from preventing a miscarriage of justice, in which an innocent man is found guilty of a crime he did not commit.'

'And they think it likely in this case?'

'As I say, ma'am, they have reservations.'

Victoria sat in pensive silence for a moment, then turned to Abdul Karim and asked: 'What do you think, Munshi?'

Karim, for his part, turned and asked Thurrington: 'These people they call the Museum Detectives have been involved in police investigations before, I believe.'

'That is correct, Munshi,' said Thurrington.

'And I understand, from what was said in the pages of the press, that on some of those occasions, the Museum Detectives proved that the police had made an error in arresting a suspect, who these Museum Detectives subsequently proved to be innocent?'

'Again, that is correct.'

'Has this led to ill-feeling between the police and these Museum Detectives?'

'There is no ill-feeling on the part of Mr and Mrs Wilson, nor from most of the police force towards the Wilsons. I have made enquiries and it appears that there is a great deal of respect and friendship between Mr and Mrs Wilson and Inspector Feather of Scotland Yard.'

'But this Chief Superintendent Armstrong?' asked Karim. 'I recall seeing in the press on those previous occasions that he was compared unfavourably to the Museum Detectives.'

'Yes, that is true.'

Karim turned to the Queen. 'I believe it is worth allowing these Museum Detectives to continue with their investigation, Your Majesty. If they confirm that Mr Ward is guilty, that will be fine. If, on the other hand, they are able to show that another person committed the murder, then an innocent man will have been saved from death.'

'Wise words, Munshi,' said Victoria. She turned to Thurrington. 'You have my instructions, Sir Anthony.'

CHAPTER FIFTEEN

Chief Superintendent Armstrong stared at Sir Edwin Bratt, Commissioner of Police, in a mixture of horror and stupefaction.

'She's *what*?' he said.

'*She* is the cat's mother,' Bratt corrected him sharply. 'We are talking about Her Majesty the Queen.'

'Yes, all right. But you're saying the Queen still wants that pair of amateurs, the Wilsons, to carry on poking their nose into the case? Even though we have the culprit under lock and key!'

'Her Majesty summoned me to her presence not an hour ago and expressed her wish that Mr and Mrs Wilson be allowed to continue with their investigation.'

'Why? It's an open and shut case!'

'Not in the Queen's view. She has asked that we do not proceed further with the case against Mr Ward until the Wilsons have satisfied themselves that he is, indeed, guilty.'

Armstrong did his best to contain the rage that boiled inside him.

'So we, the official police force, Her Majesty's own constabulary, are being overridden by this pair of amateurs! It's intolerable!'

'Nevertheless, Chief Superintendent, those are Her Majesty's wishes, and we must abide by them.'

With that, the commissioner left. Armstrong glared at the closed door, anger raging through him.

'When this is over and Ward goes on trial and hangs, I shall make sure every paper in this country knows that pair interfered with our investigation in this way. I shall have them shown up for the amateurs they are! I will tear their reputations to shreds!' He gave a harsh scornful laugh. 'The Museum Detectives? When this is over they won't be allowed near a museum of any sort.'

Abigail opened the envelope that had just been hand-delivered by messenger.

'It's from Sir Anthony Thurrington,' she told Daniel. 'He says Her Majesty has approved our continuing with our investigations.'

'I wonder if Chief Superintendent Armstrong has been informed,' mused Daniel.

'I'm sure he has,' said Abigail. 'Sir Anthony adds that Her Majesty has advised the Commissioner of Police, Sir Edwin Bratt, of this decision.' She smiled as she handed the letter to Daniel for him to read. 'I'm sure Sir Edwin has told the chief superintendent.' She laughed. 'I bet Armstrong almost exploded when he heard the news.'

'The trouble is we've now made a rod for our own backs,'

said Daniel doubtfully. 'If we're wrong and the press get wind of it, and Armstrong will make sure they do, our reputation will be shot.'

'You don't think we were wrong to express our doubts?' asked Abigail.

'No,' said Daniel. 'I think Armstrong was being too premature. But the police might be right. Ward might be the one who killed him. And now we're going to have to spend a lot of time on looking into whether Ward is guilty or not.'

There was a ringing of their doorbell.

'John Feather?' hazarded Abigail. 'He must have been told.'

She opened the door, and found herself looking at a frightened and agitated girl of about seventeen.

'Mrs Wilson?' asked the girl.

'Yes,' said Abigail.

Daniel appeared behind Abigail, caught by the panic in the girl's voice.

'This is my husband, Mr Wilson.'

'I'm Mary Ward. Stephen Ward's daughter. I've come to beg you to stop my dad being hanged. He didn't do it. He didn't kill Mr Page.'

'I'm sure if there's any evidence of his innocence it will come out at his trial.'

'That's the thing, he shouldn't even be put on trial! He didn't do it. And I can prove it!'

They looked at the girl, then exchanged wary looks. She seemed sincere, but of course she would do if she was set on obtaining her father's freedom.

'It'd be better if you came in and we talked in comfort,' said Abigail.

They showed Mary Ward into their living room.

'Would you like anything?' asked Abigail. 'Tea?'

'No,' said Mary. 'I just want to tell you my dad's innocent. He didn't do it.'

'You said you could prove it,' said Daniel, sitting down opposite the girl. 'How?'

Mary hesitated, looking at them both nervously, as if weighing up if she could trust them. 'If I tell you something, I want you to promise you won't tell anyone else.'

'If it's evidence that will save your father, that's going to be difficult,' said Daniel. 'The police will have to know, for one thing. They're the ones who've arrested him.'

Mary hesitated, biting her lip, worried, then she said: 'But only the police. No papers, nothing like that.'

'Why don't you tell us and we'll see what we can do,' said Abigail. 'There are ways round this.'

Mary hesitated, then she said: 'The police say that Dad killed Andrew – Mr Page – and then put his body by the foundation stone and then pretended he'd found it when he went to work.'

'Yes,' nodded Abigail. 'That's what they believe.'

'Well, he couldn't have!' exclaimed Mary. 'He was at home all the night before he went to work, and when he went …' She hesitated, then said awkwardly. 'He took someone with him.'

'Who?'

'Mabel Jenks, next door.'

'Mabel Jenks?'

'She's our next-door neighbour. Dad's keen on her, although he don't say as much. But he can't really, seeing as she's married. Her husband's a sailor away at sea. The last thing he'd do is say that he took Mabel with him when he went to work because word was sure to get back to Ernie, that's her husband, and there'd be hell to pay.'

Daniel and Abigail again exchanged glances, then Daniel said: 'Let me make sure I've got this right. The night before your dad found Mr Page's body at the museum, he was at home all night with you.'

'That's right,' said Mary. 'He went to bed before I did, and he was there all night.'

'The following morning, he went next door to call for Mabel Jenks and took her to work with him?' asked Daniel, just to make sure he had things right.

Mary nodded. 'He wanted to show her the foundation stone. He knew she'd be impressed because so far only the high and mighty and posh people had seen it.'

'So she was with him when he went into the marquee and found Mr Page's body?'

'Yes.'

'And what did Mrs Jenks do?'

'She ran off. Dad told her to. He said it wouldn't be good for her, or for him, if it was found that he'd brought her to see the stone and she was with him when he found the body. He told her to go home and forget she'd ever seen it. He knew there'd be big trouble if it got out he'd brought her with him. Ernie would think there'd been something going on between them.'

'And had there been anything going on between them?'

'Oh no!' said Mary. 'I know Dad would have liked there to be, and I think Mrs Jenks wouldn't have been unhappy about it. But Ernie would have been, and when Ernie gets mad, he gets dangerous.'

'We need you to tell this to a policeman friend of ours, Inspector Feather,' said Abigail.

'Oh no!' said Mary, horrified at the thought. 'Can't you tell him?'

'It'll have more impact coming from you,' said Daniel.

'And we can promise you, Inspector Feather is a kind man,' added Abigail. 'He won't shout at you or anything like that.'

'And he's the person who's got to be convinced of what you've told us if we're going to get your father released,' said Daniel.

Abigail looked at the clock on the mantlepiece. 'He should be at home now. We'll take you to him.'

Feather was at home alone when Daniel and Abigail arrived with Mary.

'Vera's taken the kids to see her cousin,' he told them. 'Come in.'

As they walked into the house, he looked at Mary and asked: 'Who's this?'

'Mary Ward,' said Daniel. 'The daughter of Stephen Ward.'

Feather stopped and stared at them, then at the girl, then back at them again.

'Why?' he asked.

'Because she's got something to tell you,' said Abigail.

'In that case you'd better come into the kitchen and I'll put the kettle on while we sit down.'

'No, thanks,' said Mary. 'I don't want anything.'

'She just wants to tell you her story.'

They went through to the kitchen where they sat down, and

Mary told Feather what she'd told Daniel and Abigail. When she'd finished, Feather let out a groan. 'If this is true, the chief superintendent is going to go mad.'

'It is true,' said Mary passionately.

'I'll have to talk to this Mrs Jenks,' said Feather. 'To get confirmation.'

'I don't know about that,' said Mary uncertainly.

'It's necessary if you want to get your father out of prison,' said Daniel. 'It'll be the one thing that will do it.'

'We'll come with you,' said Abigail. 'We'll talk to her.'

Feather let out a heartfelt sigh. 'We might as well go and see her now. Get it over with.'

Out in the street, they hailed a hansom cab, which took them to Paddington and Mrs Jenks's house. Mary knocked at the door, which was opened by a middle-aged plump woman wearing an apron dusted with flour. She'd been obviously in the middle of baking.

'Mary!' said Mrs Jenks in surprise. She looked at the two men and one woman with Mary, puzzled. 'Who's this?'

'Inspector Feather, ma'am, from Scotland Yard,' said Feather, doffing his hat.

'Daniel and Abigail Wilson,' said Daniel. 'We've been commissioned by Her Majesty, Queen Victoria, to look into the murder at the Victoria and Albert Museum.'

'They know you went with Dad to the museum on the morning he discovered the body,' said Mary.

Mrs Jenks looked flustered. 'He said he'd never tell!' she burst out in alarm.

'He didn't,' said Mary. 'I did.' She looked appealingly at the woman. 'They'll hang him, Mrs Jenks, if you don't speak up.'

'But-but-but . . .' she burbled helplessly, obviously frightened.

'Your name won't be revealed,' said Feather. 'Unless you want it to be.'

'No!' she said firmly. 'I only went along because Stephen said he'd show me the foundation stone. Only the toffs and nobs had seen it before.'

'Was the curtain locked when you arrived?' asked Feather.

Mrs Jenks nodded. 'Stephen had to use a key to open it and take the bar off.'

'And then you went in?'

She nodded again. 'Yes. My God, it was horrible!' She shuddered at the memory. 'That poor man lying there, his throat cut.'

'What did you?' asked Abigail.

'I just stood there. I didn't know what to do. It was Stephen who told me to go home straight away and not tell anyone. He said he'd report it, but we'd keep secret the fact that I was there.'

'Because of your husband?' asked Feather.

Mrs Jenks glared angrily at Mary, then said defiantly: 'We weren't doing anything wrong. Only Ernie wouldn't see it that way.'

'Thank you, Mrs Jenks,' said Feather. 'Mary's quite right. By you telling us this you've saved an innocent man from being put on trial and possibly hanged. And this way your involvement doesn't have to go any further; whereas if it had gone to trial, his lawyer would have used it in Mr Ward's defence, and the tale would have come out in a glare of publicity.' He doffed his hat to her. 'We'll leave you in peace.'

'Thank you,' added Daniel.

Mrs Jenks hesitated a moment, then went in and closed the door.

'Thank you, Mary,' said Feather.

Mary turned to Daniel and Abigail. 'Thank you, Mr and Mrs Wilson, for passing it on.' She looked at Feather. 'What happens now? Will you let my dad go?'

'I have to go and see my superior and tell him this first,' said Feather. 'But once we've done the formalities, he'll be released.'

'Can I see him?'

Feather hesitated, then said apologetically: 'I really need to see my superior first. But, once that's done, we'll have your dad returned to you.'

'What about the papers?' asked Mary. 'They all had the story saying he was the murderer.'

'We'll deal with that,' said Feather. 'We'll have a retraction published.'

'A what?' asked Mary.

'A notice saying he didn't do it.'

'When will you see your boss?' asked Mary.

'I'll go to his house now and tell him,' said Feather. He turned to Daniel and Abigail.' I'd rather you weren't there when I see him.'

'Understood,' said Daniel. 'Actually, we were about to ask Miss Ward if we could talk to her.' He smiled at Mary. 'Is that all right?'

'What about?' asked Mary. 'Dad's going to be free.'

'There's still the real culprit to be found,' said Daniel. 'We'd like to talk to you about Mr Page.'

'I don't know,' said Mary doubtfully.

'If we don't find the real person who killed him, there's

always going to be talk and suspicion about your dad after the story in the papers,' said Abigail gently. 'None of us want that, and the only way to stop it is finding the real killer.'

Mary nodded. 'Yeh, All right. Come in.' She made for the door of her house, taking the front door key from her pocket. 'Now I can put the kettle on.' She turned to Feather and said: 'You will tell my dad it's going to be all right won't you, Inspector?'

'I promise,' said Feather.

CHAPTER SIXTEEN

Inside the small terraced house, Daniel and Abigail settled down with the cups of tea that Mary had made. To be frank, the tea was too strong for Daniel, who preferred his weak, but he supped at it as part of putting Mary at her ease.

'Mary, we have to ask, what was the extent of your relationship with Mr Page?' asked Abigail.

Mary blushed, then said in a quiet voice, almost defiantly: 'We were close.'

'How close?' asked Abigail.

'You're asking if we were lovers?'

'Yes,' said Abigail.

'No,' said Mary. She looked down at her hands in her lap, obviously awkward, then said: 'He wanted us to be.'

'Your dad told a friend of his that he said he was going to get a divorce and marry you.'

'Yes, that's what he said to me. But … But I said I wouldn't do that with him while he was still married.' She gave an unhappy sigh. 'I think that might be why he dropped me. Because I wouldn't let him make love to me.'

'You wanted to?' asked Abigail.

'Oh yes!' said Mary. 'But I know what some men are like. They make promises to get what they want, and once they've had it, they leave you. That's what happened to two friends of mine. In one case she was left with a baby. I decided that wasn't going to happen to me.'

'Did you love him?'

'I thought I did, but now I'm not sure. If he'd really loved me, like he said he did, he'd have got a divorce so we could be free. He said the only way he could get a divorce was if he committed adultery, and that's why he wanted to do it with me.'

'But you had doubts?'

'Yes.'

Abigail nodded. 'In my opinion, you did the right thing.'

'Even though I lost him because I wouldn't?'

'Yes,' said Abigail. 'Many men say such things at the time, and they may even believe it, but when things get difficult, when it comes to seeking a divorce, they change their minds.'

Feather felt as miserable as he'd ever felt as he rang the bell of the Chief superintendent's house. He'd seen the chief superintendent in rages before, but this one would be the equivalent of a bomb going off. And he, Inspector Feather, as the one informing him of this latest news, would be the one in the explosion range.

The door opened, and Armstrong looked at him in surprise.

'Inspector?' He looked up and down the street to see if he

could see the reason for this visit, but the inspector seemed to be all on his own.

'What's happened? Nothing's happened to Ward, has it? He hasn't escape, or anything like that?'

'No, sir, nothing like that.'

'Thank God for that!'

'But there is some new information about the case.'

'What information?'

Feather told him: about Ward and Mrs Jenks, and how Mrs Jenks had verified the story. Armstrong stared at him, stunned.

'You mean … he didn't do it?'

'He couldn't have, sir. It's the strongest alibi anyone could ever have.'

'But why didn't Ward say anything about this Mrs Jenks before?' Armstrong burst out angrily.

'He was afraid of what her husband would do if he found out.'

'And because of that he was prepared to go to the gallows?!'

'I don't think it would have come to that, sir. Mrs Jenks and his daughter, Mary, would have spoken up if that looked likely.'

For a moment Armstrong stood on his doorstep, opening and closing his mouth like a stranded fish. Then he said, in an agonised voice. 'I got the police commissioner to tell Her Majesty we'd got the person who did it. We told *the press* Ward was guilty! They'll crucify us!'

'Yes, sir,' said Feather unhappily.

Suddenly losing his temper, Armstrong pointed his finger accusingly at Feather.

'Someone's going to carry the can for this, Inspector, and it's not going to be me!'

'Yes, sir,' said Feather. 'Shall I release Ward?'

The only response from the chief superintendent was a swear word and the door being slammed shut.

'I guess that's a yes,' said Feather sagely.

Once back at home, Daniel made tea for them, weak for him, normal strength for Abigail, and they discussed Andrew Page and Mary Ward.

'He tried to sweet-talk her into bed. She wouldn't, so he dropped her,' said Abigail. 'I wonder how many other women he tried that with?'

'Plenty, according to Adrian Hegley,' observed Daniel. 'Which brings me back to jealousy or revenge as a possible motive. Mary Ward said no, other women may have said yes. Daughters, wives, with angry husbands or fathers or brothers.'

'We need to look into that aspect of his life properly.'

'We also need to look into this business of the Boers and the Germans.'

'That might be trickier with Special Branch being involved,' pointed out Abigail.

'True,' said Daniel. 'There's always the money. The possibility he discovered some kind of financial chicanery at the museum.'

'Would he have noticed? He was a very wealthy man. Which raises the same question over the allegation of blackmail. If he was doing it, it wasn't for the money.'

'It's still worth asking questions about it.'

'We've asked questions. Magnus Evans, remember?'

'But there was nothing reassuring in what he told us,' Daniel pointed out. 'He simply reinforced that it was possible. I think it's worth making enquiries at the museum. If there has been anything untoward going on there financially, the fact we're asking questions might put the cat among the pigeons.'

'So we ask, and see if anyone flinches.'

'Yes.'

Abigail nodded. 'Then let's make that our next course of action. I suggest we begin with Mr Tweed. After all, as the man in charge of the curators' department, he must have some knowledge of the museum's finances. And after him, we'll talk to Mr Wilton.'

CHAPTER SEVENTEEN

The museum was closed on Sundays, so it was the Monday before Daniel and Abigail could make their call on Herbert Tweed in his office at the museum. Tweed looked both relieved, but also very disturbed.

'Mr Wilson, Mrs Wilson. So, the murderer has been caught.' He shuddered. 'And to think it was the very man who has been working here! And he came into my office after he'd killed Mr Page, pretending to have just discovered the body! That violent dangerous man! I could have been killed!'

'There was never any danger of that, Mr Tweed,' said Daniel. 'In fact, we've just established that Mr Ward is innocent. The police should have released him by now, and we assume they'll be issuing a retraction confirming he was not the guilty party.'

Tweed stared at them, stunned. 'He was not? But the newspapers said…' He stammered silently, uncomprehending, before managing to say: 'Chief Superintendent Armstrong…'

'The chief superintendent misinterpreted some information he received,' said Abigail. 'We can assure you that Mr Ward did not kill Mr Page.'

'So … he can resume work?'

'Yes,' said Abigail. 'And I hope everyone here will be sympathetic to the awful experience he has endured, quite unfairly.'

'Absolutely,' said Tweed. 'I do thank you for coming here to inform me of this development.'

'That's not the only reason we came, Mr Tweed,' said Daniel genially. 'We've been given some information that means there's another avenue we need to explore.'

'Oh?' asked Tweed uncertainly.

'We're sure it means nothing, but, as you can imagine, as we are under instruction from the Queen herself, we have to look at every possibility.'

'Of course,' nodded Tweed. 'And what is this other avenue?'

'Who do we contact to examine the museum's finances?' asked Daniel. 'There must be an accounts department, we assume, who handle all payments and other financial transactions.'

Tweed stared at them, now obviously very uncomfortable. 'F-financial transactions?' he stammered.

'Yes,' said Daniel. 'I assume there is a department that handles the money the museum receives from the government and distributes it to various departments. The building department that handles payments to builders and other contractors. For the current construction costs. And purchases for the different departments. The exhibits the museum has acquired over the years when it's been known as the South Kensington Museum.

The expenses paid to the curators who were out gathering the exhibits from abroad.'

'And also purchasing some of the exhibits from British companies,' added Abigail.

Tweed gulped nervously. 'That means a vast amount of records to be gone through,' he said. 'The museum has been here for many years as it evolved into its present form.'

'There's no need to go that far back,' said Daniel. 'The accounts for the last year up to the present will suffice. After all, if there should be anything in the financial activity which could be behind Mr Page's death, it must be something of recent date.'

Tweed gulped again and forced an obsequious smile. 'Of course,' he said, adding apologetically: 'Although it may take me some time to locate all the records.'

'We understand,' said Daniel sympathetically. 'That's why, rather than add to your already heavy workload, we'll be happy to examine the records.'

'That may not be that easy,' said Tweed nervously. 'They're quite difficult to decipher, especially for the lay person. I, personally, wouldn't be able to understand them.'

'But you administer the funds for the curators?' queried Abigail.

'Oh yes,' said Tweed.

'Then we'll start with those. After all, as Mr Page was a curator, if there was anything amiss that he'd spotted and was reporting on—'

'He never reported anything of that nature to me,' cut in Tweed hastily.

'Perhaps he mentioned it to someone else,' said Daniel amiably.

'But the accounts really are a complicated set of documents,' said Tweed. 'As I said, they're not easy for the lay person to understand.'

'That's all right,' said Abigail with a smile. 'We'll bring in an accountant to examine them.'

'We have accountants!' protested Tweed.

'We know, but we have been asked to conduct an independent enquiry,' said Abigail.

'And it is by order of the Queen herself,' added Daniel apologetically. 'I'm sure you understand.'

'Yes, yes, of course,' said Tweed.

'We'll get back to you and arrange a date for our accountant to come in once we've seen him,' said Abigail.

Once outside the museum, Daniel and Abigail exchanged looks of amusement.

'Well, we talked about setting the cat among the pigeons,' smiled Daniel.

'I've never seen a man act more guilty,' chuckled Abigail. 'What do you think he'll do?'

'Destroy the accounts, possibly. An accidental fire.'

'He could only do that for the accounts for his own department,' said Abigail. 'The curating section. And there will be copies elsewhere in the main accounts.'

'You're very knowledgeable about account ledgers,' observed Daniel.

'I was involved in the curating accounts while I was at the Fitzwilliam,' said Abigail.

'And who's this accountant you mentioned that we'd be bringing in?'

'I thought we'd see Magnus Evans for his advice on the best person to ask. After all, it's a royal command. We'll be able to get the best.'

'The question is: if Tweed is involved in some financial skulduggery, did Page find out about it, and is Tweed capable of killing him?'

'Everyone's capable of killing someone,' said Abigail. 'And the body was found on the site inside the marquee, right next to his office. Tweed could easily have killed Page and left his body there for Ward to find.'

Daniel and Abigail had barely arrived home when a ring of their doorbell announced a visitor.

'Reporters?' queried Daniel.

'The announcement of Mr Ward's release hasn't appeared in the papers yet,' said Abigail. 'I hope John was able to persuade the chief superintendent of Mr Ward's innocence.'

The answer came as she opened the door and came face to face with Stephen Ward.

'I've called to thank you,' he said. 'Mary told me what you'd done. I can't thank you enough.'

'Do come in,' invited Abigail, and she led him to the kitchen where Daniel was catching up with the morning's newspapers.

'It's Mr Ward,' she announced. 'He has been released.'

'Excellent,' said Daniel. He got up and shook Ward's hand with a smile. 'Congratulations.'

'The congratulations have to go to you and your wife, sir,' said Ward.

'More particularly to Mary for coming to us,' said Daniel.

'Ah yes, but Mary wouldn't have been able to persuade the

police to let me go.' He looked uncomfortable as he added: 'And thank you for keeping Mabel's name out of it. We wasn't doing anything wrong, but people might get the wrong impression.'

'We understand,' said Abigail. 'And, on that subject, we talked to Mary.'

'Oh?' said Ward, suddenly wary.

'We can reassure you that nothing actually took place between her and Mr Page. Nothing of an intimate nature.'

Ward looked at them, uncertain. 'She told you that?'

'She did,' said Abigail. 'She'd have told you the same if you'd asked her.'

'I couldn't talk to her about things like that,' said Ward. 'I'm her father.'

'Even more reason why you should have,' said Abigail. 'She cares for you very much.'

'I know,' said Ward. 'And I care for her. She's all I've got since her mother died. If her mother was still here, she'd have talked to Mary about it.' He again looked unhappy as he said: 'I've now got the problem of going to work and facing the others. With nothing about me not being guilty in the papers, I might not be welcome.'

'We've been to see Mr Tweed this morning,' said Daniel. 'We've told him that you're innocent and the police will be releasing you, and publishing an apology for your wrongful arrest.'

'I still think I'll leave it till tomorrow before I go back,' said Ward, still concerned. 'By then it should be in the papers, and it'll save me getting a lot of funny looks.'

'To reassure you, just in case the police are slow in getting the information out, now we've seen you've been released, we'll send a note about it to a reporter friend of ours on the *Daily Telegraph*,' said Abigail. 'That'll make sure it gets in tomorrow morning's papers.'

'Thank you,' said Ward. He reached out a hand to shake both of theirs. 'I've never known such kindness. If I can ever do anything for you, you only have to ask.'

After he'd gone, Daniel said: 'Well, I guess that counts as our good deed for the day.'

'It will be when you write the letter to Joe Dalton telling him about it.'

'I'll do it now,' said Daniel, taking a sheet of paper from a drawer. 'And I suggest we drop it off at the *Telegraph*'s offices. If he's there, we can tell him in greater detail, and if he's not I'm sure he'll pester Armstrong for the story. And while we're in Fleet Street we can call on Magnus Evans and get the name of an accountant who might help. And then I suggest we celebrate Mr Ward's release as a victory of justice with a meal at the One Tun.'

Herbert Tweed sat at his desk looking through the sales ledger for the past twelve months, a look of such distress on his face that it bordered on panic. At first glance everything looked in order, but if an accountant began to examine them in detail and compared them with the main accounts books, he knew there would be some questions raised, especially over some entries itemised as cash payments to unnamed third parties 'for services rendered'. Fortunately, no one had ever looked at the accounts books in detail and asked him what these referred to. If they had, he'd had his story ready: the payments were for information received about an item that would make a good acquisition for the museum.

That excuse might satisfy the casual enquirer, but if anyone asked for details – namely, which particular item did it relate to; who was eventually paid money for the item to be purchased; how much was paid to that vendor, and where was the signed receipt regarding the purchase – then a competent inspector would find shortcomings. A lack of official receipts. A lack of names. A lack of a detailed description of the items in question.

I've been too casual, thought Tweed, a sick feeling coming into his stomach. When he'd first started taking money from the Curating Fund – to which he felt he was rightly due to make up for what he considered to be the unfairly low salary he was being paid, especially in view of the work he was doing as Senior Manager of the Curating Department – he'd just entered these items as unidentified 'services rendered', intending to add details later. But when it became obvious that no one was examining the ledgers in any great detail at the annual audit – after all, it was *public* money, not coming out of someone's individual pocket – he just continued the practice, confident he'd be able to satisfy any questions that might be raised. After all, the unidentified payment 'for services rendered' only appeared infrequently. At least, at first.

The problem was he'd got used to the good things the extra money could buy. So had his wife. He'd explained this extra money they had to spend as bonuses from the museum as a reward for efficiencies he'd made. For two years now things had gone smoothly. No questions, and the money had made life for him and his wife comfortable.

And now those damned Wilsons had decided to poke their noses in. An external accountant! The thought filled him with fear. What could he do? He couldn't go back now and alter the figures, especially if this independent accountant checked Tweed's accounts with the museum's main ledgers.

As he looked at the pages a feeling of desperation came over him. He'd already sent a message to his wife to tell her he'd be working late that night, but what could he do?

'Working late, Mr Tweed?'

He jumped, startled. The figure of the nightwatchman, Ross Egmont appeared in his doorway.

'Er … yes.' He gave an awkward smile. 'Paperwork. Always too much of it.'

'Can I help in any way?'

'No, I'm afraid it's things that only I can deal with.'

'Will you be here long, do you reckon?'

'I hope not, but you never know when it comes to paperwork.'

'In that case, sir, I'll get on with my rounds.' His face took on a wry expression as he said: 'It's a big old place, this museum. Or, museums, really, with so many different buildings to be gone through. And it's going to be even bigger when the work's done outside.'

'Indeed,' said Tweed. Inwardly, he thought: *Go away, you idiot. I don't want to engage in idle chatter. I've got desperately important things to do.*

'How long's the work going to take, do you reckon?' asked Egmont, and he sat down on a chair.

'I have no idea,' said Tweed. 'And you must excuse me, but I do have important work to do here, and I need to finish it tonight.'

Egmont shrugged and rose to his feet.

'It's a busy time for all of us,' he said sagely.

Then, to Tweed's relief, he ambled out of the office. Tweed

hurried to the door and locked it, stopping any other casual visitors dropping in. Not that there should be any at this time of night.

He looked again at the ledger. It was impossible. The only answer was to stop the Wilsons from getting in touch with an accountant. It was the only thing that could save him.

CHAPTER EIGHTEEN

The next morning, with breakfast eaten and the dishes washed, Daniel and Abigail were preparing to call on Wensley Pithy at his offices in the City of London, the accountant that Magnus Evans had commended to them the previous day, when there was the sound of their doorbell ringing. Abigail returned from opening it with an envelope, which she'd opened and was reading the letter inside.

'That was a messenger from Buckingham Palace,' she told Daniel. 'Sir Anthony Thurrington has invited us to come to the palace today, if it is convenient.'

Daniel indicated the front page of the newspapers, which all contained the same story: 'Victoria & Albert Museum Murder: Innocent man arrested by police is released.'

'I'm guessing he wants to talk to us about this,' he said. 'I suggest we go there first before we call on Mr Pithy.'

'Absolutely,' agreed Abigail.

On their arrival at the palace, they expected to be shown to Sir Anthony's office. Instead, Thurrington himself came to the main entrance to greet them.

'Her Majesty wishes to confer with you in person,' he said. 'She is in her private chambers.'

Daniel and Abigail exchanged looks of surprise.

'What is the protocol for seeing her in her private chambers?' asked Daniel warily.

'The same as when you met her at the audience in the throne room,' said Thurrington. 'Except today she wishes to ask you questions, so you'll have more of an opportunity to talk to her.' He smiled. 'I shall be there with you, so if you are in any doubt about anything, just look at me and I'll come to your assistance.'

'How?' asked Daniel.

'A nod or a slight shake of my head will suffice, I'm sure. But I'm equally sure that it won't be needed. The Queen is pleased with you.'

Daniel and Abigail followed Thurrington down a long corridor, then into a side corridor, finally stopping before a dark oak door, at which Thurrington knocked.

'Enter!' came a young woman's voice from within.

They walked in. Victoria was sitting in a stiff-backed large wooden chair, with Beatrice and the Munshi sitting slightly apart from her. They all gave welcoming smiles towards Daniel and Abigail, and the Queen motioned towards two chairs that had been placed opposite her.

So, today we sit, thought Daniel.

Daniel bowed and Abigail did a curtsey bob before they both sat.

'Your Majesty,' they said.

'I have summoned you because we wish to express our gratitude for work you did in saving this poor man from a grave injustice. I refer to the man who was falsely accused of the murder.

'Thank you, Your Majesty.'

'Why were you so sure of his innocence?'

'To be honest, ma'am, we weren't sure. But, at the same time, we weren't sure he was guilty,' said Daniel.

'We felt that his arrest was somewhat premature without a fuller investigation being carried out,' added Abigail.

'Which I assume you both did,' said Victoria. 'Although I notice the newspapers do not mention your part in this.'

'We could not tell the newspapers our part in this without revealing where we got our information from, ma'am,' said Daniel. 'And we had promised certain people that the information they passed to us which enabled us to aid Mr Ward's release would remain confidential.'

'You are a credit to your profession,' said Victoria. She smiled at Karim. 'As is the Munshi in his role as my adviser. It was his advice I sought when I was first advised that you had doubts following the arrest of the poor man and asked to be allowed to continue your investigation. The Munshi recommended I let you proceed.'

'We are very grateful to you, Your Majesty, and to the Munshi,' said Abigail.

'Are you any nearer to identifying the real culprit?' asked Victoria.

'We have several lines of enquiry that we are pursuing at this moment,' replied Daniel. 'I'm afraid we cannot be more specific at this time just nowbecause we don't want to raise false hopes.

But there is one that appears to have promise. We shall keep you informed through Sir Anthony, ma'am, if it seems to be leading to a satisfactory conclusion.'

'Very good,' said Victoria.

There was a bit of social chit-chat, in which the Queen enquired after their health, and then Daniel caught Sir Anthony's eye, the Queen's adviser pursing his lips and raising an eyebrow, then giving a small smile.

I hope I'm interpreting this correctly, thought Daniel. *I'm guessing our audience is over.*

By way of confirmation, Thurrington spoke in his gentle and polite tones: 'Your Majesty, I believe Sir James Reid is here.'

The Queen nodded. 'Very well,' she said. To Daniel and Abigail she said: 'Once again, I thank you for your work and hope you will be successful.'

Daniel and Abigail rose, did their slight bow and curtsey, and followed Thurrington out of the room and along the corridors to the palace entrance. They passed a man in his early fifties, balding but with a full moustache that joined his sideburns, well-dressed with a high starched collar and carrying what looked like a leather doctor's case.

'Sir Anthony,' nodded the man.

'Sir James,' Thurrington returned the greeting with a nod of his own. 'Her Majesty is expecting you.'

Daniel waited until the man had passed out of earshot, then asked: 'Sir James?'

'Sir James Reid, the Queen's personal physician,' replied Thurrington. 'He examines her every day at about this time.' He smiled at them as they walked. 'Her Majesty was genuinely impressed by your work on proving that unfortunate man innocent.'

'It seems we have the Munshi to thank for allowing us to continue,' said Abigail.

'Indeed,' said Thurrington. Then a half-smile crossed his face as he added: 'Though I don't feel he was driven by concern that an injustice was being perpetuated as much as his desire to annoy certain members of the family.'

'Oh?'

'Yes. I think I mentioned before, there are different opinions about the Munshi. Some of the family don't like him. With this poor man released after being found innocent, you are free to continue poking your noses into their business, and so annoy them.'

'Who in particular?' asked Abigail.

'Oh, I think once you start questioning them, you'll soon identify those who would prefer you not to be involved.'

Daniel and Abigail elected to catch the underground train to the City of London, in part because it was so noisy it would be hard for fellow passengers to hear their conversation. Their main topic of discussion was their visit to Buckingham Palace, and the fact it had been a far less formal meeting with the Queen than their previous one.

'We should feel flattered that she spent the time with us and praising us in person, instead of just letting Sir Anthony do it.'

'It was interesting what Sir Anthony said about the Munshi,' said Daniel. 'By the family, I assume he means the Queen's children.'

'We've already been told that Prince Albert Edward doesn't

like the Munshi, and nor does Prince Arthur,' said Abigail. From her bag she took a sheet of paper on which she'd made a list of the Queen's offspring. 'Let's look at the others. In order of age the eldest is Princess Victoria. She married German royalty and lives there. After her comes the Prince of Wales, then there was Alice, but she died in 1878. Next is Prince Alfred, who's also Duke of Saxe-Coburg and Gotha. He's been living in Germany for some years, so he can be discounted. Then there's Helena, who also married a foreign royal and is now Princess of Schleswig-Holstein.'

'Is she also living abroad?'

'No, she and her husband, Prince Christian, live at Windsor on the Queen's estate. Their address when they're in London is Buckingham Palace. Apparently, she wanted to stay in London to assist her mother, along with her sister, Beatrice.

'Next is Louise. She married the Duke of Argyll, who became Governor General of Canada. They've been living in Canada for many years.'

'So she can be excluded. How many more of them are there?'

'There was Leopold, but he died in 1884. So that leaves Arthur, who we've already mentioned as being no admirer of the Munshi; and finally, Beatrice, the youngest, who was there with the Queen again today.'

'Is Arthur still living in England?'

'Yes, in Bagshot in Surrey. Although he's spent many years going around the Empire representing the Queen on royal business: Canada and India, in particular. He also spent a great deal of time travelling around the Empire in his army role. He was Commander-in-Chief of the Bombay army, and a colonel in one of the Canadian regiments.'

'His marital situation?'

'Married to Princess Louise Margaret of Prussia. By all accounts, a happy and devoted couple. They've got three children.'

'Did any of the family know Andrew Page, as far as we know?'

'If so, there's nothing in any reports. The only one with a possible connection is the Prince of Wales, if it's true they shared a mistress.'

'I still can't believe that someone like the Prince of Wales would risk getting rid of someone because they were a love rival.'

'People do strange things when love is involved.'

'But is the prince in love with this Lady Vanessa Horden, or is she just another of his alleged conquests?'

'I suppose the only way to find out is to ask him.'

'He'll deny it.'

'Yes, but it's *how* he denies it that'll show how he feels about her. And you're good at reading people's true feelings.'

'So are you.'

'Yes, but in this case, I don't think it's a good idea for me to quiz him. I think this is one for you.'

'Why?'

'Man-to-man talk. He's going to be embarrassed as it is. He'll be even more so if a woman's there. As it is, I think there's a very good chance he'll have you thrown out on your ear once he realises the personal nature of your questions. Which, in a way, will give you an idea of the strength of his feelings.'

On their arrival at Monument station, they made their way to Wensley Pithy's offices.

'I'm sorry, but Mr Pithy is away today,' his secretary informed them after they'd shown her the letter from Buckingham Palace. 'He will be in tomorrow.'

'In that case, we'd like to make an appointment with him for tomorrow,' said Daniel.

'Certainly.' She checked the appointments dairy, then said: 'Would eleven o'clock tomorrow morning be convenient?'

'That will be fine,' they told her.

'So,' said Abigail. 'What's our next move?'

'I suppose it'll be me going to corner the Prince of Wales,' said Daniel ruefully. 'I suppose the worst he can do is have his servants throw me out.'

'Not while you have that letter giving you his mother's authority,' said Abigail. She smiled. 'Isn't it wonderful having a letter like that. It opens all doors to us.'

'Except those of Special Branch,' Daniel reminded her.

'No, they opened their doors to us because of it,' countered Abigail. 'It's just that they don't want us poking around in areas they consider sensitive.'

'Heinrich Kurtz,' agreed Daniel. 'However, if Herbert Tweed turns out to be a false course, we're going to have to talk to Mr Kurtz whether Special Branch like it or not.'

CHAPTER NINETEEN

Daniel had checked and learnt that although the Prince of Wales and his wife, the Princess Alexandra of Denmark, usually lived at Sandringham in Norfolk, while his mother was in London, the prince had decided to reside at their London residence at Marlborough House in St James's in Westminster. As Daniel approached the building, he reflected that it was a misnomer to call it a 'house'. He'd been told that it was officially listed as a mansion, but even that did not do this building justice. It was enormous, larger than a palace.

Before coming to Marlborough House he'd returned to Buckingham Palace and sought out Sir Anthony Thurrington to get the answers to some questions, namely: Would the prince be at home this afternoon? Would Princess Alexandra be at Marlborough House? Thurrington seemed the best person to answer these questions because he would know why Daniel wanted to know, and also because Sir Anthony seemed to know what all the members of the royal family were up to on a daily basis.

'Your first introduction to the prince will be meeting his private secretary, Michael Shanks. His *very* private secretary. Shanks is the prince's protector in every sense. Without that letter of authority I gave you, you would have no chance of getting past Shanks. I assume you may have questions to ask His Highness that may be of a personal nature?'

'Yes, that is so,' said Daniel.

'If, by any chance, the prince refuses to dismiss Shanks while you meet him, rest assured that there is no secret of the prince's that Shanks is not aware of.'

'Thank you. One other question: will the Princess Alexandra be at Marlborough House today?'

'No, she is currently at Sandringham.'

'That's a relief. I'd feel very uncomfortable asking her to leave while I talk to the prince in private.'

There were a variety of uniformed flunkeys on duty in the reception hall of Marlborough House, and Daniel chose the one who seemed to be in charge and showed him the letter from Sir Anthony.

'I'm here at the authority of Her Majesty the Queen to talk to His Highness, the Prince of Wales,' said Daniel.

'Yes, sir. If you will wait here.'

The man disappeared into the depths of the huge house, and reappeared a few moments later accompanied by a bulky man who sported a luxuriant pair of whiskers rather similar to those worn by the prince.

'I'm Michael Shanks,' said the man. 'The prince's private secretary. May I see your letter, Mr Wilson?'

Daniel handed the letter to Shanks, who read it, then handed it back.

'What do you wish to speak to the prince about?' he asked.

'It concerns the recent murder of Mr Andrew Page at the site of the new Victoria and Albert Museum,' said Daniel. 'My wife and I have been asked by Her Majesty, the Queen, to investigate. To that end she has authorised this letter in order that we may ask questions of everyone, including, I am advised, members of her family. But I can assure you any such conservations will be carried out with the greatest discretion and the least possible intrusion.'

This seemed to reassure Shanks, because he said: 'Very well. Follow me.'

As Daniel followed the man through the maze of corridors, he reflected that from the inside it was on a scale with Buckingham Palace, but without the pervading smell of damp.

They entered what appeared to be a large library, although Daniel noted that the books on the shelves did not appear to have been used much. Much of the decor seemed to be the stuffed heads of wild animals along with paintings of hunting and battle scenes.

The Prince of Wales was instantly recognisable to anyone who'd seen photographs of him in the newspapers, an event which seemed to happen frequently. He was a large man of almost sixty, given to fat rather than muscle. Daniel wondered if the wide sash he wore across his chest had been put on for effect, or if he regularly wore it about the house. He looked at Daniel with obvious disapproval.

Shanks moved to a large table on which papers were spread out and sat, watching Daniel and his master with a worried intensity. Daniel remembered what Sir Anthony had told him, that Shanks was the prince's protector, and wondered how far that meant. Would Shanks attack him if he felt he was being uncivil to his royal master? His expression certainly suggested that.

'You've examined this letter, Shanks?' he demanded.

'I have, sir. It is indeed an authority from the office of Her Majesty the Queen, signed by Sir Anthony Thurrington.'

The prince turned his attention to Daniel.

'Wilson, isn't it?'

'It is, sir. Her Majesty has asked me to look into the murder of Mr Andrew Page, whose body was discovered at the site of the new Victoria and Albert Museum.'

'Yes, I know about it,' snapped the prince. 'There's no need to embark on the whole history of the thing. What can I do to aid you?'

'Did you know Mr Page, Your Highness?'

'No.' The answer was not just short, it was curt, hostile.

Daniel looked towards the watching Shanks.

'May I talk to you in confidence, Your Highness?' asked Daniel.

'I thought that's what you were doing,' snapped the prince.

'I meant just us two.'

The prince glowered at Daniel. 'Anything you have to say, you can say in front of Shanks.'

'Even if the question could be interpreted as indelicate?' asked Daniel. 'Although I can assure you it is not meant to be.'

'Shanks stays,' growled the prince. He looked at his private secretary. 'That's all right with you, Shanks?'

'Yes, sir.'

The prince looked at Daniel. 'Say whatever you have to say.'

'Thank you, sir. I've been advised that you and Mr Page both shared the acquaintanceship of Lady Vanessa Horden.'

The prince's face flushed an angry red and he barked 'How dare you! Get out of my sight at once.'

Daniel nodded and made a polite bow.

'Of course, Your Majesty.'

He turned and made for the door. The prince watched him and, just as Daniel was about to exit, he shouted 'God blast you! Come back here!'

Daniel returned and stood looking at the prince, unabashed but wary, waiting for what would happen next.

'You're going to tell my mother about this, aren't you?' he snapped. 'My turning you away?'

'Her Majesty the Queen has tasked us with asking questions about Mr Page, and has informed us that she would like to be kept informed of our enquiries.' He paused, then said politely: 'I will have to tell her you were reluctant to answer.'

The prince glared at Daniel, obviously seething. Then he said: 'Go on, then, blast you. Ask your damned questions.'

'Did you know of Mr Page's acquaintanceship with Lady Vanessa?'

The prince hesitated, then said reluctantly: 'No.'

Daniel turned to the watching Shanks and asked: 'How about you, Mr Shanks. Were you aware of a companionship between Mr Page and Lady Vanessa?'

Shanks glared at Daniel, then very reluctantly forced out the words: 'Yes.'

The prince turned to look at his secretary, obviously shocked. 'You knew?'

'Yes, sir.'

'Why didn't you tell me?' demanded the prince.

'It didn't seem relevant, sir,' said Shanks through gritted teeth, his vengeful gaze on Daniel the whole time.

Daniel made a slight bow with his head.

'Thank you, sir,' he said to the prince. 'I won't trouble you any further.' He then turned to Shanks and said: 'I would appreciate it if we could talk, Mr Shanks, and you could enlighten me on your knowledge of Mr Page.' He turned to the prince and added: 'With your permission, Your Highness.'

'Yes, but not now!' barked the prince. 'Shanks and I have business to attend to.'

'Of course, sir,' said Daniel. 'I wish you good day.'

With that, he bowed again, and was about to leave when the prince stopped him.

'Wait!' he said. 'You need to be escorted. Can't have people we don't know wandering about the place. Shanks, ring for one of the servants to show Mr Wilson out.'

Daniel waited as Shanks, rang the bell pull, then issued orders, and the servant duly led Daniel out of the room and along the corridor to the entrance.

'You never told me about Page and Lady V,' said the prince accusingly.

'My apologies, sir. I refrained from telling you in case it caused you distress.'

'So the minx was playing both of us,' grunted the Prince.

'It would appear so, sir.'

'I think we have to consider removing her from our social circle,' the prince mused.

'That might be advisable, sir,' agreed Shanks.

The prince sat in deep and thoughtful silence for a few moments, then said, his voice carrying a hint of bitter anger: 'I've just remembered when I encountered that Daniel Wilson before.'

'You've met him before, sir?'

'No, Shanks, I *encountered* him before. It was during that dreadful thing where they tried to involve my poor son, Albert Victor, ten years ago. Horrible!'

'That was before I entered your service, Your Majesty,' Shanks said tactfully.

'The Cleveland Street Scandal, the newspapers called it. You don't remember it?'

'No, sir.'

'Abberline and Wilson were the investigating officers. It just came back to me when I saw him. They had Wilson's picture in the papers at the time.'

'Yes, sir.'

'It was a travesty and a tragedy,' said the Prince. 'There was a brothel in Cleveland Street that catered to men of … alternative tastes. Oscar Wilde types. It turned out that my then equerry, Lord Henry Arthur Somerset, was a client.' His face darkened as he said: 'The bastard tried to bargain his freedom by naming names, and among them he gave the police my son's name. Completely false, of course. Somerset only did it to give himself time to escape to the Continent, along with the brothel keeper. Charles Hammond, his name was. Another slimy bastard.

'Of course, the police never brought any charges against my poor son, there was nothing to Somerset's allegations. But the trauma he suffered as a result of being named, and investigated, damaged his health. He was never the same again.' He looked at Shanks, his expression grave, serious. 'He died three years later. Caught pneumonia. Broke my heart. My eldest son, Shanks. Born to be king after me.' He shook his head, angry and bitter. 'They killed him, Shanks. Somerset and Hammond with their lies. Then Abberline and that damned Wilson with their questions.'

'The police questioned him, sir?' asked Shanks, shocked.

'Not directly, but he knew questions were being asked. It broke his health. He was never strong after that.' He glared angrily at his secretary. 'And now that damned Wilson is back, plaguing and badgering me the same way he did my poor son. I will not have it, Shanks. He must be stopped. Poor Mama is very old and frail. Her physician has expressed his doubt to me that she will last another year. When that unfortunate event happens, I will be king; but I do not want my coronation to be marred by scandal and innuendo because of this Wilson character. I repeat, he must be stopped.'

'Yes, sir,' said Shanks.

'You know what I mean, I'm sure. I trust you, Shanks. You are a loyal servant. Have him stopped. For me, and for the memory of my poor departed son.'

Abigail was agog to hear how Daniel had got on at Marlborough House.

'Well?' she asked as he walked through the door. 'What happened? Did he have you thrown out?'

'No, but he thought about it[illegible],' said Daniel. 'Fear of his aged Mama made him think twice.'

'Did you ask him about Page and Lady Vanessa?'

'I did. He didn't like it, but he told me he didn't know Page, or that he was involved with Lady Vanessa Horden.'

'Do you believe him?'

'I do,' said Daniel. 'The interesting one was his private secretary, Michael Shanks, who was with us during our meeting. The prince insisted he stay. It turns out that Shanks *did* know about Page and Lady Vanessa, which came as a shock to the prince.'

'The prince could have been pretending,' suggested Abigail.

'No, I don't think so,' said Daniel. 'I'm sure his surprise was genuine. But Shanks is an awkward character. He looked at me with total malevolence the whole time. Sir Anthony Thurrington called him the prince's protector. He struck me as more like his attack dog.'

'Could Shanks have killed Page?'

'He's certainly capable of it, in my opinion. I've seen that look on his face on other men who will do anything to protect their lord and master – including murder.'

Pug Mason and Percy Smith sat in the Plume of Feathers pub in Kentish Town and clinked their beer glasses together in celebration before letting the taste of the mild ale roll over their tongues. It had been a good evening. A bloke had approached them, a well-dressed bloke. A toff, in Smith's words. He'd ordered beers for them, and then made his pitch.

'A friend of mine is having trouble with a pair of nosey people. He wants them to stop interfering in his business, but so far they don't seem to be persuaded. I've been told that you two gentlemen have a history of successfully dealing with awkward people. Would you consider being involved with them? For a price, of course.'

'Talk to them?' asked Smith.

The toff gave an unhappy sigh. 'They've been *talked* to, but it doesn't seem to have done the trick. We were thinking of something more *physical*. Something that would stop them doing what they're doing.'

'Scrag 'em,' nodded Mason.

The toff regarded him with a look of uncertainty. 'Er. If scragging means what I think it does…'

'Physical,' confirmed Smith. 'A bash over the bonce. That usually does the trick. People don't do a lot once they've had a taste of the old leaded stick.'

No,' said the toff. 'Well, that sounds acceptable.' He then produced a roll of pound notes and counted off five, which he handed to Smith.

'Each,' said Smith.

'Each?' queried the toff.

'You want the job done properly,' said Smith. 'You want 'em out of action. We're professionals at what we do. You might get someone to do it cheaper, but would they be any good? Would this couple be put off?'

The toff hesitated, then he took five more pound notes off the roll and handed those to Mason.

'Thank you,' nodded Smith. 'Now. Who is it you want scragged?'

'Their names are Daniel and Abigail Wilson. They live in a house overlooking Primrose Hill.' He gave them the address. 'My friend would like them … dealt with as soon as possible.'

'Leave it to us, guv'nor,' smiled Smith. 'Consider it done.'

With that, the toff had doffed his hat to them and left the pub.

'Just scragging?' asked Mason. 'We don't even have to take their wallets or anything?'

'Of course, we'll take whatever they've got on them,' said Smith. 'Wallet, watches, purse, whatever there is. After all, that's our dibs.' He raised his glass. 'Here's to scragging.'

CHAPTER TWENTY

The following morning, Daniel and Abigail discussed their plans for the day.

'First, we have our appointment with Wensley Pithy,' said Abigail. 'Then I suggest we talk to Lady Vanessa Horden.'

'That should be an interesting conversation,' said Daniel. 'I think it will be politic to see her without her husband in attendance.'

'Yes, so we need to find out where she goes when she's not at home,' said Abigail thoughtfully. 'Perhaps Adrian Hegley might be able to help us there.'

'The odious man,' Daniel reminded her with a smile.

'Odious but useful,' conceded Abigail.

As they were about to leave the house and walk across Primrose Hill, Abigail looked up at the sky.

'It looks like it's going to rain,' she said.

She picked up her rolled umbrella from the umbrella stand

and they set off.

'I love this place,' said Daniel. 'Living here, right next to all this open space, the grass, the trees, the fresh air. When I think of all those years living in the smoke and dust of Camden Town.'

'But you loved it,' said Abigail. 'I remember you said you felt safe there.'

'Only because it was where I'd grown up. It was familiar. But here—'

Suddenly Abigail was aware of a flurry of movement close behind them out of the corner of her eye. She turned as a heavily built man brought a leaded stick down hard on Daniel's head and he crashed to the ground with a groan. Another man, also armed with a heavy stick, brought it down towards her, but she was able to dodge to one side. As the man tried to straighten up to strike again, she rammed the pointed end of her umbrella hard into his stomach.

The man dropped his stick and fell to the grass, howling and writhing in agony. His friend looked down at him in horror, then he turned towards Abigail, an angry snarl on his face and raised his leaded stick to attack, but this had given Abigail time to pull the police whistle she always carried from her pocket, put it to her lips and let go with a series of loud shrill blasts.

'Hoy!' came a yell.

The man turned and saw the figure of a police constable running towards them, truncheon at the ready. Immediately, the man ran across the open ground, making for the road.

The constable arrived by Abigail and the fallen Daniel.

'Are you all right, miss?' he asked.

'Yes, but my husband isn't,' said Abigail. She dropped to

her knees and urgently began to check on Daniel. He was unconscious and deathly pale.

'He needs an ambulance,' she said. 'And quickly.'

The constable looked down at the moaning man who was clutching his stomach and writhing in agony.

'I know him!' he exclaimed. 'Pug Mason!'

'The ambulance!' urged Abigail desperately.

'Yes, ma'am,' said the constable. He looked down at the groaning Pug Mason.

'What about him?'

'Leave him to me,' said Abigail grimly. 'He won't get away.'

Another constable appeared, brought by Abigail's police whistle. This one was on a bicycle.

'What's happened?' he asked.

'We need an ambulance, urgent,' said the constable. 'Get to the cottage hospital.'

The constable nodded and pedalled off, while the first constable bent down and put handcuffs on the groaning Pug Mason.

Abigail knelt beside Daniel, checking to make sure his tongue wasn't blocking his airways. He was breathing, but barely.

'Stay alive, my love,' Abigail whispered urgently.

It seemed an interminable wait before the ambulance arrived. A doctor was on-board and he made a brief examination of Daniel, who still lay unconscious on the grass.

'That's a nasty gash on the head,' said the doctor. 'I'm worried in case there's been a bleed on the brain.'

The ambulance driver and the constable on the bicycle, who'd returned, lifted Daniel and carried him into the ambulance. Abigail turned to the first constable who was still standing guard over Pug Mason, and said: 'Can you get a message to Inspector Feather at Scotland Yard and tell him what's happened. I'm Abigail Wilson and this is my husband, Daniel Wilson. We're working with Inspector Feather on a case.'

'I will, ma'am. I'm just waiting for a police van to arrive so I can take Mason in. When I get to the station, I'll make sure a message is sent.'

Abigail hurried to the ambulance and joined the doctor inside. Daniel lay on a bench, pale and still unconscious.

'The hospital, driver!' shouted the doctor.

The driver cracked his whip and the horse set off at a trot, the ambulance shaking and shuddering as it rolled across the grass towards the main road.

Inspector Feather hurried into the reception area of the Hampstead Cottage Hospital, where he found Abigail sitting. She leapt to her feet as he approached her.

'I came as soon as I heard,' he said. 'How is Daniel?'

'Still unconscious,' said Abigail, biting her lip. 'The doctor's worried he might have a bleed on the brain. Do you have anything on the men who attacked us?'

'The one you caught with your umbrella has been identified as a thug called Pug Mason. He's currently behind bars, complaining about you attacking him. He's got a record of robbery with violence as long as your arm. He usually operates with another thug called Percy Smith, who I guess is the one who struck Daniel. We've put out a search for Smith. As soon as we've got him, we'll let you know.'

'This didn't come across like a robbery,' said Abigail. 'That usually means they threaten you with violence if you don't hand over your valuables. This seemed to me like a straightforward attack.'

'We'll be able to find out what was behind it once we can get Pug Mason talking,' said Feather. 'Do you think it's connected with your investigations into the murder of Andrew Page?'

'I do,' said Abigail. 'Which means we're upsetting someone badly enough for them to hire a couple of thugs to attack us.'

'Have you got any ideas who might be behind it?'

Abigail thought it over.

'There's Herbert Tweed at the Victoria and Albert. He's in charge of the curating department. We told him we'd like an accountant of our choosing to go through the ledgers because we suspected some financial skulduggery might be the motive for Page's murder. That threw him into a panic. We're fairly sure he's been skimming money off from the museum's finances.'

'And Page might have found out about it, and Tweed killed him to shut him up?'

'It's possible. And Tweed's office is right next door to the site where Page's body was discovered. Then there's Mrs Page and her brother.'

'The very wealthy widow.'

'Not just that. When we were warned off by Special Branch, we became aware that Special Branch have been keeping Mrs Page's brother Heinrich Kurtz under observation. They suspect him of being involved in some Boer plot against Britain. If Kurtz thought that Page had discovered what the plot was they'd need to silence him to protect their plans. And then there's the Prince of Wales.'

'The Prince of Wales?' echoed Feather, bewildered. 'How does he fit into things?'

'He and Andrew Page shared a mistress. Daniel went to see him to ask him about it, and he was pretty angry. At first, he tried to have Daniel thrown out. It was only when Daniel used the fact that his mother, the Queen, had given us carte blanche to question him that he very reluctantly admitted it was so. But we got the impression he didn't like the fact that we'd found out about it. We believe he's concerned about a scandal happening when he's about to become king.'

'You surely can't think that the Prince of Wales ordered the attack on you?'

'No, but Daniel thought his private secretary, Michael Shanks was perfectly capable of doing something like that. He said he was a man capable of murder.'

'But why would he want to kill Page?'

'To eliminate his lord and master's rival.'

Feather weighed this information up with a thoughtful frown.

'So, out of those three, who do you suspect is most likely behind the attack on you and Daniel?'

'I can't see it being Heinrich Kurtz and his sister. If they wanted to do something about us, they'd do it using their own people, not hire a couple of unreliable Cockney thugs. So that leaves Herbert Tweed and Michael Shanks.'

'I'm wary to do anything about either of them yet after what happened with Stephen Ward,' said Feather. 'If we have to release yet another man we've arrested, the chief superintendent will go berserk. I think it's better to wait until we get Mason talking.'

'Mason may not talk.'

'He will do once he realises he's going to be charged with the murder of Andrew Page.'

'You think this pair did that?'

'It's possible. We'll certainly use it as a lever over him.'

'It's a stretch from coming at us with leaded sticks and cutting someone's throat.'

'It's a pity we got Mason not Smith,' said Feather unhappily. 'Mason's the sharp one of the pair. Smith's the one who isn't the brightest penny in the box. I'm sure we could have persuaded Smith he's in the frame for the murder of Andrew Page. In which case he would have given us Tweed or Shanks for the attack on you and we could have hauled him in and questioned him about Page's murder. But it's going to take a bit more to get Mason to cough up.' He looked at Abigail, concerned. 'Is there anything I can get you?'

'Yes,' said Abigail. She proffered a piece of paper. 'This is a note for Wensley Pithy. He's in the City. The address is on it. We were on our way to an appointment with him when we were attacked. It's to explain the reason for us not being at his offices this morning.'

'No problem,' said Feather taking it. 'I'll see that it gets to him. What about food? Can I get you a sandwich or something?'

'Yes please,' said Abigail. 'I don't want to leave here while Daniel's still unconscious.'

'What would you like? There's a cafe just round the corner.'

'Anything,' said Abigail. She began to rummage in her purse for money to pay, but Feather stopped her. 'If I can't get you a sandwich, I'd be a pretty poor friend. I'll be back in a moment.'

He left and Abigail returned to her chair, her eyes on the stairs that led up to the wards. She so much wanted to be with him, but hospital rules forbade visitors except during certain hours, and the next visiting time was some hours away.

Oh, Daniel, she groaned silently. *Just when we've finally got the life we wanted.*

CHAPTER TWENTY-ONE

Inspector Feather sat in the interview room in the basement of Scotland Yard facing Pug Mason across a bare wooden table. Mason, in his mid-twenties, looked at the inspector with a mixture of arrogance and defiance.

'Right, an easy question to start,' said Feather. 'Who hired you and Percy to attack the man and woman?'

'I never attacked them!' retorted Mason indignantly. He frowned and asked. 'Percy who?'

'Percy Smith.'

Mason shook his head. 'Never heard of him.'

'You were seen by a police constable to attack the woman when she poked you in the stomach with her umbrella.'

'Exactly!' burst out Mason. '*She* attacked *me*.'

'Because you were trying to hit her with your stick.'

'No. I was going to her assistance.'

'What do you mean? You and Percy Smith attacked them.

Percy hit the man and the woman put you out of action.'

'I don't know who this Percy is you keep talking about. What happened, I was walking over the Hill when I saw this bloke – who I'd never seen before – smack the bloke on the head and he fell over. So I ran over to hit the bloke before he could strike the woman. But she turned round and poked me in the belly with the point of her brolly. Nearly killed me! She should be in jail, not me.'

'Why were you carrying a heavy stick?'

'I always carry one when I'm out in case I'm attacked.'

'You've been attacked before?'

Mason nodded. 'Lots of times. There are some very dangerous people out there. Like that woman.'

'So you've never seen the other man before? The one who hit the bloke and then ran off.'

'No. And how come the woman had a police whistle? That's against the law, surely. She should be in jail for that.'

'So your story is that you were coming to their help?'

Mason nodded energetically. 'That's right. That's how it was. I ought to get a medal.' He looked aggressively at Feather. 'When are you gonna let me go?'

The Prince of Wales sat in his library in a state of shock as he saw the late news item in the paper. It had caught his eye as he was about to turn to the back pages and the racing news. 'Museum Detective attacked. At death's door.'

He read the item again, and then rang the bell pull beside his chair. There was the briefest of delays, then his private secretary, Michael Shanks, appeared.

'You rang, sir?'

'Have you seen this? That Wilson fellow. Attacked. Badly hurt.'

'Yes, sir. I saw the item.'

Prince Albert looked uncomfortable. 'I'm afraid I must have misled you, Shanks.'

'Sir?'

'In what I said. I was angry at the time. Very angry. The memory of my poor son flooding back to me.' He brandished the newspaper at his secretary, clearly upset. 'But I didn't mean *this*. I'm not that kind of man, Shanks, and I won't be that kind of king. The Henry the Second kind. You know, that saying about Thomas Becket: "Will no one rid me of this troublesome priest?" I didn't mean that kind of thing. When I said he had to be stopped—'

'Excuse me, sir,' interrupted Shanks, politely but firmly. 'That was not me. I did not arrange for them to be assaulted.'

'You didn't?'

'No, Your Majesty. I interpreted you to mean for him to be stopped using legal means. Protocol.'

'Yes, exactly. That's what I meant.' He looked at the newspaper again, then at his secretary. 'I have to offer my apology, Shanks, that I even thought you had been responsible for this assault on Wilson.'

'No apology necessary, Your Majesty. Your reaction was quite understandable. I was at fault for not making clear how I meant to carry out your wishes.'

'I don't wish to know, Shanks,' said the prince quickly. 'Just as long as it is done without violence. No man deserves violence brought upon him.'

'Yes, sir.'

The prince looked again at the newspaper and said in awed

tones: 'She overpowered one of them, Shanks. Mrs Wilson. The man who attacked her. Just with a brolly. By God, what a woman!'

Percy Smith felt alone and frightened. He'd spent all day hiding in a series of sheds and outhouses in and around Kentish Town, each time being shouted at and moved on when the owner found him. He didn't know what to do. Normally, Pug said what they were going to do. Pug was the one with the brains. But Pug had been snaffled after that woman had hit him with her umbrella, and then the police turned up.

He wondered what had happened to Pug. He'd seen from a distance the second copper arrive on the bike. He'd thought of going back and dealing with the coppers and the woman and getting Pug away, but he knew he couldn't do it on his own.

It was getting late now. He'd missed his dinner and now it looked like he was going to miss his tea. His mother would be angry with him. She always had his tea on the table for him at six o'clock.

He'd been afraid to go into one of the cafes he regularly used to get something in case the police were looking out for him. But if they were, he hadn't seen them.

His stomach rumbled. He was hungry. He thought of his mum putting the tea on the table. Something hot. It was nearly always something hot. And tasty.

He needed to get some food in him, and do it somewhere safe. And the safest place he could think of was his home.

He made his way through the narrow streets of terraced houses, looking around every corner before he moved to a different street. So far so good. No sign of police. He came to the corner of his own street and peered carefully round the corner of the end house. No sign of any coppers watching.

He edged his way along the street, alert for any sign of a blue uniform, but the street was clear.

He reached the front door of his house, put the key in the lock and walked in.

'Mum! I'm home!' he called out.

In the front living room of the house on the other side of the road, Police Sergeant Fred Dewsbury watched Percy enter his house and smiled to himself. He turned to the elderly lady sitting in her armchair, knitting.

'Thank you, Mrs Shipton,' he said. He produced some coins from his pocket and put them on the dresser. 'Very much appreciated.'

He went out into the passageway and called to the kitchen: 'Constable, put down that cup of tea, it's time for action!'

In the same interview room in the basement of Scotland Yard where Inspector Feather had sat and listened to Pug Mason declare his innocence and offer to enter into negotiations over the compensation he believed he ought to receive for wrongful arrest and assault with a deadly weapon, now Feather faced the worried-looking outsized heap of muscles that was Percy Smith. Sergeant Cribbens sat at one side of the table, puffing on his pipe.

'You're here for two reasons, Percy,' said Feather. 'One, for hitting a man on the head with a leaded stick and there is concern that he might die. So that will be either murder, or – if he lives – attempted murder. The second is the death of a man called Andrew Page at the Victoria and Albert Museum. That is also murder.' He stopped and fixed Smith with a hard look. 'If you're lucky you'll go to prison, possibly for life. If you're not, you'll hang. You and Pug Mason.'

'We didn't murder anyone!' burst out Smith in agonised tones. 'All we did is scrag that couple, like we was told to. I didn't mean to hit him that hard.'

'Who told you to do it? I assume he paid you?'

'Up front,' confirmed Smith.

'For both jobs?' asked Feather. 'Cutting the throat of the man at the Victoria and Albert Museum, and attacking that man and that woman.'

'We never cut anyone's throat! Neither of us!'

'But you hit the man on the head with your leaded stick?'

Smith lowered his face and mumbled something, then nodded.

'Who was he?' asked Feather. 'The man who paid you to do it?'

'He didn't give his name,' said Smith. 'He paid us up front, which was good enough.'

'What did he look like? Give me a description.'

'Tall bloke. Very tall. Big belly on him. In his fifties, I reckon. Bit of a toff.'

'A toff?'

'Yeh. The way he spoke. His smart clothes.'

Feather eyed Smith thoughtfully, then said: 'If you help us, I might be able to help you. Maybe get you a lighter sentence. But that depends.'

'Depends on what?'

'Tomorrow morning I'm going to take you to the Victoria and Albert Museum.'

'Where's that?' asked Smith.

'It's the new one that's being built in Kensington. You're going to get out of the van and stand beside it. You'll be handcuffed to Sergeant Cribbens. I'm going to bring a man out of the museum offices to look at you. I want you to tell me if this was the man who hired you to attack the couple on Primrose Hill.'

'I don't know,' said Smith doubtfully. 'I ain't never grassed on anyone.'

'This ain't grassing, Percy. This is just saying yes or no. And at the same time, stopping you and Pug from being hanged.'

Sergeant Cribbens waited until Smith had been taken back to the holding cell before asking the inspector: 'D'you reckon this bloke Tweed did it, sir? Had the Wilsons attacked?'

'I hope so,' said Feather. 'The description Smith gave us tallies, but you never know. There's plenty of other people walking around looking like that. But if it isn't Tweed, we've got a whole big headache.'

Abigail was sitting in the reception area at the cottage hospital. She'd been sitting there for about six hours. Visiting time had come and gone, but she'd been refused admission to see Daniel because of his condition, which a ward sister had told her was 'still precarious'.

She heard footsteps ringing out on the marbled floor near the entrance. She looked up and was surprised to recognise Sir James Reid, the Queen's personal physician, accompanied by three men in dark suits and a woman in a nurse's uniform.

'Sir James!' she cried, springing to her feet and hurrying towards him. Her heart thumped with fear. Had something bad happened with Daniel that had resulted in him being summoned?

'Mrs Wilson,' Reid nodded politely. 'I have been despatched by Her Majesty to take Mr Wilson to a private clinic. When Her Majesty heard about the attack on Mr Wilson, and the seriousness of the damage to him, she immediately contacted me and instructed me to take over his medical care. She feels that the attack was to prevent you and Mr Wilson enquiring further into the murder of Mr Page, and as such she feels a certain responsibility.'

'Sir James, I cannot tell you how grateful I am to you, and to Her Majesty for this. I have been sitting here for six hours and received no information about my husband's condition. I am at my wits' end.'

'Unfortunately, although these public hospitals do a great service, they can only operate by running to a rigid set of rules. At the clinic where I shall take Mr Wilson, we can operate with more flexibility.'

'May I accompany you?' asked Abigail.

'Certainly,' replied Reid. 'And you will be able to have access to the private room where he will be cared for. There will even be a bed for you in the room.' He looked towards the reception desk, where the staff were looking towards these new arrivals with a mixture of excitement and trepidation. Sir James's picture had appeared frequently in the newspapers whenever the Queen's health was being discussed. 'I will make arrangements to transfer Mr Wilson,' he told Abigail. Then walked towards the reception desk, followed by his entourage.

CHAPTER TWENTY-TWO

It was ten o'clock the following morning when the police van pulled up outside the marquee that housed the site for the new Victoria and Albert Museum. Inspector Feather left Percy Smith handcuffed to Sergeant Cribbens and standing next to the police van outside the marquee, while he went into the offices of the Victoria and Albert Museum and sought out Herbert Tweed.

'Mr Tweed,' he said, 'we need your assistance. We've caught one of the men who attacked Mr and Mrs Wilson.'

'Were they attacked?' asked Tweed, looking surprised.

'It was in the newspapers.'

'Ah, I haven't had time to read the newspapers lately. I've got such a backlog of work.'

'The thing is, we wondered if you might have seen these men hanging around by the marquee where Mr Page's body was found.'

Tweed looked alarmed. 'You think they might be the people who murdered Mr Page?'

'At this moment we're still conducting our enquiries,' said Feather. 'But it would help us if you would take a look at one of the men we've apprehended and see if he looks familiar.'

Tweed looked uncertain. 'I doubt very much if I can be of help.'

'All you have to do is look at him from a distance. You won't need to go anywhere near him, or talk to him.'

'I'm not sure . . .' said Tweed doubtfully.

'Of course, if you'd rather do it in official circumstances, we can always take you to Scotland Yard for you to look at him.'

'Scotland Yard!' exclaimed Tweed in alarm. 'No, no.'

'In that case, if you'd accompany me outside and we'll stand by the marquee. You'll see the man handcuffed to my sergeant a short distance away. All you have to do is say whether you recognise the man.'

Tweed hesitated, then nodded. He took a heavy overcoat from a peg, along with a hat, then put them on, turning up the coat collar and pulling the brim of the hat partly over his face.

'You won't need those, Mr Tweed,' said Feather genially. 'It's quite warm outside.'

'Yes, but I'm concerned that if I recognise him, he'll know it was me who did it. And if he's as violent as you say he is, I'll be in danger.'

'You'll be in no danger at all. He's handcuffed to a police constable. You'll be at a distance from him. And he'll be going to jail, where he'll be safely under lock and key.'

'Bu—' Tweed began to protest.

Feather cut him off by removing the hat from his head and

turning down the collar of his coat.

'We need you to be able to see him clearly,' he said. 'Otherwise a good defence barrister will insist you didn't get a good view of him.'

Tweed again hesitated, then gave a gulp and a nod, and followed Feather down the stairs and out of the building. Percy Smith was standing about ten yards away, handcuffed to Sergeant Cribbens.

'There,' said Feather. 'Do you recognise this man?'

'No,' said Tweed. 'I've never seen this man before.'

'Thank you, Mr Tweed,' said Feather. 'We'll continue with our investigations elsewhere.'

He doffed his hat in farewell and walked towards Smith and the constable; while Tweed scurried back into the building.

'Well?' Feather asked Smith.

Smith nodded. 'That's him. That's the bloke what paid us.'

Abigail sat beside Daniel's bed in the room in the private clinic. He was still unconscious, but Abigail felt that his breathing had become more measured and some colour had returned to his face. She didn't know what sort of treatment Sir James Reid had carried out, she'd only been allowed into the room once the medical staff had finished their work, but she was sure Daniel seemed to have improved. Or was it her imagination, her desire for him to recover so deep that it was leading her to fancy improvements?

She looked around the room and reflected that it was as good as any room in a top-class hotel.

This is what money buys you, she thought. *Or, at least, an acquaintanceship with Her Majesty, the Queen.*

The door opened and Sir James entered the room.

'How does the patient appear to you, Mrs Wilson?' he asked.

'Stable, and in fact there seems to be more colour to his face and his breathing is less laboured,' replied Abigail. 'Although it might be just my wishful imagination.'

Sir James smiled. 'On the contrary,' he said. 'He is definitely improving. Fortunately, my examination shows no fracture of the skull, nor of any bleeding on the brain. In my opinion, the shock to his system as a result of the blow led to his body and his mind shutting down. Now his life signs are returning, I anticipate he should wake fairly soon. However, I believe he should stay here for a few days more yet to ensure a full recovery.' He gave a knowing smile as he added: 'From what I've learnt about Mr Wilson, I imagine he will not be happy about that, he will be eager to get out of bed and resume his work. But, as his physician, I cannot permit that; which is why I will insist he stays here. If he was allowed to go home it would be much harder for you to insist on him resting, rather than pursuing the current investigation.'

'Yes, Sir James, your assessment is very accurate,' said Abigail. 'Daniel can be very stubborn and a law unto himself, believing he has some kind of invincibility.'

'An attitude which can be very risky,' said Sir James. 'I will tell him firmly when he wakes that if he attempts to leave this clinic before I say he is ready, he could well collapse and die.'

'Could he?' asked Abigail, alarmed.

'That's what I will tell him,' Sir James said. He gave a small smile. 'It is not a complete lie, but it will ensure he doesn't overexert himself until he is ready. I believe he will not want to leave you a widow, and I hope he will have faith in the opinion of such an eminent physician as myself.' He took another look at the sleeping Daniel. 'If you wish to take a break and go out for some fresh air, one of the nurses will take your place.'

'Thank you, Sir James, but I'll stay here until he wakes.' She rose and held out her hand to him. 'I cannot thank you enough.'

'The Queen is the one you should thank,' said Sir James, shaking her hand. 'It is Her Majesty who gave the order. We only carried it out.'

Herbert Tweed sat in his office and mulled over the man in handcuffs. The inspector had said the purpose of the event was for Tweed to see if he recognised the man, but Tweed suspected it was the other way round: to see if the man recognised Tweed. And he was sure the man had. Damn that police inspector for not letting him put on the hat and turn his coat collar up. In Herbert Tweed's mind, that's what had given the inspector's game away. But he couldn't refuse to go through with the charade, not after the inspector's threat of taking him to Scotland Yard.

The net was closing in on him.

Suddenly determined, he got up, put on his hat and coat and went into the secretaries' room.

'If anyone wants me, I am going out for a short while,' he announced.

The secretaries looked at him and nodded.

With that, he left.

Chief superintendent stared at Inspector Feather, reflecting on what Feather had just told him.

'So you got positive identification that Herbert Tweed was

the one who hired Mason and Smith to attack the Wilsons.'

'Yes, sir,' said Feather. 'I believe he did it in an attempt to cover up the fact that he's been skimming money off the museum. But does it mean he was also involved in the murder of Andrew Page? It does if Page found out about his financial dealings and threatened to go to the authorities and Tweed killed him to silence him. But at the moment we can't prove it. We could bring him in—'

'No,' said Armstrong sharply. 'Not after the fiasco over that Ward character. We're going to need concrete proof the next time we bring someone in. I'm not going to be dragged up in front of the commissioner again for another tongue-lashing.'

'We can at least charge Tweed with being behind the attack on the Wilsons. Percy Smith identified him.'

'Percy Smith?' said Armstrong scornfully. 'That idiot. A good defence barrister – and Tweed will have one – will chew Smith up and spit him out in court. We need something stronger. Has Mason confessed yet? He's the brighter of the two. If he says it was Tweed, we've got a chance. Then it'll be the words of two men against one. And if we get accountants to look at the books and get proof that Tweed was fiddling, then we can bring him in. But only about the attack on the Wilsons, not the murder of Page.'

'Mason's still being difficult, sir,' said Feather. 'I think he's looking for a deal.'

'What sort of deal?'

'Being let off.'

'After they put Daniel Wilson in hospital and nearly killed him?' said the chief superintendent, outraged.

'It was Smith who struck Mr Wilson, sir. Mason didn't hit anyone.'

'Only because Mrs Wilson clobbered him.' He thought it over. 'Is Mason prepared to let his pal, Smith, take the rap?'

'Knowing Mason, I expect so. They may be old pals, but Mason's main concern is himself.'

Emily Tweed made her way up the short path of the semi-detached house, smiling to herself with a sense of satisfaction as she looked at the neatness of her front garden, the neatly cut lawn, the array of flowers. She'd just come from visiting her sister, Annette, whose own garden she considered a disgrace. Annette didn't look after it at all. Nor did that lazy husband of hers, Horace. The grass of their lawn was too long, dropping, and riddled with weeds. The plants, what few there were, looked dead. How lucky Emily felt to have a husband like Herbert, a man who could afford to hire a gardener to maintain their garden. Trim the hedge, cut the grass, look after the flowers and the wild cherry tree with its beautiful pink blossom once a year.

She let herself in the house and was surprised to see Herbert's overcoat and his hat hanging on the rack in the hallway. At this hour? Herbert never came home during the day. In fact, he was more likely to be late home, as he had been the other night.

Such a hard worker, and a dedicated servant of the museum.

'Herbert!' she called.

There was no answer.

She was about to take her own coat off and go into the living room, when she realised there was something hanging from the bannisters. It looked like a tailor's dummy, or something similar. Puzzled, she approached it, and then stopped,

It was Herbert, suspended from the bannister by his tie,

which had caught under his ear. His mouth and eyes were wide open and … And he was dead.

She screamed. She couldn't help herself. She screamed, and carried on screaming.

CHAPTER TWENTY-THREE

Chief Superintendent Armstrong sat in his office, a smile appearing on his face as he listened to Inspector Feather telling him about the discovery of Herbert Tweed's body.

'Excellent!' he beamed when Feather had finished. 'So it was Tweed who killed Page!'

'We don't know that for sure, sir,' said Feather warily.

'Oh yes we do!' said Armstrong confidently. 'Everything fits. Motive. His character. Tweed had his hand in the museum's till and was skimming money off. Page found out about it and challenged him. Possibly used it to try and get a promotion.'

'Page didn't need a promotion,' said Feather. 'He was wealthy.'

'Everyone wants a promotion,' said Armstrong. 'If it's not the money, it's the status. Anyway, Tweed kills Page and dumps his body in the marquee. We've seen that Tweed's capable of it because he hired those two thugs to attack the Wilsons. Daniel

Wilson was nearly killed, and Abigail would have been if she hadn't belted Pug Mason.

'Once Tweed realised we'd got our hands on Mason and Smith, he knew it wouldn't be long before they gave him up. So, unable to face the shame and the state hangman, he decides to do it himself. Case closed. And this way there's no way anyone's going to come up and say we're wrong, not like they did with that bloke Ward. Tweed's dead. It's perfect.'

'If you think so, sir.'

'I do! And so will the commissioner when I tell him. And this time when he tells the Queen there'll be no second thoughts. No humming and hawing.'

'Yes, sir,' said Feather. 'I thought I'd go and tell Mrs Wilson.'

'Where is she? Still at the Hampstead hospital keeping watch over Wilson?'

'No, sir. The Queen had him transferred to a private clinic in London, where he's being treated by Her Majesty's private physician, Sir James Reid.'

Armstrong looked stunned.

'Her Majesty's private physician?'

'Yes, sir.'

'How do they do it? The Wilsons, I mean. All these perks. If you or I got bashed over the head we'd be lucky to get anything, but there's Wilson living it up in some private clinic.'

'I hardly think he's living it up, sir,' said Feather disapprovingly. 'He's still unconscious, and there was some doubt if he'd pull through.'

'Yes, I'm sorry. I was forgetting you're a friend of his. Go and see him and … er … tell him I was asking after him.'

Just in case the Queen makes enquiries about him from her

private physician, thought Feather cynically.

'Yes, sir,' he said.

When Feather arrived at the private clinic he was struck by the luxury, as someone whose experience of hospital care had been of large drab buildings with long echoing corridors, a regime of strict silence on a level with Trappist monasteries, and wards with the metal-framed beds close together and grim-faced nursing staff on the watch for any transgressions by patients or visitors. Not that there was much scope for visitors to break any of the many rules in place – visiting hours were strictly limited and controlled. The private clinic, by comparison, was of the standard of a luxury hotel. The staff were welcoming rather than forbidding. There seemed to be no restrictions on visiting, unless a medical procedure or inspection was taking place. The walls were painted in cheerful cream and yellows, rather than the gloomy browns and dark greens of the public hospitals. However, Feather felt a sense of foreboding as he walked up the stairs to the first floor, and the room where Daniel was. He was worried how Abigail would react to the news of Tweed's suicide. Knowing her, he was concerned that she might feel guilty over it, feeling that it had been their action in telling Tweed they were going to get an accountant in to look at the account books – which they felt he was fiddling in some way – that had led him to kill himself. He'd expressed that concern to Sergeant Cribbens before leaving Scotland Yard to come to the clinic.

'She's got nothing to feel guilty about,' Cribbens had declared. 'Tweed tried to kill them both. And he was on the fiddle. You tell her that, Inspector. Because I can see she might think like you said. She's that sort of thoughtful person!'

The big surprise for Feather was finding Daniel lying back on a pile of pillows in the bed, his eyes open and awake. Abigail sat beside him, reading to him from the day's newspapers. She stopped and got to her feet when Feather knocked at the door and then came into the private room.

'John!' she exclaimed.

Feather smiled at her, and at Daniel.

'It's good to see you with your eyes open,' he told Daniel. 'How are you?'

'I suppose I'm as well as can be expected,' said Daniel. 'I've been told I was hit over the head with a leaded stick, but I can't recall it. All I remember is Abigail and I walking across Primrose Hill.'

'Sir James says that's normal, not remembering the actual event,' said Abigail.

'How soon do you think you'll be able to leave?' asked Feather.

'I feel ready now,' said Daniel. Then, wryly, he admitted: 'Well, maybe tomorrow.'

'Not a chance,' said Abigail firmly. 'Sir James says you have to make a full recovery before he'll let you go. He's concerned there may be some residual damage to your brain that might suddenly cause you to collapse. He wants to keep you under observation for a while yet.'

'Well, I've got news,' said Feather. 'We caught the second man, the one who actually hit Daniel, and he identified Herbert Tweed as the man who paid them to attack you.'

'I knew it was him!' said Abigail. 'Have you arrested him?'

'We were about to, when he killed himself.'

Both Daniel and Abigail stared at Feather. 'Killed himself?' echoed Abigail.

'He went home from the museum immediately we'd got the positive identification from Percy Smith, and hanged himself from his bannisters.'

'My God!' said Abigail, shocked.

'As a result, Chief Superintendent Armstrong is sure it links Tweed to the murder of Page. Tweed was fiddling the books, Page found out about it and was going to expose him, so Tweed killed him. You two had your suspicions about financial skulduggery going on at the museum, so he tried to have you dealt with to stop you investigating further. So, for him, that's it. Case closed,' said Feather, his tone slightly rueful.

'It's all supposition,' said Abigail. 'Just as it was with poor Stephen Ward.'

'Yes, but unlike Stephen Ward, Tweed is dead and so unlikely to dispute it.'

Abigail looked at Daniel, shocked. 'You know what this means,' she said unhappily. 'Because we put that pressure on Mr Tweed, he killed himself. It's our fault he's dead.'

'No,' said Feather firmly. 'He killed himself because he was caught out fiddling the books, and also because he was identified as the person who paid for the attack on you. He knew he'd be going to jail and he couldn't face it. It's his fault, not yours.'

Inspector Feather returned to Scotland Yard and found Sergeant Cribbens eagerly anticipating his return.

'What's happened, Sergeant?' he asked. 'You look pleased.'

'Well, I don't know if pleased is the right word,' said Cribbens. 'But if Mrs Wilson was worried about it being her who made

Tweed hang himself, she doesn't have to worry any more.'

Feather frowned, puzzled. 'Why?'

'Dr Proctor called in. The one who did the autopsy on Herbert Tweed. He said it wasn't suicide, it was murder.'

'What?'

'He said there was a contusion on the back of Tweed's head which he hadn't spotted before. He said he was knocked unconscious and then hung from the bannisters.'

'He's sure?'

'Dead sure, sir.'

'Tweed couldn't have had a fall and banged his head, and then got up and hanged himself?'

'Dr Proctor says not, sir. There was a bit of scientific jargon he used, but he says Tweed was unconscious when he was hung up.'

Chief Superintendent Armstrong sat at his desk feeling very pleased with himself. This was going to be a major mark in his career. The commissioner had been pleased when he'd told him the news and had immediately hurried off to see the Queen at Buckingham Palace. Once they had royal approval the story could be passed to the newspapers. He could see the headlines now: 'A triumph for traditional policing.'

There would be accolades afterwards. royal approval. There might even be … honours bestowed. Perhaps even – if he dared to dream – *Sir* Giles Armstrong. It wasn't impossible. There had been other examples before of public servants finding favour with Her Majesty receiving a knighthood.

He was interrupted in his reverie by the door of his office opening and the Commissioner of Police entering. The commissioner closed the door, locked it to make sure they weren't disturbed, then sat down.

'I saw the Queen,' he announced.

'And?' asked Armstrong. 'Was Her Majesty pleased?'

'She was, Chief Superintendent. However…'

It was the 'however' that sent a warning chill down Armstrong's spine.

'However, sir?' he asked nervously.

'Her Majesty does not want this outcome publicised.'

'Pardon, sir?' asked Armstrong, bewildered.

'The fact that the murderer was a senior member of the staff of the museum. She feels it will taint the museum, and therefore the late prince's memory.'

'Well, what are we going to tell the press?'

'Nothing, Chief Superintendent. The crime will remain officially unsolved.'

'No, sir! I must protest! This is a triumph for police investigations.'

'I'm sorry, Chief Superintendent, but those are our instructions from Her Majesty. The reputation of this museum is too important to her for it to be damaged with negative publicity about possible fraud.'

Armstrong sat in a daze after the commissioner had left. It was so unfair! A major crime, solved, and instead it would be considered a crime unsolved, a failure on the part of Scotland Yard.

There was a knock at his door and then Inspector Feather appeared.

'I saw the commissioner leave just now, sir,' said Feather. 'Had he been to see the Queen?'

'Yes,' growled Armstrong sullenly.

'What was her reaction?' asked Feather tentatively.

Armstrong told him. 'She doesn't want it publicised,' he said bitterly. 'Our greatest triumph and she wants it kept under wraps.'

'Perhaps that might turn out to be fortunate, sir,' said Feather.

'Fortunate!' exploded Armstrong. 'In what possible way can that be said to be fortunate?'

'Because it seems that Mr Tweed was actually murdered.'

Armstrong stared at Feather, stunned.

'Murdered?'

'That's what Dr Proctor says. He says that now he's examined Tweed's body properly, he's found a contusion at the back of the skull.'

'All right, so he fell over before he hanged himself.'

'That's what I thought, sir, but Dr Proctor says not, He says all the evidence points to Tweed being knocked unconscious, then hanged from the bannisters.'

Armstrong looked at Feather, concerned. 'This is a weird one, Inspector.'

'Yes, sir.

'I have to let the commissioner know.' Armstrong scowled. 'It won't make any difference to the Queen not wanting to tell the public about it, all this business of protecting the museum's reputation. Tweed was on the crook, after all. But it means the case isn't over.'

'That's right, sir.'

'Maybe it's a good thing the Queen won't let the press know what's going on. This makes any investigations much more complicated.'

'Yes, sir.'

'So, what theories have you got?'

'At this moment, none, sir. I've only just learnt that Tweed was murdered rather than having committed suicide.'

'Yes,' said Armstrong thoughtfully. 'There might be something to our advantage in this.'

'How, sir?' asked Feather, puzzled.

'If we can unmask the person who killed Tweed, we can chalk that up as a success. We might even be able to avoid any mention of the fraud that Tweed was up to.'

'Unless he was killed by an accomplice to shut him up,' pointed out Feather.

'Yes, there's always that thought,' admitted the chief superintendent. 'But we can cross that bridge when we come to it. If it is connected to the fraud that was going on, we keep it quiet. If, on the other hand, if there was some other reason, we can publicly claim the credit for solving the crime.'

'I don't think this will be an easy one to solve, sir,' said Feather doubtfully. 'I still believe it's connected with the fraud at the museum, or the death of Andrew Page, and it seems as if we're being discouraged from looking into either too deeply on the orders of Her Majesty.'

'There'll be ways round it,' said Armstrong dismissively. 'You find them, Inspector. The first thing to do is keep it quiet that Tweed was murdered. We don't want the press picking that up.'

CHAPTER TWENTY-FOUR

Once word had spread that Daniel was conscious again, visitors began to descend on the private clinic. The first was Sir Anthony Thurrington.

'I am delighted to see that you are conscious again,' he said. 'As was the Queen when she heard the news. How are you feeling?'

'Strange,' admitted Daniel.

'That often happens with a case of concussion,' said Thurrington. He turned to Abigail. 'But it's Mrs Wilson I've come to see. Her Majesty has been informed by the Commissioner of Police that the case has been solved. As a result, she feels able to return to her house on the Isle of Wight, but she's expressed a wish to talk to you before she goes. I have a carriage waiting outside.'

Abigail cast a questioning look at Daniel.

'I'll be fine,' he assured her. 'If I relapse even in the smallest degree – which I think is highly unlikely – I'm surrounded by the very best medical staff. And this is a royal command. You can't refuse.'

Abigail kissed him goodbye, then accompanied Sir Anthony to his waiting carriage and they drove to Buckingham Palace. Once there, Thurrington escorted Abigail to the Queen's private rooms. As before, her daughter, Princess Beatrice and the Munshi were in attendance on Victoria.

I wonder if she does anything without them? Abigail questioned silently.

'Mrs Wilson,' said the Queen, nodding politely to Abigail's curtsey bob.

'Your Majesty,' responded Abigail.

'I understand your husband has recovered consciousness.'

'He has, Your Majesty, thanks to you allowing Sir James Reid to take charge of his medical care. We are both very grateful for your generosity in this matter. I have no doubt at all that without the specialist care of Sir James and his nursing team my husband would not have recovered, at least not as speedily and as well as he has.'

'I'm delighted to hear that,' said the Queen. 'Now, to the reason I asked Sir Anthony to bring you here. I'm told that one of the senior staff at the museum was responsible for the attack on you and your husband, and there is evidence that implicates him in a misuse of museum funds, and also the tragic death of Mr Page.'

'So we understand, Your Majesty.'

'I do not wish this information to be made public,' said Victoria, and there was no mistaking the firm glint in her eyes as she looked at Abigail. 'This museum is dear to me, dearer than any other such establishments, because it was the creation of my much-missed late husband, Prince Albert. I will not have the museum tarnished in any way. Is that understood?'

'It is, Your Majesty. That information will remain secret with us.'

'Good. I have already made sure that the police will also keep this to themselves. When the Victoria and Albert Museum finally opens its doors, I want there to be no stains on its reputation of any sort, only praise lavished on it, the praise the museum and Prince Albert justly deserve for bringing it to fruition.'

'I'm sure the museum will be lauded in his memory, Your Majesty. And in yours.'

Victoria nodded, obviously satisfied.

'Thank you. This means that I can now return to my house on the Isle of Wight. In truth, I have found the past few weeks somewhat taxing.' She turned and smiled affectionately at Princess Beatrice and the Munshi. 'I doubt I could have borne it without my constant companions to support me.' The Munshi bowed and Beatrice bobbed in recognition of the compliment. 'And without the sterling work that you and your husband did on this case,' said Victoria, turning back to Abigail.

'It was our pleasure, Your Majesty. And my husband and I both wish you well on your journey to the Isle of Wight.'

As Thurrington escorted Abigail towards the entrance of the palace, he murmured: 'There is now just the matter of your fee. I must warn you that Her Majesty can be quite parsimonious when it comes to spending money.'

'She has been more than generous in providing medical care for Daniel,' said Abigail. 'The cost of the stay at the private hospital and the nursing staff would have been out of our financial reach.'

'I am sure the Queen will take that into consideration when she approves the payment,' smiled Thurrington. 'When it comes to her personal spending, she is very much penny wise.'

'Murdered?' said the Commissioner of Police, a stunned expression on his face as he sat behind his desk.

'Yes, sir,' said Armstrong. The chief superintendent had sought out the commissioner to tell him the news. 'The pathologist has confirmed it. The hanging was done to confuse the situation.'

'Well, it certainly confused you and your Inspector Feather,' snapped the commissioner, unimpressed.

'With respect, sir, neither of us have been medically trained,' said Armstrong in a mild protest. 'We had to take the situation as we saw it.'

'Yes, I appreciate that, but following the fiasco over the arrest of Stephen Ward—'

'Again, sir—,' interrupted Armstrong to defend himself, before being cut off with the commissioner's curt: 'Two mistakes, Chief Superintendent. I cannot go to see Her Majesty with this latest news, that Mr Tweed was murdered, in case that, too, turns out to be an error.'

'The doctor is very firm on the point, sir.'

'That may be, but as Her Majesty has seen fit to call the case closed, I think the safest course of action is to keep this latest development to ourselves. If you manage to get to the bottom of this case and the miscreant is identified and charged, then, and only then, will I inform Her Majesty.'

'Yes, sir.'

'Until then there will be no passing this information onto anyone, especially not the gentlemen of the press.'

'Yes, sir.'

When Feather arrived at the clinic, he was pleased to see that Daniel, although still wearing a dressing gown over pyjamas, was sitting on a chair. The thick crepe bandage that had been wrapped around the top part of his skull had been replaced with a light gauze one.

'This looks like an improvement,' he said.

'It feels like an improvement,' said Daniel. 'I'm not suffering from headaches now, thank heavens. I'm just waiting for Sir James to say I'm ready to be discharged.'

'Which he will not do until he feels confident enough,' said Abigail.

'And then you'll be able to go home,' said Feather. 'I'm sure for both of you it must feel a bit like being in prison in here, in this one room. Have you had any opportunities to go out for a break, Abigail? I'd be happy to come and visit to give you a chance to get outside.'

'I went outside this morning,' said Abigail. 'To Buckingham Palace.'

'Sir Anthony Thurrington?' asked Feather.

'Her Majesty herself,' said Victoria.

Feather gave a rueful grin. 'Such exalted company you keep, Abigail. I'm surprised you can bear to be with mere mortals like myself.'

'Give me your company over the Empress of the World any time, John,' said Abigail. 'Anyway, this will be the last such meeting between us. Her Majesty is going home to the Isle of Wight. She summoned me to ensure our secrecy about the circumstances surrounding Mr Tweed's suicide, his fraudulent activities, and his attack on us.'

'Yes, that's why I've come to see you. Tweed did not commit suicide.'

Abigail and Daniel stared at the inspector, stunned.

'What?'

'He was murdered. The pathologist confirmed it. He was struck on the head and knocked out before being hung from the bannisters.'

'So the murderer's still out there,' said Daniel.

'That's how it looks,' Feather nodded.

'Obviously no one's told the Queen,' said Abigail.

'No, and I get the impression from the chief superintendent that they're not going to. As far as she's concerned, the case is over.'

'But what are you going to do?' asked Abigail. 'Does this mean you'll be conducting an investigation in secrecy?'

'It does,' said Feather unhappily. 'Which means no contact with the press. No passing the fact on to the public in any way. And the chief superintendent's put me in charge.' He sighed. 'To be honest, I'm groping in the dark. And the fact that I've got to keep everything secret is going to be hard with the press dogging my heels. I still feel it's connected to what happened at the museum, either to Page's murder or the fraud that Tweed was carrying out. Have you still got that letter of authority from the Queen, Abigail?'

'I have,' said Abigail. 'While Daniel's in here I keep it with me. Although, now she considers the case closed, I don't know how much use it will be.'

'It will be, I can assure you,' said Feather. 'There'll be no mention of Tweed's involvement, or his death, in the papers. The Queen has expressly forbidden it. So, as far as the general public are concerned, the case is still active.

'My intention is to see Mrs Tweed and ask if she knows anything or anyone Tweed might have been involved with. I'll also ask the neighbours if they saw anyone going into the Tweeds' house on the day he was murdered. Meanwhile, Abigail, if you don't mind going to the museum and root around there, using that letter to gain access to everything there is to look at. I'm thinking that if there is anything to find, it'll be in the desks of Tweed and Page.'

'I thought you'd looked into Page's desk and papers?'

'Yes, but not as thoroughly as I'd have liked. And can you find out what time Tweed left the museum on the day he died?'

Daniel looked at Abigail. 'Are you all right with this?' he asked. 'Maybe I should see if I can talk Sir James into letting me get out and start digging.'

'Absolutely not,' said Abigail firmly. 'I'm perfectly capable of doing this. And discreetly. You're not leaving here until Sir James authorises it.'

CHAPTER TWENTY-FIVE

Abigail was surprised and perturbed when she arrived at the museum secretaries' office to be met with the women sitting at their desks inside the room all looking at her with naked hostility as she opened the door and entered. One of the women, a tall thin red-haired woman, got up from her desk and walked to Abigail and gestured for her to step outside into the corridor. Surprised, Abigail did so. The woman followed her into the corridor and pulled the door shut behind her.

'Yes?' asked the woman, her manner curt and seething with barely concealed anger for some reason, which puzzled Abigail.

'My name's Abigail Wilson. I was here very recently.'

'Yes, I remember you,' said the woman. 'What do you want?'

'I'm here to examine Mr Tweed's desk.'

Abigail produced the letter of authority from Buckingham Palace and held it out to the woman. The woman barely glanced at the letter, not even taking it from her to look at.

'You'll need permission from Mr Wilton,' said the woman curtly.

'I already have authority from the Queen herself. As this museum is named after her, I should imagine she is the highest authority there is.'

The woman glared at her. 'You'll still need permission from Mr Wilton.'

Suddenly Abigail realised what was behind the woman's hostility: she believed that Tweed had killed himself and, in some way, Daniel and Abigail's were responsible.

I need to deal with this, she thought. But first she tried using reason.

'I've already met Mr Wilton with my husband and showed him this letter,' said Abigail. 'He had no objection then. And on what basis does he have a higher level of authority than Her Majesty the Queen?'

'Mr Wilton is the senior director,' said the woman, ignoring the last part of Abigail's question.

'I know that,' said Abigail. 'As I've told you, we've already met him. But, as you insist, please take me to Mr Wilton.'

The woman hesitated, then said defiantly. 'Mr Wilton is very busy. You will need to make an appointment.'

Abigail looked at the woman, at the hardness and anger for Abigail in her eyes.

'I don't understand what the problem is here,' she said. 'I am here to try to ascertain why Mr Tweed died,' she said.

'We know why he died,' snapped the woman, almost snarling. 'Because you and your partner hounded him to his death.'

'That's not true,' said Abigail firmly. 'We told him that we'd heard allegations that some kind of financial skulduggery may have been happening. We did not say he was involved. We said that we would like an independent accountant to examine the ledgers.'

'And he killed himself!' the woman barked.

'He did not kill himself, he was murdered,' said Abigail.

As soon as the words were out of her mouth she mentally kicked herself. *I promised the Queen we'd keep that secret*, she thought angrily.

The woman stared at her, horrified. 'But … we were told he'd hanged himself.'

'What I'm about to tell you must not be made public,' said Abigail. 'The police and Her Majesty have insisted it not become common knowledge because it could seriously damage the reputation of the museum, and that of Mr Tweed. I'm sure that's a point of view you can sympathise with.'

'Absolutely,' said the woman.

'Mr Tweed was struck over the head and then hung from the bannisters to make it look like he'd committed suicide. We have that information from Scotland Yard. Inspector Feather told us that today.' Before the woman could reply, Abigail leapt into the attack, letting her own anger show. 'And even if Mr Tweed had committed suicide, it would not be because of anything we did. It would have been because he was identified as the man who paid two thugs to attack myself and my husband. An attack so serious that it was thought my husband would die. Fortunately, the Queen's personal physician, Sir James Reid, took charge of his medical care and he is slowly recovering. If Mr Tweed had killed himself – and I say again, he did not – it would have been because Inspector Feather of Scotland Yard had got one of the assailants to positively identify Mr Tweed as the man who paid them to attack us. I will be happy to bring Inspector Feather here to confirm that to you. The question being asked is: why did Mr Tweed hire two thugs to try to kill us once he realised we were bringing in someone to look at his accounts? The police believe it was because he wanted to stop the fact that he was skimming money illegally off this museum being discovered by us. Or do you have an alternative theory?'

The woman stood, helpless, stunned by this verbal onslaught.

'I-I-I didn't realise,' she stammered. 'We thought he killed himself because you hounded him.'

'And now I hope you realise this wasn't the case,' said Abigail, still tense from her outburst.

The woman nodded. 'Yes,' she said. She hesitated, then said: 'In view of that, I don't think there's any need to involve Mr Wilton. I'll show you where Mr Tweed's desk is.'

'I believe there is a need to involve Mr Wilton,' said Abigail firmly. 'If you believed that we were responsible for Mr Tweed's death, then so will he. Therefore, I need to explain to him the truth of the matter. While I see him, I would appreciate it if you would tell your colleagues in the secretaries' room what I've just told you, if you think they can be trusted to keep the information to themselves.'

'Of course,' said the woman. 'You know where Mr Wilton's office is?'

'I do,' said Abigail.

The woman hesitated, then said awkwardly: 'I apologise for my attitude towards you, but we were all fond of Mr Tweed, and we genuinely thought that you had driven him to his death.'

'I understand,' said Abigail. 'And I, too, apologise for the terseness of my tone to you. It has been a trying time recently.' She held out her hand. 'We are on the same side. We both want to protect the reputation of the museum.'

The woman took her hand and shook it.

'Thank you,' she said. 'I'll now pass on what you've told me to the secretaries, and insist they do not tell anyone else.'

'You think they'll stick to it?' asked Abigail doubtfully.

'I can assure you they will remain silent about it. Like all of us here, they care deeply about the museum and its reputation. After you've seen Mr Wilton, if you have any questions, don't hesitate to ask me. My name's Margaret Huss and I'm the senior secretary.'

'There is one question,' said Abigail. 'Do you know what time Mr Tweed left the office yesterday?'

'I do, actually, because I remember looking at the clock. Mainly because it was so unusual for Mr Tweed to go home early. Usually he worked later, after we'd all gone home. It was half past eleven in the morning when he left.'

Inspector Feather and Sergeant Cribbens sat in the very neat living room of the Tweeds' house and looked at Mrs Tweed as she wept, a handkerchief to her face.

'Why?' she cried. 'It was bad enough to think that Herbert had … Had ended it himself. But for you to tell me that someone murdered him!'

Once again she subsided into tears, sobs racking her body.

'That's why we've come, Mrs Tweed,' said Feather. 'We really hate to disturb you at this time, but the sooner we can find out who may have done this to your husband, the better. Did he have any enemies that you know of?'

'No. Everyone liked Herbert.'

'Did he have any problems at work?'

This time she glared at him through her tears.

'You asked me that when you came before, after his … his body was discovered. You insinuated that there was something wrong at the museum, and Herbert was involved in it.'

'There may have been something wrong there. I'm just wondering if Mr Tweed had found out about something and had been talking to anyone about it.'

'What sort of something wrong?' she demanded. And now her grief had definitely been replaced by an angry defence of these slurs she felt the inspector was making about her husband.

'That's what we're trying to find out, Mrs Tweed—' began Feather.

He never finished. Mrs Tweed interrupted him, her voice full of anger and venom.

'Herbert was one of the most honest men who walked this earth,' she stormed. 'How dare you try to blacken his name this way.'

'Mrs Tweed, I can assure you that is not our intention.'

'No? Last time you said there were questions being asked about money going missing from the museum.' She stood up, angry and defiant. 'And now you're saying it again! How dare you?' She pointed at the door. 'Get out!'

'Mrs Tweed—' tried Feather.

'Out!' she shouted.

Wearily, Feather got to his feet and gestured for Cribbens to get up as well.

'We'll talk to you later when things are a bit calmer,' said Feather.

'Not as long as you keep accusing my poor dead husband of something. He's the victim here! He was murdered! Why aren't you out looking for the person who killed him?'

'We are, Mrs Tweed.'

'Well you won't find them in this house! Get out!'

Feather and Cribbens looked at one another ruefully as they left the house and the front door was slammed shut hard behind them.

'Grief,' observed Cribbens. 'It does funny things to people.'

'She's certainly not interested in entertaining the idea that Herbert may have been involved in some sort of fraud,' agreed Feather.

'What's our next move, sir?' asked Cribbens.

'As we're in the area, we go knocking on doors and see if anyone saw anything on the day he died.'

'We don't know what time he left the museum,' pointed out Cribbens.

'No, so we'll just ask if anyone came to the house at any time during the day,' said Feather.

Inwardly, he thought: *I wonder how Abigail's getting on at the museum?*

When Abigail entered Wilton's office she recognised the same glare of hostility from him towards her that she'd encountered from Miss Huss. Before sitting down, she stood in front of his desk, looking down at him.

'Before we begin, Mr Wilton, I think it's important that you know the truth of Mr Tweed's death,' she announced. 'Contrary to what seems to be the story circulating in these offices, he did not kill himself because we hounded him, as I've heard it said. He was murdered.'

Wilton stared at her, bewildered.

'Murdered? But we were told he'd hanged himself.'

'That was what everyone thought at first, until a Scotland Yard pathologist examined his body and discovered that, in fact, he'd been murdered and then hanged from his bannisters to look like suicide.'

She then went on to give Wilton the further details: the suspicion that Mr Tweed was defrauding money from the museum, him hiring two thugs to attack Abigail and Daniel; and the fact that Daniel was at death's door before the Queen's physician aided him in his recovery.

'I must stress that all of this must be kept secret by order of the Queen herself,' added Abigail.

'I was not aware of those details,' said Wilton awkwardly. 'Your being attacked and Mr Tweed being behind it.'

'Were you aware that he was stealing money from the museum?'

'No,' admitted Wilton.

'Who was his supervisor here?'

There was a pause, then Wilton admitted awkwardly: 'I was.'

Got you! thought Abigail. In the same conciliatory tone she'd used to Margaret Huss at the end of her previous conversation, she said: 'Mr Wilton, it's not my intention to bring any unpleasantness to the museum. I can assure you that if we find there had been any financial awkwardness on the part of

Mr Tweed, it will not be made public. It will be kept between ourselves. My remit from Her Majesty was to find out who killed Mr Page. To that will now be added to discover who killed Mr Tweed, and why.'

'Thank you,' said Wilton. 'And if there's any way I can help, please just ask.'

I will, thought Abigail. *Including how you as Tweed's boss didn't notice he was stealing money from the museum.*

However, instead of saying that she smiled and said: 'Thank you, Mr Wilton. The first thing I need to do is examine both Mr Tweed's desk, and Mr Page's. Miss Huss has agreed that I can do this with help from her.'

'By all means,' said Wilton. 'And if there's anything I can do to assist you, do please just ask.'

Inspector Feather and Sergeant Cribbens had gone up and down both sides of the street talking to the residents, asking if they'd seen any callers at the Tweed house on the previous day. Without exception, one after the other, the people they met had the same response; either they hadn't been in that day, or they'd been too busy to notice anything. It was at a house directly opposite the Tweed house that their luck changed with an elderly invalid lady called Mrs Networthy, who spent most of her time sitting in an armchair in her living room looking out at the street.

'I've got bad arthritis, you see, so I can't move about much,' she told them. 'So I spend most days sitting here looking out of the window, watching the world go by. Watching people. Since my husband died, I haven't got anyone for company. There's my daughter, Alice, but she lives up the Edgeware Road and I don't see her much. She comes round when she can, but it's difficult for her with three young kids.'

'Did you see anyone going into the Tweeds' house?' asked Feather.

'Well, there was Mr Tweed himself. That was late morning. I don't know the exact time because I haven't got a clock in this room. When you get to my age and you can't move around, the last thing you want is a clock staring at you, reminding you that time is passing so slowly.

'It was some time in the afternoon that this man and woman appeared.'

'A man and a woman?'

'Yes. They walked up the path to the door and rang the bell. Mr Tweed opened the door and invited them in.'

'Can you describe the people who called?' asked Feather.

Mrs Networthy frowned, thinking hard.

'I didn't really see him when he went in. I could only see him from the back. But I saw him when he came out. He looked very respectable. He had an overcoat on buttoned right to the top, a nice good-quality overcoat. And a scarf pulled up over his nose and mouth. He also had a bowler hat. He looked every inch the gentleman.'

'But you didn't see his face?'

'No, not with the scarf pulled up like that. It was quite cold.'

'How tall was he? '

'He was about the same height as Mr Tweed. That struck me when I saw them together at the door.'

'And the woman?'

'Again, like the man, she was wrapped up against the cold. A big coat with the collar turned up, scarf pulled up, a big hat, so I couldn't see her face.'

'How tall was she?'

'Shorter than the man, but tall for a woman.'

'How long were they in the house?'

'I would think about half an hour. I didn't really check the time.'

'Did anyone else call?'

'No. The only other person who arrived was poor Mrs Tweed. She came about a couple of hours after the man and woman had gone. Like I say, I don't know what time she came home because I don't have a clock.' She shook her head, sadly. 'It was terrible. I heard her scream from here. Next moment she came rushing out of the house shouting "Help! Police!" She was in a right state. I saw Mr Grant come rushing out of his house. He lives next door to the Tweeds. He asked her something, but she didn't answer. She was all shaking and crying. He ran into the house, then came out a moment later.

'By then another neighbour, Mrs Peasworth, had come out to see what all the shouting and screaming was about. Mr Grant said something to her, then he hurried off, leaving Mrs Peasworth to look after Mrs Tweed. About half an hour later, Mr Grant came back with a policeman. Then a bit later another policeman came.

'After that there were lots of people coming to see what was going on. One of the policemen went off, and sometime later I saw you and this sergeant arrive in a van and go in.'

Feather gave her a grateful smile.

'Thank you, Mrs Networthy. You've been enormously helpful.'

'Do you know why he did it? Killed himself, I mean.' She looked bewildered at the thought. 'He always seemed a happy soul. Him and her both.'

There were six desks in the curator's room: one that had been for Andrew Page's use, one used by Gideon Oakley, the others belonged to Jeremy Purbright, who was in America, Peter Kenton, Frederick Fellowes and Ian Tavistock. None of the surviving curators were in. Abigail had been told by Miss Huss that the curators rarely came into the office, they spent most of their time talking with manufacturers or artists, examining their products and mulling over whether they would be suited for the Victoria and Albert.

Mr Tweed's desk had been bereft of secrets. In fact, it had been bereft of almost everything: it looked as if most of the correspondence had been removed, presumably after Daniel and Abigail had mentioned to him that they would be bringing in an accountant of their own.

Andrew Page's desk, on the other hand, was packed with papers, letters, notes, and catalogues from different firms. She went through the contents of the desk drawers methodically. Many of the catalogues, and quite a few of the letters, were in German. The ceramics catalogues included one from Meissen, and others whose names were unfamiliar to her. There were also catalogues from ceramics companies based in France and Belgium.

She checked through the catalogues and the papers, looking to see if there were any pieces of paper that stuck out as incongruous, but everything seemed to be there by right.

It was as she was pushing against one of the drawers to

ease it back into place that her fingers felt something beneath it. Curious, she bent down and looked underneath and was intrigued to find a thin envelope had been stuck to the underside of the drawer.

Carefully, she unpeeled it from the wood. She opened the envelope and took out a sheet of paper. It appeared to be a report written in German.

She'd studied German as one of the modern languages when she'd been at Girton, but lack of regular practice meant that she could only admit to an understanding of parts of the language. However, a cursory look at the words on the sheet of paper suggested that this was nothing to do with ceramics. She recognised the word '*Gewehr*' as being German for rifle; and '*munition*' meaning the same as its English equivalent, 'ammunition'. She also recognised the name of Krupp, who she knew from recent newspapers and magazine articles to be a leading manufacturer of German armaments. One thing was certain, whatever this document was about, it was nothing to do with German ceramics. On the contrary, it seemed to be a list of weapons. And the word 'Transvaal' occurred more than once.

Hastily she put the sheet back into the envelope, then the envelope inside her bag.

If this document was what she thought it was, she felt she'd just discovered the reason for Page's murder. And the sooner she shared it with Daniel, and with John Feather, the better.

CHAPTER TWENTY-SIX

Abigail stopped at their house in Primrose Hill just long enough to pick up a German vocabulary before making for the clinic. In view of the urgency, she took a hansom rather than wait for a series of buses. She needed to get this to Daniel as soon as she could.

On her arrival at the clinic, she arranged for a messenger to take a note to Inspector Feather at Scotland Yard, asking him to come and join them there. 'We have some important information', she wrote.

'How did you get on?' asked Daniel as Abigail entered the room.

Abigail produced the envelope from her bag and handed it to Daniel. He scanned it, then looked at her, puzzled. 'It's in German,' he said. 'I don't read German. What does it say? And where did you get it?'

'I found it stuck to the underside of one of the drawers

of the desk that Andrew Page used. At first sight it looks as if it's detailing weapons, and you'll note the word "Transvaal" pops up a few times.' She produced the German vocabulary from her bag. 'This has always been useful for me when I've tried translating articles in archaeological pieces in German magazines – the Germans have always been very prominent in studying the pyramids of Egypt. I thought I'd use it to see if we can see what this piece of paper is actually about.' She took a notebook and pencil from her bag, and retrieved the sheet of paper from Daniel. 'I've also sent a note to John Feather asking him to join us. It certainly feels as though whatever it is, it's crucial to the murder investigation.'

'Which we're no longer involved in, officially,' Daniel pointed out. 'The Queen has finished with our services.'

'Don't you want to know who killed Page and Tweed, and why?' asked Abigail.

'Yes, I do,' admitted Daniel.

With the aid of her basic German, and the vocabulary, Abigail set to work to translate the document. She had just finished as Inspector Feather appeared in the room.

'I got your note,' he said. 'I got the impression it was urgent.'

'It is,' said Daniel. He handed the sheet of paper to Feather, who looked at it blankly. 'It's in German,' he said.

'Abigail's just finished translating it,' said Daniel.

Feather looked towards Abigail, who announced: 'Andrew Page was supposedly looking into machines for the making of ceramics for the museum. But this document is about weapons being manufactured in Germany and being sent to South Africa.

'According to this, the Germans have supplied the army of

the Transvaal with 37,000 Mauser Model rifles with 50 million rounds of ammunition. The note goes on to say that 7,000 Guedes rifles had been sent to the Transvaal. It also mentions Krupp artillery. Along with 73 heavy guns, including four Creusot fortress guns and twenty-five Maxim Nordenfelt guns.'

'Someone's getting ready for a war,' observed Feather.

'Why was this hidden in Page's desk rather than being kept at his home?' asked Daniel.

'Because he didn't want his wife or his brother-in-law to find it,' said Abigail. 'Which indicates he was not working for the Germans or the Boers.'

'He must have been spying on them for our side,' said Daniel. 'Remember, he was in Germany four months ago, ostensibly on behalf of the museum. This suggests he had a spy ring there who kept him informed of what the Germans were up to. They must have sent him reports, like this one.'

'But who did he pass them on to?' asked Feather. 'Special Branch?'

'I'm not sure, but we're not going to take the chance of asking them,' said Daniel. 'First, they'll lie, because they always do. And secondly, they'll confiscate these papers, which will then just vanish.'

'So where do we go with them?' asked Feather.

'Not to Armstrong,' said Daniel. 'He'll just pass them on to Special Branch.'

'Then who?' asked Feather.

'Simeon Benton,' said Abigail.

'Exactly,' smiled Daniel.

'Who's Simeon Benton?' asked Feather.

'A friend who knows about these things,' said Daniel. 'And, in your position, John, as a detective inspector at Scotland Yard, it's not advisable that you get involved with him. If Special Branch hear about it, and they might well, you'll be in a very tight spot.'

'But you won't?' asked Feather sarcastically.

'We're already in a spot with them,' said Daniel. 'But we can do things unofficially. You can't. By the way, how did you get on with Mrs Tweed?'

Feather explained that the widow Tweed was upset, but could offer no reason why anyone should want to kill her husband.

'Did you find out what time Tweed left the museum?' he asked.

'Yes,' said Abigail. 'Half past eleven in the morning.'

'So he would have arrived home at about noon,' mused Feather. 'Mrs Tweed arrived home and found him dead at half past three. And we have a witness who saw a man and a woman arrive at Tweed's house sometime in the early afternoon. A man about the same height as Tweed and a tall-ish woman. They were in the house with him for about half an hour. And this witness didn't see anyone else calling at the house that day.'

'So she saw the killers!' said Abigail excitedly. 'A man and a woman!'

'Unless someone else crept into the house from the back,' said Feather. 'But yes, that's my opinion. This couple were the ones who killed Tweed. And Tweed and they knew one another, because Tweed invited them in.'

'Have you any idea who this mystery man and woman are?' asked Daniel.

Feather shook his head.

'Unfortunately, no. He wore a bowler hat, a scarf wrapped round his face, and his overcoat buttoned right up.'

'Bowler hat,' said Daniel. 'So, not just some casual thug.'

'No, the witness said he looked every inch a gentleman.'

'Kurtz is about as tall as Tweed,' said Abigail thoughtfully. 'Kurtz and his sister, perhaps?'

'But did Tweed know them well enough to invite them in?' asked Feather.

'He might have recognised Mrs Page,' said Daniel.

The door opening made them all look round. Sir James Reid entered and surveyed the gathering with disapproval. He took in the papers on the bedside table, and Abigail's handwritten notes, then said in censorial tones: 'This is not what I had in mind when I advised Mr Wilson to rest. You're turning this place into an office. I must ask your visitors to leave, Mr Wilson, while I examine you.'

Abigail gathered up the papers and the German vocabulary and replaced them in her bag.

'Come on, John,' she said. To Sir James she said: 'We'll be downstairs in the wating room.'

Abigail and Feather went downstairs to the luxurious waiting room, where they talked about the document that Abigail had found, and its implication.

'It certainly looks like a motive for murder,' said Abigail, looking at the letter again. 'If the Germans had discovered the existence of this spy ring of Page's in Germany, they'd want to find out the extent of information that had been passed to Page.'

'So you think they killed him in their efforts to find it?' asked Feather doubtfully. 'That's a bit counterproductive.'

'Perhaps they didn't intend to kill him,' suggested Abigail.

'Perhaps they threatened him, and things went too far.'

They were interrupted by the arrival of Sir James Reid, who told them: 'I've examined Mr Wilson, and in my opinion he has improved enough to be discharged.'

'Thank you, Sir James,' said Abigail. 'That is a great relief.'

'My decision was also reached because I feel that all this activity involving you all is disturbing the orderly and quiet running of this clinic. But I will examine him here in my consulting room every other day, at least for the next week.'

CHAPTER TWENTY-SEVEN

As they left the clinic, Daniel said: 'Right, let's go and see Simeon Benton.'

'Don't you want to go home first and relax?' asked Abigail. 'Sir James still seems to feel you should be careful about overdoing things.'

'I've been relaxing for what seems like ages, while all this has been going on,' said Daniel. 'I need to get back into action.'

They made their way to the Foreign Office, where Simeon Benton appeared delighted to see them.

'Mr Wilson, you are back among the land of the living,' he smiled. 'With a clean bill of health, I hope?'

'Clean-*ish*,' said Abigail. 'He's only just been released from the clinic. I wanted him to go home first to recover, but he insisted we came to see you.'

'And here's why,' said Daniel, giving Benton the letter in German. 'Abigail found this hidden in Andrew Page's desk at the museum. She's made a translation of it.' He produced Abigail's translation, but Benton waved it away. 'No need. I understand German.' He read the letter, then said: 'You know what you've got here?'

'Concrete evidence that the Germans are arming the Boers in Transvaal.'

Benton looked thoughtful.

'As it's in German I think we can safely assume it was sent to Mr Page from Germany.'

'Where we believe he was running a spy ring,' said Daniel. 'We know he went there on a number of occasions. He must have sought out people who were sympathetic to Britain, and they in turn sent him inside information about Germany arming the Boers.'

'And other things, I assume,' said Benton thoughtfully.

'So who's behind it?' asked Abigail. 'Who was Page working for? Special Branch?'

Benton shook his head. 'Special Branch's activities are restricted to British soil.'

'They were active in Ireland, I recall,' said Daniel.

'Ireland is still British, despite the activities of the Home Rule lobby,' pointed out Benton.

'So if it's not Special Branch, who is it?' asked Abigail.

'I suspect it's connected to military intelligence,' said Benton. 'To be specific, the Directorate of Military Intelligence.'

Daniel frowned. 'I've never heard of them.'

'Very few people have.'

'Are they part of Special Branch?'

'Not at all. Very separate. In fact, I believe there is quite some jealous rivalry between the two.' He looked at the documents. 'I'd put my money on Page working for the Directorate, gathering information about the link between Germany and the Boers.'

'Could that be a motive for him being killed?' asked Abigail.

'Absolutely. If the Germans discovered the existence of this spy ring, they'd be ready to move heaven and earth to discover what they knew, and what had been passed on to the British government.'

'Why kill Page?' asked Abigail. 'Surely it would make more sense to keep him alive and pressurise him into telling them about it.'

'Torture?' asked Benton. 'Perhaps that's what happened, and cutting his throat was the final act.'

'Herbert Tweed was murdered,' Abigail reminded him. 'My guess is the Germans knew a message had been sent to Page. They tried to get it off him, but failed, for some reason. Perhaps one of the questioners was too overzealous. So Page is dead, and the Germans are no nearer to finding this message. They know it's not at his home. Kurtz must have searched there for it. Or his sister.'

'You think they were part of the plot?' asked Benton.

'It makes sense,' said Daniel. 'So their attention turns to his office. Who might he have taken into his confidence at the office, they wonder?'

'And they come up with Herbert Tweed, his immediate boss,' said Abigail.

'Exactly,' agreed Daniel. 'So they watch him, and one day he leaves work early. They follow him home and question him. 'Where's the message in German?' But he can't tell them because he doesn't know. So they either kill him and then hang him from the bannisters, or they use that to try and frighten him into telling them, but it goes wrong and he dies. The bang on the head was part of the softening-up process.'

'Do you believe that Kurtz was one of the assassins?' asked Benton.

'He has to be,' said Daniel.

'If he was, why did Special Branch take such care to warn you off from talking to him?' asked Benton.

'Because they're gathering evidence against him themselves,' said Daniel.

'Or perhaps Kurtz is actually working for them,' said Benton. 'Or perhaps for British Military Intelligence. His job may have been to protect Page, and now he's using his contacts to find out who did kill Page. If that's the case, Special Branch wouldn't want you interfering.'

'But you told us yourself that Kurtz is working for the Boers, and before that he was working for the German government,' pointed out Abigail.

'Double agents are as old as the hills,' said Benton. 'People who appear to work for one side but actually work for the opposite.'

'So you're suggesting that instead of Kurtz possibly being the one who murdered Page, he might have been in England to protect him on behalf of either Special Branch or these Military Intelligence people?'

'It's only a possibility,' said Benton.

'But it's a feasible one,' said Abigail thoughtfully. 'The problem is, it gives us a major quandary. Who do we take this to? Special Branch? If it turns out that Kurtz isn't working for them, they'll arrest him. It could be that the only reason they're keeping him at arm's length at the moment is because they haven't got any evidence to pull him in, especially as he's a representative of a foreign government.

‘On the other hand, if we give it to these Military Intelligence people and he’s not working for them, what can they do?’

‘As I said before, Special Branch only operate on British soil. They won’t have been able to set up this spy ring in Germany. That would have been Military Intelligence. So Page must have been working for them. My suggestion would be to hand it to them.’ He smiled. ‘Or, at least, give them a copy. You could give the original to Mrs Page. She is, after all, his widow, so anything of his should be rightfully hers.’

‘Set the cat among the pigeons,’ smiled Daniel. ‘See what she does with it.’

‘She’ll give it to her brother,’ said Abigail. Then she added warningly: ‘The last time we set the cat among the pigeons, Daniel ended up almost killed.’

‘Then can I suggest you tell your friend at Scotland Yard what you’re up to.’

‘Inspector Feather,’ said Abigail.

‘He might be able to mount some kind of protective watch over you. A discreet policeman outside your door.’

‘Hardly discreet,’ said Daniel, sourly.

‘It’s up to you,’ shrugged Benton. ‘You asked for my advice.’

Daniel and Abigail returned to their home, relieved at finally being able to relax in their own familiar surroundings. Over tea they discussed what they’d learnt. Did Benton have a point? Was Kurtz’s role to protect Page, working as a double agent? In which case, if he didn’t kill Page and Tweed, who did?

‘We can’t discuss this with Kurtz in case we’re wrong and Kurtz is the killer,’ said Daniel.

‘We can’t discuss it with Special Branch in case Kurtz is

working for them,' added Abigail.

'Not according to Benton,' said Daniel. 'If Kurtz is a double agent, Benton's money's on Kurtz working for Military Intelligence.'

'*If* he's a double agent,' cautioned Abigail. She fell into a thoughtful silence, before finally saying: 'I think setting the cat among the pigeons is the only way to flush out the truth, and the killer.'

'But which one do we try it on?' asked Daniel.

'All of them,' said Abigail. 'I write out copies of the German letter, along with the translation. We give one to these Military Intelligence people that Benton was talking about. We give one copy to John Feather, just in case anything happens to us. But we ask him to keep it to himself for the moment, otherwise he'll be forced to pass it on to Armstrong, and then to Special Branch. We also give the original to Mrs Page.'

'She'll give it to her brother,' said Daniel.

'Yes,' said Abigail. 'And we watch him to see what he does with it.'

'It's a dangerous game,' cautioned Daniel.

'I know. And, because of that, I suggest we leave a copy with our bank, addressed to Joe Dalton at the *Telegraph*, to be sent to him in the event of our death.'

'You think it could come to that?' asked Daniel.

'You've already been attacked once,' Abigail reminded him.

'Yes, but I'm sure that was to do with us looking into Tweed's fraudulent activities.'

'But Herbert Tweed was killed, and most likely because someone was after this letter.'

'Hopefully, putting it into the public domain like this would take that threat away,' said Daniel. 'If Kurtz was looking for it, he'll stop once he gets his hands on it.'

'I think we might need to have a word with Raphael Wilton,' said Abigail. 'If these people killed Tweed as part of trying to get their hands on this letter, they might look at Wilton, wondering if he's got it.'

'Yes, that makes sense,' said Daniel. 'If they thought that Tweed might know where it was just because he was in the same office as Page, the same applies to Wilton.'

'So, do we make a copy for Wilton as well?' asked Abigail.

'No,' said Daniel. 'Giving him a copy will only increase any possible danger to him.'

CHAPTER TWENTY-EIGHT

Abigail made four copies of the German letter, each written in perfect script, and then a further three English translations. That done, they returned to the Foreign Office and told Benton their plan.

'Can you arrange a meeting for us with military intelligence, someone you trust?' asked Daniel.

'I'm not sure if anyone can be trusted in the world of spying,' said Benton. 'However, there is someone that almost fits the bill. I'll give you a letter to him, introducing you.'

Benton took a sheet of Foreign Office letterheaded paper, and wrote a few lines on it. While the ink on that dried, he addressed an envelope, which he handed to Daniel.

'Edgar Blenkinsop Esquire, Adjutant General's Department, Horseguards Avenue, Whitehall,' read Daniel. He looked quizzically at Benton. 'Adjutant General's Department?'

'You'd hardly expect them to have a plate outside their door saying "Military Intelligence",' said Benton.

'Who is he, this Edgar Blenkinsop?'

'He's a senior aide to Henry Brackenbury, Director of Military Intelligence. He's a good man.'

'You've known him long?'

'We were at school together.'

'Where?'

'Harrow.'

The Adjutant General's Department in Horseguards Avenue was one of the myriad government buildings tucked away in the cluster around the Houses of Parliament. There was a wait while they sat in the marble-floored reception area of the building before a tall well-dressed man appeared from down a set of marble stairs. His dress showed all the appearance of a senior civil servant, from the black patent leather shoes to the high starched collar above his immaculate black jacket.

'Mr and Mrs Wilson?' he enquired as he approached them.

'Yes,' they said, getting to their feet. 'Mr Edgar Blenkinsop, we assume?'

He inclined his head in confirmation, then said: 'Simeon suggests this is of a confidential nature, so I suggest we go to one of the smaller conference rooms.'

Abigail and Daniel followed him to a door marked 'Private'. Inside was a long table with six chairs around it.

'One of the smaller conference rooms?' asked Daniel.

'The larger ones seat thirty,' said Blenkinsop. He gestured for them to sit. 'Simeon suggests you have something I may be interested in.'

Abigail took out one of the envelopes that contained the

copy of the German letter.

'There's a translation in the envelope as well,' she said.

As Benton had done, Blenkinsop shook his head as he scanned the German script. 'I read German,' he told them. He looked at them and asked: 'Where did you get this?'

'I found it hidden beneath the desk of Mr Andrew Page at the Victoria and Albert Museum,' said Abigail. 'He was murdered recently…'

'Yes, said Blenkinsop. 'I saw it in the newspapers.'

'We've been engaged to investigate his murder,' said Daniel.

'I saw that, too,' said Blenkinsop. 'Her Majesty hires the Museum Detectives.' He tapped the letter. 'You know what this says, of course.'

'Yes,' said Abigail. 'I wrote the translation.'

Blenkinsop studied the letter some more.

'Why did you bring it to me?' he asked.

'We thought Military Intelligence were the best people to have sight of it,' said Daniel. 'In view of its contents. It would appear that Mr Page was receiving information from his agents in Germany about armaments being sent to the Boers.'

Blenkinsop looked at the letter again, and nodded.

'This is a copy,' he said. 'Do you have other copies?'

'We have one, which we are planning to deposit with Inspector John Feather at Scotland Yard,' said Daniel. 'In case anything should happen to us. He is also investigating the murder of Andrew Page.'

'Does he know about this already?'

'He does,' said Abigail.

'But we've asked him to keep this to himself at this moment and not to pass it on to his boss, Chief Superintendent

Armstrong, or anyone else at Scotland Yard.'

'May I ask why?'

'Because if he did, it would go immediately to Special Branch.'

Blenkinsop looked at them inquisitively. 'And you have reservations about that?'

'Let us just say that after discussing this with Simeon Benton, we felt that the – ah – Adjutant General's Department was more appropriate.'

Blenkinsop permitted himself a slight smile at this.

'Thank you,' he said. 'I'll look into this.'

'And you'll let us know?' asked Abigail.

Blenkinsop hesitated slightly, then said: 'Possibly. If it seems appropriate.'

'If it seems appropriate,' said Daniel sarcastically as they left the building.

'He's a civil servant,' said Abigail. 'They're trained not to commit themselves.'

'Nor to show any emotion,' said Daniel, still annoyed. 'As one of the senior protectors of our national security, you'd think he'd be overjoyed to get that information.'

'Where to now?' asked Abigail. 'Mrs Page or John Feather?'

'Neither,' said Daniel. 'Raphael Wilton, to warn him. Heaven knows, even as we speak he could be in danger.'

Inspector Feather sat at his desk and watched Sergeant Cribbens sucking on his infernal foul-smelling pipe and thought about the dilemma of Heinrich Kurtz. Normally he'd discuss the issue with his sergeant, get his thoughts on the matter, but as he'd promised Daniel and Abigail that he'd keep the contents of the letter Abigail had found to himself, he couldn't. But he decided he could be *hypothetical.* Talk about it in general terms, suggesting things that were *possible,* without giving anything away.

'Sergeant,' he said, 'I've been thinking.'

'Yes, sir?' said Cribbens.

'This business of Herbert Tweed being murdered. We know that he had his fingers in the till at the museum.'

'Yes, sir. Although Mrs Tweed didn't agree.'

'Mrs Tweed is being loyal to her late husband. No, it's possible he was killed because of information that some people may have thought he had.'

'What sort of information, sir?'

'About the death of Andrew Page.'

'You think they're connected?'

'It's a bit of a stretch of a coincidence if they're not. Both of them working at the same place, and in the same department.'

'Yes, sir, that's a good point. So do you think that Page also had his fingers in the till?'

'Unlikely, Sergeant. It turns out he inherited a quarter of a million pounds, so he wasn't hard up for money.'

Cribbens stared at him, astonished. 'A quarter of a million?' he croaked.

'My sentiments exactly,' said Feather. 'Which suggests there could be something else linking them.'

Cribbens frowned. 'Like what, sir?'

'Politics,' said Feather.

The sergeant groaned. 'Lord protect us from politics. There's always trouble when politics come into anything.'

'Very true,' said Feather. 'Like this case for instance. You know we were warned off from looking into Page's brother-in-law, this Heinrich Kurtz, by Special Branch?'

'No, sir.'

'Yes. The chief superintendent told me. He was the one they warned off Kurtz., Doesn't that strike you as suspicious?'

'It does, sir.'

'Mr Kurtz is German.'

'Yes, sir. I thought he must be with a name like that, and the fact his sister's German.'

'What I'm saying, Sergeant, is that there must be something to do with this case that involves Kurtz, otherwise we wouldn't have been warned off. Something to do with the Germans.'

Cribbens thought it over, then said: 'Are you thinking that maybe this Kurtz killed Page? And Mr Tweed?'

'I don't know, Sergeant. I might have a better idea of that if we'd been allowed to talk to him, but we've been barred. So I was wondering if it might be useful to talk to some Germans. Not about this case, but about Mr Kurtz. See if anyone has got anything to say about him that might be useful.'

Cribbens frowned. 'That ain't going to be easy, sir. I mean, there's thousands of Germans over here, most of 'em over in the East End. Little Germany.'

Cribbens was referring to the area of the east end of London around Whitechapel where most of the immigrants from Germany had settled, mainly because it was close to the docks where they'd arrived, and the housing was cheaper.

'I'm thinking that this bloke Kurtz doesn't strike me as the sort to mix with people in the poorest part of the East End. Look at the house where his sister lives, in Belgrave Square. And he worked for the German government. No, I'm thinking of the richer sort of Germans. More his social class.'

'Fitzrovia,' said Cribbens. 'That's where the rich Germans live. Some of the best German restaurants in town are in Charlotte Street.'

Feather nodded. 'Yes, I know the maître d' at Schmidt's. I think I'll go and have a word with him. He might know someone who's met this Kurtz bloke.'

'Do you want me to come with you, sir?'

'No thanks, Sergeant. You'd better stay here and hold the fort in case the chief superintendent comes looking for me.'

'Right, sir. Do you want me to tell him where you've gone?'

Feather shook his head. 'I don't think that's a good idea in view of the fact he was the one who told me we've been warned off poking into Kurtz. If he asks, tell him I'm doing some checking on Mr Tweed.'

'Right, sir.'

CHAPTER TWENTY-NINE

Raphael Wilton looked at Daniel and Abigail with curiosity as they entered his office.

'Do sit down,' he said, gesturing at two chairs. 'It's good to see you, Mr Wilson, after your recent tragic accident.'

'No accident, I'm afraid,' said Daniel.

'Yes, so I understand,' said Wilton uncomfortably. 'I can't think what possessed Tweed to hire those men to attack you.'

'An attempt to protect himself,' said Daniel.

'Yes, so it seems,' said Wilton ruefully. 'How can I help you today?'

'While I was checking Mr Page's desk I found a letter in German,' Abigail told him. 'It's been suggested to us that Mr Page was part of a spy ring, and that information from Germany was being sent to him to pass on to the authorities. Somehow or other, the Germans found out about it and want to get the information back. They killed Mr Page. When they didn't get it off him, they next tried Mr Tweed, believing he must have been involved with Mr Page.'

As they watched, Wilton sagged unhappily in his chair.

'But it wasn't Tweed, was it?' said Daniel, quietly. 'It was you. That's why you appointed Page to Germany.'

'I was forced to,' said Wilton unhappily. 'They said I had to do it to protect the nation.'

'Who said?'

'This man. He didn't give his name. He was a military type, but in a suit. He showed me a card saying he had government authority. But I didn't know what it was about, or why it was important that Page got the German position.'

'You were seen in close conversation with Page,' said Abigail.

Wilton nodded, unhappily. 'He asked if the mail for him was arriving. He'd arranged for it to be delivered here rather than at his home.'

'And was it?'

'Yes. A couple of times it was later than he expected. I believe he had an arrangement.'

'How often did letters arrive for him here?'

'There had been two since he returned from Germany. One a month ago, and the last with a German stamp arrived last week.'

'That must be the one his assassins were looking for,' said Daniel. 'Mr Wilton, we don't wish to alarm you, but we feel you should take some time off very soon, and go away somewhere safe.'

'Impossible,' said Wilton. 'The foundation stone has only just been laid by Her Majesty, and there are immediate arrangements to be made.'

'Two men from this office have recently been murdered,' said Daniel. 'The Germans don't know who has the letter, but they might suspect you. After all, they suspected it was Mr Tweed.'

'No,' said Wilton, suddenly resolute. 'I will not be driven out of the museum, not at this vital stage in its development.'

'You aren't listening to us,' said Daniel. 'You could be at risk.'

'It is my duty to be here. With Mr Page and Mr Tweed gone, someone of my position is needed here. I cannot abandon the museum.'

Daniel and Abigail exchanged looks of frustration.

'Did the military man you mentioned give you his name and where he could be contacted?' asked Daniel.

'No,' said Wilton. 'He insisted everything be done with absolute secrecy.'

'Very well,' said Daniel. 'We'll inform Inspector Feather of what's happened and ask him to put a guard on your house. We'll also talk to the people who we believe might be these military people you spoke of. We'll tell them of the danger we believe you're in.'

'If you feel that's necessary,' said Wilton, determined to stand his ground.

'We do,' said Daniel.

There was a knock on the door and Miss Huss entered.

'I'm sorry to interrupt, Mr Wilton,' she said, 'but you have an appointment with the ceramics expert at the British Museum.'

'Of course,' said Wilton. 'Thank you for reminding me.' He rose to his feet and turned to Daniel and Abigail. 'Thank you for coming to warn me. I shall certainly take it into consideration.'

They followed him out of his office into the secretaries' room. Miss Huss looked up at Wilton from her typewriter and said: 'Remember, I have a dental appointment this afternoon, Mr Wilton. I shan't be any longer than necessary.'

'Of course,' said Wilton. 'Thank you, Miss Huss.'

He left, followed by Daniel and Abigail who made their way to the outside.

'Did you see that?' asked Daniel.

'What?'

'When Miss Huss told Wilton she had a dental appointment, one of the other secretaries winked at another.'

Abigail frowned. 'You think Mr Wilton and Miss Huss are planning to meet for an illicit relationship?'

'It's possible.'

'But they are so formal to one another. Positively aloof.'

'But something's going on,' grinned Daniel. 'Don't you think that's interesting?'

'No, I think it's salacious,' said Abigail.

Inspector Feather walked down the steps of Der Gymnasium, a club for expatriate Germans located beneath a greengrocer's shop in Charlotte Street. He'd been sent there by Max Kessler, the maître d' at Schmidt's restaurant, who'd told him that Mr Kurtz had dined at their establishment a couple of times since he'd arrived in London. 'I believe on one occasion he went as the guest of Karl Venner, the man who owns Der Gymnasium, a private club. He might be able to help you.'

Feather had deliberately avoided bringing Sergeant Cribbens with him. Daniel and Abigail were anxious to keep the fact of the German letter about the arms for Transvaal away from the chief superintendent and Special Branch. Although he knew he could trust Cribbens, it wouldn't be fair to put him in that difficult position. When the appropriate time came, he'd tell his sergeant, but until then he had to do this solo.

From the title, Der Gymnasium, Feather had expected some military establishment, filled with exercise equipment. Instead, the basement area was luxuriously decorated and furnished with heavy oak furniture. The walls were adorned with paintings of German scenery, and there was a portrait of Kaiser Wilhelm II in pride of place behind the long bar, with German flags on either side of it. The signage was also in German.

At this time of day the club was virtually empty, just a barman cleaning glasses behind the bar and a man with a mop cleaning the floor.

Feather approached the barman and asked politely: 'Is Mr Karl Venner available?'

The barman looked at him warily.

'Who wishes to know?' he asked.

'Detective Inspector Feather from Scotland Yard,' said Feather, showing the barman his warrant card. 'But this is an informal visit. Nothing official. I just want to talk to him. Max Kessler at Schmidt's suggested I call.'

The barman walked the length of the bar and disappeared through a door at the end. A short time later the barman reappeared accompanied by a man wearing a suit of a large-checked material, a checked waistcoat with a red and black cravat above it, and a monocle in his right eye. Like many Germans, he favoured a large bushy moustache.

'Inspector Feather,' he beamed, holding out his hand. 'Hans mentioned Max Kessler.'

'Yes. It was Max who suggested I talk to you,' said Feather shaking his hand.

'What about?'

'As I said to your barman, nothing formal. I'm just interested in finding out about Heinrich Kurtz. I believe you know him.'

'We dined together at Schmidt's and he has been here on a couple of occasions. Why do you wish to know about him?' Venner gestured towards two large dark brown leather armchairs. 'I suggest we seat ourselves. It's more comfortable here than in my office, and at this time we will not be overheard or interrupted. Can I offer you something to drink?'

'No Thank you, Mr Venner.'

The two men sat.

'Why do you wish to know about Mr Kurtz?' asked Venner.

'We're currently investigating two deaths that have taken place involving the Victoria and Albert Museum. One of them was his brother-in-law, Andrew Page.'

'Ah yes, I saw the report in the newspaper. But how is Mr Kurtz involved?'

'I'm not sure that he is, but we're trying to get a picture of everyone who knew Mr Page.'

'Have you talked to Mr Kurtz himself?'

'Apparently that's a sensitive issue,' said Feather. 'Politics, I'm afraid. Mr Kurtz is a representative of the Transvaal government and has also represented the German government in talks here, so I'm informed, and as such the Foreign Office have advised us that he is not to be troubled. I respect that, but it doesn't help us to build a picture of Mr Page and his activities. I believe he was active in Germany on behalf of the museum, which was why I hoped that Mr Kurtz might be able to fill in some of the gaps in our knowledge concerning Mr Page's German activities.'

'Is Mr Kurtz also then involved in the museum?' asked Venner.

'Not to my knowledge. I know that Mr Kurtz is a mining engineer, and as Mr Page's area of expertise was engineering, I wondered if there was any link there. As I'm prevented from talking to Mr Kurtz directly, I thought I'd talk to people who've known him in this country.'

Venner shook his head. 'I cannot honestly say I know him. We were introduced, and I invited him to dinner at Schmidt's. Since then, he has come here to Der Gymnasium as many Germans do because here they feel at home.'

'Has he made many acquaintances here?'

'Not to my knowledge. Most of the people here talk about business, or reminisce about our homeland.' He smiled. 'Nostalgia and our homeland are very important to us as expatriates.' He sighed. 'I'm afraid I cannot help you, Inspector.'

As Feather walked up the stairs from the basement club and out into Charlotte Street, he felt a sense of angry frustration. Venner was lying, of that he was sure. Kurtz was the key to this. Either he was the assassin who'd killed both Page and Tweed, or he'd hired others to do it. The letter that Abigail had found showed a German connection. In some way the Germans had found out about Page's spy ring. Soon afterwards, Kurtz had arrived in London, ostensibly from South Africa. And shortly after that Page had been murdered.

So why was Special Branch protecting Kurtz? What was going on?

* * *

Daniel and Abigail's next visit was to Scotland Yard to deliver a copy of the letter to John Feather, but the inspector was out. Instead, they found Sergeant Cribbens in the office, puffing away at his pipe.

'The inspector's gone to see some Germans,' Cribbens told them.

'Mr Kurtz?' asked Abigail.

Cribbens shook his head. 'No. Some club or other where Germans living in London meet and talk and drink. I think he's hoping to find things out about what the Germans in London are up to.'

'When he returns, will you ask him to call on us?' asked Daniel. 'We've got some information for him.'

'You can give it to me, if you like,' offered Cribbens. 'I'll pass it onto him.'

'Thanks, Sergeant, but we really need to see the inspector to explain it.'

'Understood,' said Cribbens. He looked at Daniel, concerned, and asked: 'How are you now, Mr Wilson? That was a terrible bang on the head you took.'

'The doctor says I'm well enough to be discharged,' said Daniel.

'But he's going to be keeping an eye on him,' Abigail added. 'What's happening to the two men who attacked us?'

'They're on remand awaiting trial for attempted murder,' said Cribbens. 'You're all right to appear in court and give evidence against them, I hope?'

'I am,' Abigail confirmed.

'Unfortunately, I can't remember anything about the attack,' said Daniel. 'Hopefully it will come back to me by the time of the court appearance.'

The door opened and the bulky figure of Chief Superintendent Armstrong entered the office. He stopped when he saw Daniel and Abigail and glowered at them suspiciously.

'What are you two doing here?' he demanded.

'We've come to catch up on the Page murder with Inspector Feather,' said Daniel. 'I've been out of action for a while, as I'm sure you know.'

'Yes,' growled Armstrong. 'I see you've recovered.'

'Thank you, I have.'

'How come the Queen told her own private physician to look after you? And at a private clinic?' demanded Armstrong, obviously resenting this fact.

'I suppose she appreciated what we were doing to solve Mr Page's murder,' said Abigail. 'Especially our intervention on behalf of Mr Ward.'

'You were lucky!' snorted Armstrong indignantly. 'We would have found out that he had an alibi.'

'Of course you would,' said Abigail politely.

'It was us who worked out that Tweed was murdered,' he went on. 'We beat you on that one.'

'We're not in a competition, Chief Superintendent,' said Abigail.

'Oh no? Well, it feels like it. How many times have you interfered with a police investigation because you've got some theory of your own?'

'And how many times have we been wrong, Chief Superintendent?' asked Daniel.

Armstrong glared at him. 'That's irrelevant. And if there's nothing else, I'll trouble you to leave. We've got important work to do.'

'Of course,' said Abigail. She and Daniel got to their feet and smiled at Sergeant Cribbens. 'Please tell Inspector Feather we called, Sergeant.'

'Of course, Mrs Wilson,' said Cribbens.

CHAPTER THIRTY

Daniel waited until they had left the office and were walking across the main reception area before saying: 'Armstrong didn't mention anything about the document in German you found hidden in Page's desk. Which suggests John has been as good as his word and hasn't told him about it.'

'After what happened with Stephen Ward, John is being extra careful about what he tells the chief superintendent,' said Abigail. 'Armstrong is likely to go straight to Special Branch with it, and we don't know if that would help or harm the investigation. Next, our bank?'

'Indeed,' said Daniel.

They lodged an envelope containing another copy of the letter in German, along with Abigail's translation, and a letter to Joe Dalton. The letter said:

Dear Joe

If you are opening this then we are both dead, and

We feel our deaths are the result of an investigation we have been conducting into the murder of Andrew Page at the Victoria and Albert Museum. The enclosed is a letter we found hidden beneath Andrew Page's desk at the museum. It has led us to believe that Page had set up a spy ring in Germany and received information from his agents there about Germany arming the Boers of Transvaal. We have given a copy of this to Edgar Blenkinsop at the Adjutant General's Department at Horse Guards Avenue. They are the Directorate of Military Intelligence. Copies are also going to be left with Inspector John Feather at Scotland Yard and Andrew Page's widow, Gretchen Page.

If you do receive this it will be unfortunate for us, and it could be very fortunate for you, as it could be a major scoop.

Yours sincerely

Daniel and Abigail Wilson

That done, they returned home, where they found John Feather waiting outside their front door.

'We hope you haven't been waiting long,' said Abigail.

'Just a few minutes,' said Feather. 'Cribbens gave me your message when I got back to the Yard.'

'He said you were out chasing Germans,' said Daniel, unlocking the door.

'Yes, but with little result,' said Feather ruefully. 'I'll tell you all after you've told me what you were after.'

While Daniel put the kettle on for tea, Abigail gave Feather the envelope with the copy of the German letter and the translation.

'We're giving you this in case anything happens to us,' she said.

'You think it might?'

'We were attacked because someone felt we were getting evidence about fraud,' said Abigail. 'This is evidence about arming the Boers in readiness for another war, which is even more potent.'

'We're doing our best to protect ourselves,' said Daniel. 'The more people who know this is out and about, the less chance there is of someone getting rid of us to ensure it remains secret. We've taken a copy of this letter to a contact at the Directorate of Military Intelligence, an Edgar Blenkinsop. We've given it to them because our contact in the Foreign Office suggests if Page was operating a spy ring against the Germans on behalf of the British, that's who he'd most likely have been working for.'

'Not Special Branch?'

'No. He says that Special Branch can only operate on British soil, not in foreign countries.'

'Huh, I don't believe that for a moment,' said Feather scornfully. 'That may be the official line, but I wouldn't trust Special Branch to stick to any rules. They act as a law unto themselves.'

'Still, that's what he told us, so that's what we've done. We're also giving you a copy of it, along with the translation, in case anything happens to us. If anything *does* happen to us, we're fairly sure it'll be because of this.

'We've also advised Wilton at the museum to take some urgent leave, but he's refused. We believe that both Page and

Tweed were killed by people who were looking for this. As they haven't found it, they'll be looking at other people in the curators' department, and the obvious one is Wilton. Especially as we've now discovered that Wilton had been told by some military types to give the post of being the museum's German connection to Page.'

'Why is Wilton refusing to take leave?' asked Feather.

'We're not sure. He might have just decided to be stubborn. He talked about not letting the museum down at this time.'

'We're also going to give the original to Mrs Page,' added Abigail. 'As his widow, it's rightfully hers.'

'She'll just pass it straight to her brother,' said Feather.

'We know,' said Daniel. 'We want to see what he does with it. If he's working for British military intelligence, he'll take it to them.'

'Why on earth do you think he could be working for British intelligence?' asked Feather, bewildered. 'He's working for the Boers.'

'It's been suggested to us he could be a double agent,' said Daniel. 'Or, he might take it to the German Embassy. Or, if he's an assassin, he might pass it on to a conspirator.'

'That's lots of "maybe and ors",' said Feather doubtfully.

'That's right,' agreed Daniel. 'Our problem is that Kurtz knows us, so we can't follow him to see where he goes with it.'

'You want me to put a couple of plain clothes detectives on him?' asked Feather.

'If you can,' said Abigail. 'It shouldn't be for long. Our guess is he'll move pretty quickly once he's got hold of this.'

'Leave it to me,' said Feather. 'When are you going to hand this to Mrs Page?'

'Tomorrow morning,' said Daniel. 'About nine o'clock, before she goes out. Did you find out if Kurtz is staying with his sister?'

Feather nodded. 'Yes. We asked the postman, and he's definitely there. So you might run into him tomorrow when you call.'

'In which case it will speed things up,' said Abigail.

'I'll have someone watching their house from nine,' said Feather.

'We also think it might be worth putting someone to watch Wilton's house in case he's targeted the same as Tweed was. Our hope is that once Kurtz gets hold of this letter, he'll pass it on to other people involved, and Wilton should be safe. But you never know. Better safe than sorry.'

'Anyone else you want watched while we're using up the resources of Scotland Yard?' asked Feather sarcastically.

Daniel and Abigail smiled.

'Our hope is that dropping this into the pool, as well as protecting us, will stir things up and we'll uncover the killer. Or killers,' said Abigail.

Daniel put the three cups of tea on the table.

'Right, that's our news,' he said. 'Now, tell us about these Germans you were seeing.'

'It struck me that, in the same way that Page had a spy ring operating in Germany, his wife's brother, Kurtz, might be doing the same here in England with Germans in London sympathetic to the German cause. After all, because of this letter you found, it seems likely that the Germans killed him while they were trying to find the letter.'

'Are there lots of Germans in London sympathetic to

the German cause?' asked Abigail. 'It's struck me that most immigrants have left their own countries because they don't like their own governments. Look at the original Pilgrim Fathers going to America in the *Mayflower*, or the large number of Russian Jews who've arrived here, driven out of Russia.'

'That's generally true,' agreed Feather. 'But there are quite a few who remain patriotic to the idea of Germany even if they didn't like the society they left. Most of them are economic migrants, come here for a better life, always intending to return to Germany. London was also a stopping off point for large numbers of Germans who headed to America for a better life. It's estimated that about three million Germans have passed through London on their way to America in the last few decades. They arrived in London in small ships, and then transferred to the much larger ships for the Atlantic crossing. Many of these migrants took temporary jobs in London to get money for going to America, but for some those temporary jobs became permanent.'

'Yes,' nodded Daniel in agreement. He turned to Abigail and told her: 'When I was on the force, we encountered many Germans who'd settled here. Mostly they settled in the East End, close to the docks. There was an area of Whitechapel that was known as Little Germany.'

'It still is,' said Feather. 'Mostly it's where the poorer Germans settled. Those who earned good money and became middle class moved to areas like Fitzrovia, especially around Charlotte Street. That's where I was today. From what I gleaned about Kurtz, I thought he was more likely to socialise with the Fitzrovia crowd than the crowded tenement-dwellers of Whitechapel and Mile End.'

'And?'

'A complete dead end,' admitted Feather. 'I was told that Kurtz visited a private German club called Der Gymnasium. I went there today to talk to the owner, a Karl Venner. He was very friendly but said he couldn't help, he knew nothing about Kurtz's activities in London.'

'You think he was telling the truth?'

'No, I think he was lying. Kurtz is over here and he must be wrapped up in whatever's going on. I can't believe he's working on his own. But I can't get through this wall of silence that he's hiding behind, a wall that Special Branch have partly put up.' He looked at the envelope Abigail had given him. 'I'm hoping that this will shake things up for us once you've given it to Mrs Page.'

Heinrich Kurtz sat in Der Gymnasium and listened as Karl Venner told him about the visit by Inspector Feather.

'I think you should leave England as soon as possible,' said Venner. 'The police are looking into you.'

Kurtz shook his head.

'I cannot leave until I've discovered just how much Andrew knew. We know he received a message recently from his people in Germany, but so far it's eluded us.'

'You've got someone to check the museum?' asked Venner.

'I have. I paid one of the cleaners to go through his desk and bring me anything she found in German.' He gave a snort of disgust. 'There were just letters from German pottery makers. Nothing at all to give us a clue about what had been passed to him, or what it concerns.'

'Perhaps the letters about pottery makers are in code?' suggested Venner.

'No,' said Kurtz. 'I have verified they are authentic.'

'And you are sure he didn't hide anything in the house?'

'I have searched every inch of it, as has Gretchen. It is her house, she knows every possible hiding place. There is nothing there.'

'Perhaps there is nothing to find?' suggested Venner.

'Oh yes there is,' said Kurtz angrily. 'The suspects who were detained were examined rigorously. One of them admitted sending a letter to Andrew at the museum.'

'Did he give you any more? What was in the letter?'

'Unfortunately, he died before that information could be obtained from him,' said Kurtz.

Venner fell into a thoughtful silence for a few moments, then he asked: 'I do not understand what the British are doing? The police inspector who called said that the Foreign Office have given orders that you are not to be questioned. Why is that?'

'The Foreign Office?' repeated Kurtz surprised. 'Are you sure he said the Foreign Office?'

'Yes,' said Venner.

'I have no idea,' he said. 'Who knows why the British do the things they do?'

'And no one from the British authorities has spoken to you at all?' pressed Venner. 'Not police or their so-called intelligence services?'

'No,' said Kurtz. 'The only people I've spoken to since Andrew died are the couple who the newspapers call the Museum Detectives.'

'Daniel Wilson and his wife, the former Abigail Fenton,' nodded Venner. 'What did they ask you?'

'Nothing,' said Kurtz. 'They had called primarily to talk to my sister.'

'Strange, this lack of interest,' murmured Venner suspiciously. He looked at Kurtz and asked: 'Is there anything we should know, Heinrich?'

'Like what?' bridled Kurtz.

'If I knew, I wouldn't ask,' said Venner.

'No,' said Kurtz. 'There is nothing.' He looked at his watch and stood up. 'I must go. I promised Gretchen I would spend time with her this afternoon.'

Venner rose to his feet and the two men exchanged brief bows, then Kurtz left. Venner signalled to the barman, Hans, to come over to him.

'Hans, I believe we may have a problem,' he said.

Hans looked towards the stairs where Kurtz had disappeared.

'Mr Kurtz?' he asked.

'We need to know why the British are apparently avoiding having contact with him,' said Venner thoughtfully.

'Apparently?' asked Hans.

'We need to know where his loyalties lie,' said Venner.

Hans smiled. 'A test?' he asked.

Venner nodded. 'I'm sure you can arrange something.'

CHAPTER THIRTY-ONE

This time it was a young housemaid who opened the door of the luxurious house in Belgrave Square when Daniel and Abigail called the following morning.

'Good morning,' said Daniel. 'Would you tell Mrs Page that Mr and Mrs Wilson are calling with something to give her?'

'I'll see if she's available,' said the girl.

She was about to close the door, but Daniel swiftly pushed his foot on the step to hold the door open, but he did it with a polite smile. 'Would you tell her it's very important, and also private.'

The housemaid left, reappearing a few moments later.

'The missus says she'll see you,' she informed them in a haughty tone.

They followed the housemaid through to the conservatory where they'd met Mrs Page on their previous visit.

'She obviously has a liking for being surrounded by large

plants,' murmured Daniel.

Today Mrs Page was alone. Her brother was not with her.

'Mrs Page, forgive us for disturbing you,' said Daniel. 'But we have discovered something that we believe should be in your possession.'

Abigail opened her bag and took out the envelope containing the original letter in German, which she handed to Mrs Page.

'I discovered this in your husband's desk at the museum,' she said. 'It was stuck to the underside of one of the desk drawers. As it was his, rightfully it should go to you.'

Gretchen Page took the sheet of paper from the envelope, then looked at them, startled.

'Have you read this?' she asked, and they both caught the note of urgency in her voice.

'I do not read German,' said Daniel.

Abigail said nothing, just smiled.

'We'll leave it with you, Mrs Page. Once again, we're sorry for disturbing you.'

Gretchen Page rang the bell for the housemaid and instructed her to show Mr and Mrs Wilson out. Abigail held out her hand, and Mrs Page took it awkwardly and shook it.

Upstairs in the spare bedroom, Heinrich Kurtz looked out of the window and watched the Wilsons walk across the road. He put on a dressing gown and hurried downstairs.

'I saw the Wilsons,' he said. 'Those private detectives. Did they just call?'

'Yes,' said Mrs Page. 'They brought this.' She handed him the letter. As he read it, she added: 'They said they found it in Andrew's desk at the museum.'

'Why did they give it to you?'

'They said as his widow it was rightfully mine.'

'Had they read it?'

'I asked, and Mr Wilson said he did not read German.'

'But she does,' grunted Kurtz. 'I have seen articles of hers in magazines in which she quotes from eminent German archaeologists.' He read the letter again. 'This is some kind of trick they are playing. No one is that naive. Especially not those two.'

'Then why did they give it to me?'

'To save their own lives,' said Kurtz. 'Two people have died because people have been looking for this.'

He turned and made for the stairs.

'Where are you going?' called Gretchen.

'To get dressed. I have to take this to someone,' said Kurtz.

Hans, the barman from Der Gymnasium, stood beneath the trees in the square of garden opposite the Pages' house. He had seen the two people he knew were known as the Museum Detectives enter the house, and then leave shortly afterwards. Why had they gone there? Was Kurtz working with them? If so, what was behind it?

He felt the weight of the pistol in his jacket pocket. Only if absolutely necessary, Mr Venner had told him. If you think he is being disloyal. We can take no chances.

The door of the house opened, and the tall figure of Kurtz came out. Hans moved behind a tree to remain out of sight, but it looked as if Kurtz wasn't watching out for anyone who might be following him. Kurtz was walking at speed, obviously in a hurry, single-mindedly set on wherever he was making for.

As Hans watched, he saw a man further along the road appear from a side alley between two of the houses and set off after Kurtz. The man's manner as well as his clothes – the long overcoat, the bowler hat, the big boots – betrayed him as an official of some sort, most likely a policeman.

They knew that Kurtz was being watched by the British, here was the living proof. The question was: was Kurtz aware of the man following him? Was Kurtz leading the man somewhere? Was it part of a ruse so they could talk somewhere privately away from the house?

Hans set off after the pair: Kurtz in the lead, the British policeman following at a reasonable distance behind him, with Hans bringing up the rear.

Hans's fingers closed on the pistol in his pocket. This might mean killing them both. If that had to be done, so be it. He'd take their wallets and let people presume it had just been a robbery, although the British authorities would know. So would the rest of the German ring in London. It would be a warning to them. Stay loyal, or else.

Abigail and Daniel were just settling down to their lunch of cold meats and salads, when the doorbell rang.

'Why do people always call when you're about to eat?' asked Daniel, annoyed.

'At least we can put it in the larder until they've gone,' Abigail pointed out. 'A hot meal would have been ruined if we'd had to put it back in the oven.'

Their visitor was John Feather.

'It's all right, it's one of ours,' said Daniel cheerfully. 'We can eat.' He turned to Feather. 'You can share it. It's just salad.'

'No thanks,' said Feather. 'It's just a quick visit to say you were right about that letter making things move. Kurtz went to the German Embassy at Carlton House Terrace. He was in there for about half an hour. Then he came out and went home. He must have delivered it.'

'Who to?'

Feather shrugged. 'That we don't know. I suppose all we can do now is wait and see what the German Embassy does.'

Daniel and Abigail exchanged concerned looks.

'Well, as he went there instead of to the Military Intelligence people, that suggests he's definitely working for the Germans,' said Abigail. 'We need to tell Blenkinsop,'

'Who?' asked Feather.

'Edgar Blenkinsop,' Daniel reminded him. 'Our contact at the Directorate of Military Intelligence. The one we gave the document to.'

'What are you going to do now?' asked Abigail.

'Nothing,' said Feather. 'Remember, we're supposed to have no involvement with Kurtz. So officially I don't know anything about this. But I'd watch your back from now on, if I were you. Anything could happen.'

Venner looked up as Hans came down the stairs into the club and walked over to his table.

'Well?' asked Venner.

'Everything is fine,' said Hans. 'The Wilsons arrived at the house this morning. They must have delivered something, because Kurtz came out of the house and hurried off at speed. He went to the German Embassy. I assume he delivered whatever the Wilsons had left at the house. A British policeman followed Kurtz, but made no attempt to talk to him. Kurtz seemed unaware he was being followed, I expect because his mind was full of whatever he was taking to the Embassy.'

'So he is loyal.'

'In my opinion, he is,' said Hans.

'Good,' said Venner. 'He is a good man. I would have hated to discover he was being disloyal to us.'

When Daniel and Abigail asked for Blenkinsop at the office in Horseguards Avenue they were told he was out.

'Will he be in later, do you know?'

'I believe he will be.'

'In that case could you tell him that Mr and Mrs Wilson called and we'll call again later. We have some important information for him.'

They walked back home to give them time to take in all they'd learnt.

'Well, I guess we got our answer about Kurtz,' said Daniel.

'If he's working for the Germans, is he the assassin?' asked Abigail. 'Did he kill Page and Tweed?'

'I'm starting to wonder if we're not talking about two separate murderers?' mused Daniel.

'Why?'

'I don't know. It's just a feeling. There's the business of Page having his throat cut and Tweed being hanged to make it look like suicide. Different methods suggest different people.' He shrugged. 'But I could be wrong. I often am.'

They arrived home and were just making tea when the doorbell rang.

Daniel opened the door and was startled to see a man he recognised as Inspector Judge from Special Branch glaring at him. He was even more shocked when he saw that the two men standing behind the inspector were both holding pistols in their hands, pointed at him.

'What the hell is this?' demanded Daniel.

'This is me placing you under arrest,' smirked Judge.

'On what charge?'

'Treason. Is your wife in?'

'Why? What's this got to do with her?'

'Her name's on the warrant as well.'

Abigail appeared behind Daniel, a concerned look on her face.

'What's going on?' she asked. 'I heard voices.'

'Mrs Abigail Wilson, I am arresting you on a charge of treason, along with your husband. Hold out your hands, both of you.'

'For what?' asked Abigail.

'This is Inspector Judge from Special Branch and he intends to handcuff us,' said Daniel, looking at Judge with scorn. 'The fact they also feel the need to point pistols at us shows what dangerous characters they think we are.'

'You are dangerous,' snapped Judge. 'Both of you. Now put your hands out.'

'May we be permitted to put our coats on?' asked Abigail. 'Or do you intend us to freeze to death? It is quite cold out.'

Judge scowled, then said: 'Very well. Get your coats, but my men are coming in with you.'

'That's a pity, now we won't be able to escape through our secret tunnel,' said Daniel sarcastically.

They went into the house, collected their coats, locked the front door, then allowed themselves to be handcuffed before they were escorted to the waiting police van. They took their seats inside it and the two armed Special Branch men sat either side of them on the wooden bench, while Judge took a seat opposite.

'Is all this really necessary?' asked Daniel. 'The handcuffs? The guns?'

'Regular procedure when making an arrest for treason,' growled Judge.

'On what grounds are we supposed to have committed treason?' demanded Daniel.

'You'll find out,' said Judge. He banged on the roof of the van. 'Scotland Yard, driver!' he called.

Sergeant Cribbens was mounting the stairs as he returned from the conveniences in the basement of Scotland Yard when he stopped to let the party of people come down. He recognised them as Special Branch officers, but he was shocked to see they were escorting Daniel and Abigail Wilson who were handcuffed. He was even more shocked when he saw that two of the officers were armed, their pistols pointed firmly at Daniel and Abigail. Neither Daniel nor Abigail gave any sign of recognition to Cribbens, just stared grimly ahead. That told Cribbens this was not a game of some sorts, or a case of mistaken identity.

He hurried up the stairs and burst into Inspector Feather's office.

'Inspector! Special Branch have arrested Daniel and Abigail!'

Feather looked at him, bewildered.

'What? Are you sure they were arresting them?'

'They'd put handcuffs on them, and they were taking them downstairs under armed guard. Two officers with pistols pointed at them. What's going on?'

Feather leapt to his feet. 'I don't know, but I've got an idea.' He grabbed his overcoat from the hook. 'If anyone asks for me, I've gone out, and you don't know where.'

'I *don't* know where,' pointed out Cribbens, looking stunned.

'Then you won't be lying,' said Feather, and he hurried out of the room.

Daniel and Abigail were once more in the basement area of Scotland Yard, but where before they'd been in the relative comfort of Commander Haggard's office, now they were ensconced in a starkly bare room, virtually a cell, with just a plain wooden table in the middle. Haggard sat at one side, Daniel and Abigail on the other. Inspector Judge and the two Special Branch officers who'd arrested them stood and watched the proceedings.

'Shouldn't we have our lawyers with us?' asked Abigail. 'I thought that was the law.'

'Not if it relates to matters of treason,' said Haggard.

'This is nonsense,' said Daniel. 'We haven't committed treason.'

'We have evidence that you have,' said Haggard. 'And treason, I have to remind you, is a hanging matter.'

Inspector Feather waited impatiently by the reception desk of the General Adjutant's offices. He'd been told that Edgar Blenkinsop had been informed of his presence and would be with him shortly, but ten minutes had passed since he'd received that message.

'Can you send another message to Mr Blenkinsop?' he asked the woman at reception. 'This is very urgent. I'm a detective inspector from Scotland Yard and this concerns a matter of national security.'

The woman looked past him, having spotted something, and said: 'Here's Mr Blenkinsop now.'

Feather turned round and then hurried towards the man walking towards him.

'Mr Blenkinsop?' he asked.

'I am,' said Blenkinsop.

'My name's Inspector Feather,' began Feather.

'Yes,' said Blenkinsop. 'I know who you are.'

'I've come to you because Daniel and Abigail Wilson have been arrested by Special Branch. Handcuffed and under armed guard.'

Blenkinsop frowned. 'That's unfortunate,' he said.

'I think that's a bit of an understatement,' said Feather.

'Do you know why they've been arrested?' asked Blenkinsop.

'No, but I can make a guess. That letter they found in Andrew Page's possession, the one in German giving details of armaments being supplied to the Boers by the Germans. The one they gave you a copy of.'

'They told you about this?' said Blenkinsop, indignantly.

'As a precaution, in case anything happened to them. And now it has. They gave a copy to Mrs Page, Andrew Page's widow, and we can only guess she passed it on to her brother, Heinrich Kurtz, because he went to the German Embassy this morning. He must have given it to them.'

'In which case they'll have been arrested for treason. Passing information to an enemy.'

'They did it to see what Kurtz would do.'

'And now we know!' said Blenkinsop angrily. 'So stupid!'

'They need help,' said Feather. 'I can't free them, but you can.'

'Why should I do that?' demanded Blenkinsop. 'They've broken the trust of this organisation by passing a secret document to an enemy power.'

'They need help,' repeated Feather. 'They hold the key to this whole business.'

CHAPTER THIRTY-TWO

Haggard regarded Daniel and Abigail with undisguised hostility.

'You came into possession of a document listing arms that the Germans have been supplying to the Boers,' said Haggard.

'How do you know what was in it?' asked Abigail. 'Have you seen it?'

When Haggard didn't reply but just glared accusingly at them, Daniel said: 'They've got someone inside the German Embassy who heard Kurtz telling someone about it. Isn't that so?'

Again, Haggard ignored the question. Instead, he asked: 'Why did you pass it on to Mrs Page?'

'She's his widow. It's her rightful property.'

'Nonsense!' barked Haggard accusingly. 'You knew what it said.'

'It was in German,' pointed out Daniel.

'Which Mrs Wilson reads,' said Haggard. He turned to

Abigail and said: 'I have read articles by you about exploring the pyramids in which you quote passages from German archaeologists.'

'I had help with the translation,' said Abigail.

'Please don't take me for a fool, Mrs Wilson,' said Haggard grimly. 'You may find this amusing, but you won't be laughing when you're dangling from the scaffold.'

'I assure you I don't find this amusing,' said Abigail.

'You knew when you gave it to her, she'd pass it on to her brother!' snarled Haggard.

'We didn't know what she was going to do with it,' said Daniel.

'You've blundered into something you don't know about, but you've still committed treason. And the sentence for treason is death.'

'You'll be happy for all this to come out in court at a trial?' demanded Abigail.

'Any trial will be held in secret,' said Haggard. 'There'll be no publicity of any sort. Fortunately, we no longer have public hangings, so your deaths will be in secret.'

He looked angrily at the door as it opened and a tall figure entered the room.

'What the hell are you doing, crashing in here?' he demanded. To the officers standing by the walls he said: 'Arrest this man!'

Edgar Blenkinsop strode to the desk, flourishing his ID card.

'Edgar Blenkinsop, senior aide to Henry Brackenbury at the Directorate of Military Intelligence. I've come to recover our agents.'

'Your agents?' echoed Haggard in bewilderment.

'Mr and Mrs Wilson,' said Blenkinsop. 'They work for us.'

Inspector Feather took the envelope Daniel and Abigail given him from his desk drawer.

'I'll be back in a moment,' he told Sergeant Cribbens. 'I've got to see the chief superintendent.

As he walked along the corridor to Armstrong's office, he rationalised what he was going to do. Daniel and Abigail had been concerned, as had Feather, that if this document was given to Armstrong he'd take it straight to Special Branch. Well now Special Branch were aware of the document and the fact they'd passed it to Kurtz, which is why they'd been arrested. He hoped that Edgar Blenkinsop had been able to intervene on their behalf. It was now a question of making sure that Feather himself did not come under suspicion, and the only way to do that was to give the document to the chief superintendent. He'd tell Armstrong that the Wilsons had given it to him, and he was passing it on because it threw new light on the murder of Andrew Page.

There was a good chance that, if Blenkinsop hadn't been able to rescue Daniel and Abigail, giving it to Armstrong might do the trick.

He knocked at Armstrong's door and entered at the call of 'Come in!'

'Inspector?' asked Armstrong.

Feather handed him the envelope.

'New evidence in the Page murder, sir. Mrs Wilson found it hidden beneath one of the drawers of Page's desk at the Victoria and Albert.'

Intrigued, Armstrong opened the envelope and took out the two sheets of paper. He frowned as he saw the first.

'It's in German,' he said.

'Mrs Wilson did a translation of it. That's the second sheet.'

Armstrong read through the second sheet, then read it again. Then he looked at Feather, shocked.

'Do you realise what this is?' he demanded, horrified.

'It indicates that the Germans have been supplying weapons to the Boers in the Transvaal,' said Feather.

'What was it doing hidden in Page's desk?'

'The Wilsons think that Page was part of a spy ring operating in Germany watching out for anti-British activities. They think that he received these reports in the post.'

'But who did he pass them on to? Who was he working for?'

'They don't know, sir. They gave it to me to pass on to you because it opens up a new motive for the murder.'

'The Germans killing Page to silence him?'

'That's one possibility, sir.'

'When did they give you this?'

'Last thing yesterday, sir. I've been out on another case today, so this is the first opportunity I've had to give it to you.'

'Thank you, Inspector. You can leave this with me.'

After Feather had left, Armstrong studied the two sheets of paper. Where to take it? Not the commissioner, he seemed reluctant to act on anything since the Ward and Tweed fiascos. No, it had to be Special Branch. They'd know what to do with it.

He smiled to himself. It would also give him status with Commander Haggard.

* * *

'You were playing a damned dangerous game,' said Blenkinsop sharply to Daniel and Abigail as they left Scotland Yard.

'How did Special Branch find out about the letter?' asked Daniel. 'We suspected they were watching Kurtz, but there was no way they could know what he was going to the German Embassy for.'

'We suspect Special Branch have got someone inside the German Embassy,' replied Blenkinsop. 'He must have overheard Kurtz talking to the ambassador about it.'

'I'm guessing you've got someone inside Special Branch.'

'I deny that completely.'

'Then how did you know we'd been arrested by them?'

'Someone who knows you had heard that you'd been seen being brought in to Scotland Yard. He passed it to us.'

'John Feather,' said Daniel.

'Fortunately for you,' said Blenkinsop.

'So, what happens now?' asked Abigail. 'Special Branch know about this letter. You know about it. Kurtz knows about it, and so does the German Embassy. Is everyone going to ignore it and pretend it doesn't exist? Especially as two men have been murdered for it.'

'We don't know that for sure,' said Blenkinsop.

'Can you think of any other reason?' asked Abigail.

'No, but it doesn't make sense to have killed them. People are killed on purpose to silence them.'

'Unless it's accidental. Overzealous torture,' said Daniel.

'Neither of these two deaths look like that,' said Blenkinsop. 'You don't cut someone's throat as severely as was done with Page to threaten them. You inflict small wounds first. There were none. Just the stab wound in his heart.'

'You've seen Page's body?' asked Abigail.

'Yes,' said Blenkinsop. 'And Tweed's. There were no marks of torture on either. Ergo, they were killed deliberately. I ask again, how would that serve the Germans or the Boers? There was no reason for them to silence them. We already were aware of Page's spy ring. And Tweed?' He shook his head.

'So you don't think Kurtz was involved in the murders?' asked Daniel.

Blenkinsop sighed. 'He may well have been but for reasons that aren't clear.'

'So, what are you going to do?' asked Abigail.

'I suppose we have to talk to him.'

'Will Special Branch allow that?'

'They might. We'll just have to see.'

Special Branch's Commander Haggard looked up from his desk as Chief Superintendent Armstrong entered his office, holding an envelope which he laid on the desk.

'This has come into my possession, sir,' he announced. 'It offers a new aspect on the Page murder.'

Haggard opened the envelope and took out the two sheets of paper. He looked at Armstrong, annoyance clear on his face.

'Where did you get this?' he asked.

'From Inspector Feather.'

'And where did he get it?'

'From Mr and Mrs Wilson.'

'Before or after they gave it to Mrs Page?'

Armstrong looked at him, bewildered.

'Mrs Page, sir? You mean they also gave a copy of this to her?'

'That's exactly what I mean.'

'But … why?'

'That was exactly the question I asked them not an hour ago in this very office.'

'They were here?'

'They were.'

'Why?'

'I had them arrested on a charge of treason. Passing vital documents to an enemy power.' He looked with distaste at the two sheets of paper. 'I wonder how many more of these they've distributed, and to whom?'

'Where are they now? The Wilsons?'

'They were taken away by their apparent employers.'

'The Victoria and Albert Museum?'

Haggard glared at Armstrong in obvious frustration. 'What are you blathering about, man?'

'Well, they were employed by the museum—' He stopped as he remembered. 'No, they were actually employed by Her Majesty, the Queen. You mean Her Majesty took them away?'

Haggard looked at him with such an angry expression that for a moment Armstrong thought the commander was going to throw something at him.

'Are you a complete moron, Armstrong? Of course, Her Majesty did not come here to collect them, nor did she send any of her flunkeys to do it. I'm talking about the Directorate of Military Intelligence.'

'You mean … the Wilsons are working for Military Intelligence?'

'According to one of their senior people.' He scowled. 'This country's going to the dogs, Armstrong. When people like that, the Wilsons, can just act with complete disregard for proper procedures…'

'I've always said Daniel Wilson was a loose cannon, sir,' said the chief superintendent. 'A maverick. I remember when he worked here—'

'Thank you, Chief Superintendent,' snapped the commander curtly. 'That'll be enough reminiscing. I now have the problem of what to do with this new information, and how I can salvage what has become a very serious matter of national security.'

John Feather and Sergeant Cribbens were at their desks when the door of their office opened and a gloomy-looking Chief Superintendent Armstrong entered.

'We're moving in dark waters, Inspector,' he said in sombre tones.

'Sir?' asked Feather.

'I took that German document to Commander Haggard of Special Branch. It turns out that he already knew about it.' Angrily, he thumped the desk. 'He'd had the Wilsons in his office questioning them over it. It seems they'd also given a copy to Mrs Page, a German. And there's no doubt that she must have passed it to her brother, this Heinrich Kurtz character. So he brought them in on a charge of treason. Treason, Feather!'

'And what's he done with them, sir? Are they being held somewhere? The Tower of London?'

'No. He had to let them go because it turns out – and you won't believe this – that the Wilsons are also working for British

Military Intelligence. A senior intelligence officer came and took them away.'

'No, sir,' said Feather, doing his best to look astonished.

'Yes, sir!' said Armstrong vehemently. He shook his head in wonder. 'It's a topsy-turvy world, Inspector.'

'What do Special Branch want us to do, sir?'

'Nothing,' said Armstrong sourly.

'Nothing? But surely there are the murders of Page and Tweed to investigate.'

'The question is: how do we do that without treading all over politics? Special Branch? Military Intelligence? The government? Because if the Germans are arming the Boers then our government will be involved. Not to mention the bloody Queen!' He let out a groan. 'It's a mess, Inspector. And we're right in the bloody middle of it.' He looked at Feather and said: 'We've got to be clever about this and keep out of trouble. Because when things go bad about this, and they will, we want to be squeaky clean. So, what I want you to do is keep in touch with the Wilsons. Find out what they're up to. But unofficially. Carry on looking into the case, but avoiding Kurtz. Stay away from him. But find out what the Wilsons are doing about him.'

CHAPTER THIRTY-THREE

Commander Haggard sat at his desk, brooding. What to do, that was the problem. Yes, the Wilsons had exposed that Kurtz had been part of a spy ring, but they didn't know who else it involved. Special Branch suspected that the people at Der Gymnasium were part of it, especially the owner, Karl Venner, but so far they'd got no proof. Haggard had been hoping to use the Wilsons in some way to force entry into the ring, but that had been snatched away from him.

What to do about Kurtz? Before, their attitude had been simply to keep a watch on him and see who he made contact with while he was in England. But to date, apart from occasional visits to Der Gymnasium, Kurtz seemed to have spent most of his time with his sister.

There was a knock at his door, and a uniformed guard looked in.

'Sorry to disturb you, sir, but there's a gentleman to see you.'

'Who is it?'

'It's a Mr Blenkinsop, sir.'

Haggard frowned. What was Blenkinsop doing calling on Special Branch?

'Show him in,' he said.

He rose to his feet as Blenkinsop entered, then gestured him to a chair.

'Come to cause more trouble?' he demanded.

'No,' said Blenkinsop, sitting down. 'I've come to offer the hand of friendship.'

Haggard regarded him warily as he took his seat. 'I assume you're familiar with the warning about Greeks bearing gifts,' he said suspiciously.

'In this case, I can assure you the offer is genuine,' replied Blenkinsop. 'This message that's surfaced. The one that was found in Andrew Page's desk and now seems to be in general circulation.'

'Hardly our fault,' snapped Haggard. 'We had the Wilsons in our custody, until you had them released.'

'By then they'd already distributed the letter.'

'On your orders? You said they worked for you.'

Blenkinsop shook his head.

'No, they were acting on their own initiative. But the result is that it's now accepted that the Germans have discovered the spy ring that Page was operating in Germany.'

'*Your* spy ring,' said Haggard accusingly.

'Our remit is to protect this country from its enemies,' said Blenkinsop calmly. 'As you'll have seen from the document, the Germans are arming the Boers in readiness for a second Boer War.'

'What's happened to your spy ring in Germany now that Page is dead?' asked Haggard.

'From what we can gather, some of them have been arrested. Some have already been executed.'

'How did the Germans find out about its existence?'

Blenkinsop shrugged. 'We assume one of their own people infiltrated the ring.'

'And that's how they knew about Page?'

'Possibly.'

'Did they kill him?'

'It's a possibility, but personally I doubt it,' said Blenkinsop.

'Kurtz took the letter to the German Embassy,' said Haggard. 'He has to be involved.'

'He's definitely involved in the spying business,' said Blenkinsop. 'As such, he's a danger to this nation. In our opinion he needs to be … talked to.'

'Who by? You?'

'Well, that's the question, isn't it? We've been looking into him and he's a mining engineer, not a diplomat. He may be an adviser to the Transvaal government, but that doesn't mean he has diplomatic immunity.' He looked at Haggard, his expression serious, as he said: 'We believe a joint operation would be advisable with regard to Kurtz.'

'Special Branch and Military Intelligence?'

'If, as we believe, Kurtz is operating here for the Boers, it would send a message back to them that we know what they're up to. It might even make them back off. Our government would prefer to avoid another war in Africa, especially as it appears it could also be a war against Germany. That would make it a very expensive operation.

'The thing is, Special Branch have the authority in dealing with the country's enemies on British soil, but sometimes our areas of action spill over into one another. We feel we have a shared mutual interest in handling this.'

'So who brings Kurtz in for questioning?'

'You at Special Branch. We know you've been watching him. You know where he's been, what he's been up to, and now the revelation about him taking this letter to the German Embassy gives grounds for bringing him in. But we've been working with Page and his German spy network. Page was Kurtz's brother-in-law. We both need to know the answers to certain questions, and if we're both there asking them it will be much harder for him to lie successfully.'

Haggard thought it over, then said: 'We have to be careful on the grounds we bring him in. The politicians will be watching, with the Germans and the Boers both ready to attack us.'

'I suggest we request Mr Kurtz to meet with us to clarify certain matters that are of concern to us. One being why he took the letter to the German Embassy. We stress that this is not a formal investigation, merely he would be helping us with our enquiries.'

'But which enquiries?' asked Haggard. 'Into the crushing of our spy ring in Germany, or the spy ring the Germans and Boers are operating here?'

'The *suspected* spy ring the Germans and Boers are operating,' Blenkinsop corrected him. 'At the moment we have strong suspicions, but no proof. But no, I suggest we tell him we are asking for his help in the investigations into the murders of Andrew Page and Herbert Tweed.'

'Which are under the auspices of the police.'

'Not necessarily,' said Blenkinsop. 'We can both invoke clauses that give either of us authority over the investigation.'

Haggard nodded thoughtfully. 'Very well,' he said. 'I'll send two inspectors to bring him in.'

'But *politely*,' stressed Blenkinsop. 'Ask him to come in.'

'And if he refuses?'

Blenkinsop shrugged and gave a slight smile. 'Then *impolitely* would suffice.'

Kurtz strode agitatedly around the conservatory as his sister, Gretchen, watched.

'The Embassy feel I have to leave England,' he said. 'This business of the letter in Andrew's desk has interrupted everything. Our hope was that I would be able to find out who else besides Andrew was involved in his spy ring in this country, and given time I'm sure I would have been able to. But now the British know about it, they feel I have to leave before I'm taken in for questioning.'

'They wouldn't dare,' said Gretchen. 'You are an emissary of the Transvaal and German governments. You have diplomatic immunity.'

'I'm afraid that the appearance of this letter gives the lie to any idea of diplomacy between our countries,' said Kurtz ruefully.

'But they cannot arrest you.'

'They can make life difficult for me. In fact, impossible as far as my mission is concerned. Our people will need to send someone else.' He looked at his sister and added: 'But it will have to be someone with no connection with you, because they will be watching you as well.'

They heard the doorbell ringing, and then the figure of the butler, Wilhelm, appeared.

'You have visitors, sir,' he announced. 'I regret that they insisted on entering.'

Two men materialised behind the butler and entered the conservatory.

'Mr Heinrich Kurtz?' asked one. 'I am Inspector Meddle of Special Branch. We have come to escort you to Scotland Yard.'

'On what grounds?' demanded Kurtz.

'We're hoping you'll be able to help us with some enquiries we're making into the death of your brother-in-law, Mr Andrew Page.'

'I had nothing to do with that,' said Kurtz.

'We're not suggesting you did, sir. It's just that certain information has come to light concerning yourself that we'd like to clarify.'

'What information?'

'Our superior officers will be able to outline it to you, sir.'

'And if I refuse?'

'We do have a warrant to order you to come with us, but we'd prefer it if it was done voluntarily, in an amicable manner.'

Kurtz nodded stiffly. 'Very well.' He turned to his sister. 'Gretchen, go to the German Embassy and advise them of what is happening.'

'Yes, Heinrich,' nodded Gretchen.

'Actually, Mrs Page, I'm afraid that won't be possible,' said the inspector. 'The warrant also has your name on it. I'm afraid we must ask you to come with us.'

CHAPTER THIRTY-FOUR

Haggard glared at Inspector Meddle. Kurtz had been brought in and was currently in one of the interview rooms. Mrs Page had also been brought in and was currently in the reception area while a uniformed constable watched over her.

'You also brought Mrs Page in?' said Haggard, angrily.

'Yes, sir. Mr Kurtz told her to go to the Germany Embassy and tell them about him being detained. At this stage I wasn't sure if you wanted the Germans to know what was happening, so I acted on my own initiative and decided to bring her in. I thought we could just deposit her somewhere comfortable while you talked to Mr Kurtz.'

Haggard weighed this up, then said: 'Yes. Good thinking, Meddle. Keep her in reception and have a couple of officers with her.'

'A couple, sir?' asked Meddle, puzzled. 'Do you think she's dangerous?'

'No, but I think she should be asked if she'd like a cup of tea, and that will take one officer to get it for her while another stays and watches her. We can't take a chance on her slipping out.'

Daniel and Abigail sat on their balcony and looked out at the tranquility of Primrose Hill.

'Do you think Haggard really would have put us on trial for treason?' asked Abigail.

'Yes,' said Daniel. 'He was angry. Whether it would have come to anything is another matter, but Special Branch have pretty far-reaching powers.'

'So we were lucky John Feather interceded on our behalf.'

'The real luck was that Sergeant Cribbens saw us being taken down to the basement. Remind me to buy that man a pint to say thank you.' He fell silent, thinking things over, then said: 'I feel Blenkinsop is right.'

'What about?'

'This business of Kurtz not being the person who killed Tweed. Remember what Blenkinsop said: people get murdered to silence them.'

'But Kurtz might have wanted to silence Page if Page had found out that he was spying for Germany.'

'True,' agreed Daniel. 'Which is starting to make me think even more we're talking about two different murderers.'

'Kurtz for Page and someone else for Tweed?'

'Possibly, but I'm starting to have doubts about Kurtz being the one who killed Page. It's too close to home.'

'Most murders are committed by people who live with their victim,' pointed out Abigail.

'Yes, but I get the feeling that isn't the case here.'

'Why?'

'At the moment I can't put my finger on it,' admitted Daniel.

'So if it's not Kurtz, who would want to silence Page and Tweed?' asked Abigail.

'Look at the one criminal activity going on at the museum that we know about,' said Daniel.

'Herbert Tweed fiddling the books.'

'Exactly. Say Page found out about it and Tweed was worried he'd report it. Tweed worked at the museum. He'd have the opportunity to kill Page and hide his body in the marquee. We know that Tweed sometimes worked late. I'm sure that Page did as well. Tweed arranges to meet Page inside the marquee after the late guard has gone. Page agrees because Tweed wants to appeal to him. But instead, Tweed kills him and dumps his body.'

'Yes,' said Abigail. 'That would fit. But why would someone want to kill Tweed?'

'Tweed was a crook. His main drive was making money on the side. Say he'd discovered something about someone. Something they wouldn't want known.'

'Blackmail?'

Daniel nodded.

'But who might he blackmail?'

'I think that it would take two people to hang an unconscious and heavy body from the bannisters. One to lift it, one to tie the rope in place.'

'Yes, that makes sense.'

'Two people who've got something to hide. But it's not connected with fraud, because Tweed was already doing that, and he wouldn't want to put himself at risk.'

'A secret love affair?' suggested Abigail. 'Both married to other people?'

Daniel nodded. 'Or, one who's married, the other single. Remember that secretary winking about Miss Huss and Raphael Wilton?'

'An illicit affair.'

'And we know the attitude of the museum bosses towards people who are found guilty of immorality.'

'But Page was an adulterer. An absolute Lothario.'

'Yes, but a blind eye was turned to that because the women he had his escapades with weren't associated with the museum. Margaret Huss and Raphael Wilton both work for the museum.'

Abigail thought it over.

'At the moment it's only your suspicious mind accusing them of having an affair,' she said. 'We need to get confirmation.'

'I agree,' said Daniel. 'So that's our next piece of work.'

Heinrich Kurtz glared at the two men sitting opposite him on the other side of the bare wooden table, Commander Haggard and Edgar Blenkinsop.

'What have you done with my sister?' he demanded. He looked around him with distaste at the stark, plain brick walls of the subterranean interview room where they were sitting, watched with eagle-eyed intensity by three officers in plain clothes. 'Have you subjected her to these same intolerable conditions?'

'Mrs Page is in the reception area, enjoying a cup of tea,' said Haggard. 'She is quite comfortable.'

'You have no right to arrest her,' snapped Kurtz.

'She has not been arrested. She is helping us with our enquiries. As you are.'

'This is illegal. I am a representative of the German government. As such, I have diplomatic immunity.'

'The German government, or the government of Transvaal?' asked Haggard.

'I refuse to answer any questions except in the presence of my ambassador.'

'So again, I would ask you: which ambassador? The German or from the Transvaal?'

'The government of Transvaal does not have a diplomatic representative here in England, as you well know,' retorted Kurtz.

'So, that'll be the German ambassador, then,' said Haggard. 'However, we've checked the list of those with diplomatic status associated with the German Embassy in London, and your name doesn't seem to feature. We shall check further, and indeed check with the embassy, but as I'm sure you know, if you are not on that official list it takes time for someone's name to be added. Checks have to be made, as do official enquiries into any person being put forward for official diplomatic status. Sometimes that can take weeks.' He looked purposefully at Kurtz. 'Or we can hopefully wrap this up in under an hour. After all, this is not an official interview, we're just asking you to help us with our enquiries.'

'Your inspector said there was a warrant. That sounds official.'

'Did he really? He must have been confused.' He gave an apologetic sigh. 'However, if you insist on waiting for someone from the German Embassy to be present' – he sighed – 'even though you do not have official diplomatic status, that will be fine. We will make arrangements for you and Mrs Page to be accommodated at one of our remand centres until the formalities have been completed.'

'Prison?' demanded Kurtz, angrily. 'You are planning to put us in prison?'

'For your own protection,' said Haggard. 'As I'm sure you are aware, two people have been murdered in relation to this case. We want answers to some questions to assure ourselves of your safety. We could never forgive ourselves if we let you go before we'd established that your positions were safe and something happened to you.'

'This is intolerable!' raged Kurtz.

'Your safety is our only concern,' said Haggard.

Kurtz sat, fuming silently, torn with indecision. Finally, he said, through gritted teeth: 'Ask your questions.'

Daniel and Abigail waited across the road from the entrance to the Victoria and Albert's entrance – or, more accurately, the existing entrance to the South Kensington Museum prior to the new entrance being constructed – and watched as the staff left the building for the day.

'That's her,' said Daniel, nodding towards a short slightly dumpy woman in her twenties who had walked out among the group of women who worked in the secretaries' office, and now separated from them and was making her own way home.

'Miss Winchcombe,' Abigail informed him. 'I found out the names of all the secretaries when I last was there and found the letter hidden in Andrew Page's desk.'

They hastened their pace and caught up with the secretary.

'Miss Winchcombe!' called Abigail.

Miss Winchcombe stopped, turned, and caught sight of

Daniel and Abigail coming towards her.

'Mrs Wilson' she exclaimed. 'And Mr Wilson. I'm glad to see you're up and about again. Mrs Wilson told us what happened to you. How dreadful!'

'Fortunately, the doctor tells me I've recovered,' smiled Daniel.

'We're sorry to trouble you, Miss Winchcombe, but as you know we've been asked to look into the tragic deaths of Mr Tweed and Mr Page,' said Abigail. 'However, an issue has arisen that we're sure is not at all connected to these tragic deaths, but we've been asked to make enquiries.'

'Oh?' said Miss Winchcombe, intrigued.

'It concerns the nature of the relationship between Mr Wilton and Miss Huss.'

Immediately, Miss Winchcombe's face flushed red and she looked discomfited.

'I don't know what you mean,' she said, flustered, and they could see the alarm in her eyes.

'Please, we're not asking you to tell us anything that isn't already known, but we need confirmation. There'll be no comeback, no one will know what you've told us, but it's one small part of our investigation that we just need to answer so we can strike it off. This conversation between us is completely private. We never asked you anything, and you never told us anything. Just a nod or a shake of your head will do. As far as you are aware, do Mr Wilton and Miss Huss see one another outside of work? In a … social manner?'

Winchcombe hesitated, unsure what to say, then, slowly and reluctantly, she gave a small nod of her head.

'Would you say their relationship is of an … emotional nature?'

This time she gulped nervously, before again, nodding.

'They have been seen?'

'Miss Picton saw them,' whispered Miss Winchcombe. 'It was an afternoon when Mr Wilton went off to an appointment, he said, and Miss Huss said she had a dental appointment. But Miss Picton had to go down to the marquee to ask the guard on duty something, and she saw them. They were holding hands and kissing, and then they walked off.'

'Separately?'

'No, together.' Miss Winchcombe hesitated, then said in awed tones: 'Miss Picton was puzzled so she followed them. She knew that as both of them were out of the office she wouldn't get into trouble.'

'Where did they go?'

'To a hotel. The Bradbury. It's not far from the museum. She saw them go in.'

'And then?'

'She waited a few minutes, but they didn't come out. So she came back to the office. Miss Huss returned after about an hour and a half, and Mr Wilton shortly after.'

'Has that happened often?' asked Daniel.

'A few more times,' said Miss Winchcombe. 'Not the hotel, as far as we know. Just that they left the office shortly after one another, saying they had appointments, and then they returned within a quarter of an hour of one another a few hours later.'

'Is Miss Huss engaged?'

'Oh no,' said Winchcombe.

'But Mr Wilton is married?'

Awkwardly, Miss Winchcombe nodded. 'Yes,' she said quietly.

* * *

Although there was no clock in the basement room, Kurtz estimated he'd been in this room with the two men for at least an hour. Commander Haggard had left the room ten minutes ago, and had just now returned. A toilet break, Kurtz assumed. Something he could do with himself, but he wasn't going to give them the satisfaction of asking for permission to use the toilet.

'Where is my sister?' he demanded. 'Is she still being held in your reception area? This is outrageous.'

'No,' said Haggard. 'I've sent her home, with a police escort just to ensure she doesn't make contact with the German Embassy or anyone else.'

'This is still outrageous,' repeated Kurtz.

Haggard ignored the comment.

'This morning Mr and Mrs Wilson gave your sister a document in German which they had discovered hidden in your brother-in-law's desk at the Victoria and Albert museum,' he said. 'You then took that document to the German Embassy. Why?'

Kurtz studied them both carefully, then he said: 'I assume you know what the document contained?'

'Proof that the Germans are arming the Boers of Transvaal.'

Again, Kurtz looked at the two men, weighing up the situation, before he said: 'Yes.'

'So why did you take it to the German Embassy?'

'To lodge a protest,' said Kurtz.

'A protest?' queried Haggard. He looked at Blenkinsop questioningly, but Blenkinsop appeared not to notice. Haggard turned back to Kurtz. 'Why did you feel the need to make a protest?'

'Because this action is inflammatory,' said Kurtz. 'It is aggressive and could be a precursor to war. I do not believe that Britain and Germany should be at war. Equally, I do not believe that the Transvaal should become involved in a war with Britain. Wars are costly, both in human terms and in financial terms. I wished to make my feelings known.'

'How did the German ambassador react to your protest?' asked Blenkinsop.

'He was not pleased by it. He suggested I was interfering in areas that I had no right to take part in. He reminded me that my sphere of operations was as a mining engineer. I pointed out to him that in the Transvaal we had established a good relationship between the local Boer population and the British miners, the Uitlanders, which had led to economic prosperity for the Transvaal. Any action as suggested in this document could put that at risk.'

Blenkinsop nodded thoughtfully, then asked: 'Where were you the night before your brother-in-law's body was found at the museum?'

'I was at my sister's house. We spent the evening together, playing cards, and then I retired to bed.'

'Your brother-in-law was not at home?'

'No. But then, that was not unusual. Often, he stayed to work late at the museum, or visited potential exhibitors.'

'Did he often stay out all night?'

'I was only in England for one week before his death,' said Kurtz. 'He was out all night on two of those nights, one being the night when I assume he was killed.'

'Was he at work on both nights?' asked Haggard.

Kurtz hesitated, then said: 'My brother-in-law was not a

faithful man. He had affairs and mistresses. I believe on some of the occasions when he was away from home, he spent the nights with his paramours.'

'Did your sister know of this?'

'She did.'

'Where were you on the afternoon of 1st June?' asked Blenkinsop. 'Last Thursday.'

Kurtz looked at him, puzzled at the question.

'Why?' he asked.

'Let's say we need to fill in some gaps in our knowledge.'

'About my movements?'

'Just this one particular date,' smiled Blenkinsop.

CHAPTER THIRTY-FIVE

Daniel and Abigail made their way to the Bradbury Hotel, where they introduced themselves and asked to see the manager. A short while later a dapper short man in his early fifties, smartly but fussily dressed and with a small moustache, appeared.

'Hector Crabbe,' he introduced himself. 'I understand you wish to see me?'

There was an apprehension in his manner, as if he was expecting a complaint. Daniel did his best to allay his fears with a friendly smile.

'Good afternoon, Mr Crabbe. My name is Wilson, and this is my wife. We are private investigators.' He produced the letter of authority from Sir Anthony Thurrington and handed it to the man. 'As you will see, we've been commissioned by Her Majesty to look into the death of a Mr Page who worked as a curator at the Victoria and Albert Museum. We have now also been asked to look into the recent death of a Mr Tweed, another curator at the museum.'

'How may I help?' asked the receptionist handing the letter back, still wary.

'We've been led to believe that Mr Raphael Wilton, the Senior Director at the Museum, occasionally uses your hotel for meetings.'

'Yes, Mr Wilson, that is correct,' said the man proudly and looking slightly relieved. 'We have an arrangement with Mr Wilton.'

'What sort of arrangement?' asked Daniel.

'It seems there are certain issues that arise sometimes at the museum that need to be kept very confidential,' said Crabbe. 'As a result, Mr Wilton comes to the hotel with his secretary now and then to deal with very confidential correspondence, which he can discuss without fear of being overheard, which would be the case if he was at the museum.'

'I see,' said Daniel. 'How often do these meetings take place?'

'About once a week,' said the receptionist.

'On the same day each week?'

'No, it varies.'

'Does he always bring the same secretary?' asked Abigail.

'Oh yes, his own personal secretary. Miss Huss. It's because she's the only one he can trust with the confidential papers they're dealing with.' He frowned, puzzled. 'But how does this relate to the deaths of Mr Page and Mr Tweed?'

'Possibly not at all,' smiled Daniel. 'It was just one more gap in our knowledge that needed to be filled.'

'But why didn't you ask Mr Wilton about it?' asked Crabbe.

'We will, now we know the facts,' said Daniel. 'We wanted to make sure of everything before we approached him. He is, after all, a very busy man.'

'He is indeed,' nodded Crabbe energetically. 'And a gentleman.'

Haggard and Blenkinsop stood on the steps of the main entrance to Scotland Yard and watched Kurtz leave. With him he carried a note from Commander Haggard ordering the officer currently with his sister to return to Scotland Yard. Kurtz had been offered a police van to drive him home, but he had refused.

'Did you believe that business about him lodging a protest over the German arming the Boers?' asked Blenkinsop.

'Not a word!' snorted Haggard. 'He took that letter to them to let the Germans know what we knew.'

'What about the murder of Andrew Page? Do you think he did it?'

'He's perfectly capable of it. And that so-called alibi of his, at home with his sister…' He snorted derisively. 'It means nothing. Just like his alibi for the time Herbert Tweed was murdered.'

'That he was at the German Embassy,' sighed Blenkinsop. 'They'll vouch for him, of course. I suppose there's nothing we can hold him on?'

'Not without making a bad political situation worse,' grunted Haggard.

'A busy man, and a gentleman,' mimicked Abigail as they left the Bradbury. 'So now we have confirmation of their affair, but what do we do with it?'

'See how this is for a theory,' said Daniel. 'Page finds out Tweed is fiddling the books. He says something, maybe warning Tweed to be careful. Possibly even threatens to expose him unless he stops. Tweed kills Page. That's murder one.

'Tweed has found out that Wilton and Miss Huss are having an adulterous affair. If it's exposed it will ruin Wilton's career at the museum. Tweed blackmails Wilton and Huss. Wilton and Huss decide to kill him. They are the man and woman who call on him and kill him. That's murder two.'

'And Kurtz and the Germans arming the Boers?'

'Is nothing to do with the murders,' said Daniel. 'I let myself get too caught up in that.'

Abigail thought it over, then nodded. 'It certainly makes more sense than involving Kurtz and his sister. But how do we prove it? Tweed's dead. Wilton and Huss are unlikely to come forward and confess.'

'No,' admitted Daniel. 'We need to provoke them in some way.' Then an idea struck him, and he said excitedly. 'No, we provoke someone else!'

'Who?' asked Abigail.

'We set a cat among the pigeons again,' enthused Daniel. 'The last time it flushed out Kurtz and exposed him and his fellow spies. This time a letter that will flush out our two killers.'

'How?' asked Abigail. 'A letter to whom?'

'To Mrs Wilton,' said Daniel. 'An anonymous one.'

'Daniel, that's horrible.'

'Not if it works.'

'But we don't know for sure they're the killers!' protested Abigail. 'Guilty of adultery, perhaps; but not necessarily of murder. It's a hideous idea.'

'Hideous or not, it will flush everything out. I'm convinced it's they who killed Tweed.'

'If you're wrong and you ruin their lives, I … I'll never speak to you again,' said Abigail.

'Then I'd better be right,' said Daniel. 'Otherwise, we're going to have a very silent marriage.'

John Feather was at home and about to sit down to his supper when Daniel and Abigail arrived.

'We're sorry about this,' apologised Abigail. 'We'll go and come back in half an hour.'

'No,' said Feather. 'Otherwise I'll be wondering the whole time what you want and it'll spoil my appetite. I'll ask Vera to pop my plate back in the oven.' He called 'Vera!' and his wife appeared from the kitchen.

'Good evening, Daniel. Abigail,' she said.

'We're sorry to interrupt at mealtime,' said Abigail. 'We should have thought.'

Vera gave a wry smile. 'It's one of the things you get used to being married to a policeman. I'll put our plates in the oven, John.'

'There's no need for you to miss out on supper,' said Feather.

'I won't be,' said Vera. 'I'll give the kids theirs and have mine with you when you're finished.'

'What have you got?' asked Daniel.

'Steak and kidney pie,' said Feather.

'In that case we'll be as quick as we can,' said Abigail.

Once again, she apologised to Vera, who gave her a reassuring smile and then disappeared to the kitchen. John Feather took

Daniel and Abigail into the sitting room.

'So?' he asked. 'What have you found out? And about what?'

Daniel imparted his theory about Wilton and Huss working together to murder Herbert Tweed to avoid the blackmailer revealing the fact of their adulterous affair.

'Hmm, I can see it might be possible,' said Feather. 'You say they were seen kissing?'

'And once a week they take a room at the Bradbury Hotel,' said Daniel.

'There are two things wrong with this,' said Feather. 'One, we don't know for sure that Tweed was blackmailing them, and we have no proof that it was them who killed him. Nor any way to get it. The woman who saw the couple go into Tweed's house couldn't identify either of them. And I think it's highly unlikely we'll get Wilton and Miss Huss to voluntarily admit to the affair, and even less likely to confess to killing Tweed. We can bring them in for questioning, but without any evidence all they have to do is deny it.'

'I'm hoping we might get that evidence.'

'How?'

'I'm going to write an anonymous letter to Mrs Wilton tonight telling her what her husband and Miss Huss have been up to, and tomorrow morning, once Wilton has left for work, I'll pop it through their letter box. I'm calling it my "cat among the pigeons" strategy, stirring things up and seeing what happens.'

Feather gave a thoughtful smile.

'That's very clever,' he said.

'No it's not,' said Abigail sharply. 'It's a filthy tactic. Despicable. Say they're innocent of the murder? Their lives will be ruined, and all because they fell in love with one another.'

'Well, yes, I can see your point,' Feather admitted awkwardly. 'But I can also see Daniel's point. This could force the fact of the affair into the open, and if it turns out that Tweed was blackmailing them—'

'*If*,' stressed Abigail. 'I've told Daniel I want no part of it.'

'Anyway, we wanted you to know, just in case anything happens tomorrow.'

'You expect it to?'

'That depends on what sort of woman Mrs Wilton is,' said Daniel. 'And now we'll let you get back to your steak and kidney pie.'

That evening, Daniel wrote a letter in block capitals, to Abigail's strong disapproval.

> *If you want to know what your husband and his secretary, Miss Huss, get up to when they're not at work, show his photograph to reception at the Bradbury Hotel in Kensington and ask them.*

'There,' he said, putting it into an envelope. 'That should set the cat among the pigeons.'

'The last time you set the cat among the pigeons you ended up in hospital at death's door,' Abigail reminded him. 'Let's hope that neither of the Wiltons carries a leaded stick.'

'That's why I'm sending it anonymously,' said Daniel.

CHAPTER THIRTY-SIX

It was at half past ten the following morning that the door of the secretaries' office at the Victoria and Albert Museum opened and a tall, elegant and well-built woman strode in, a grim expression on her face.

'Which of you is Miss Huss?' she demanded.

Margaret Huss rose to her feet, annoyance clear on her face at the rudeness of the woman's attitude.

'I am,' she said. 'What can I do for you?'

Suddenly the woman swung her right hand hard into Miss Huss's face knocking her backwards so that she fell against the desks and clattered down on top of the typewriters.

'Hussy!' screamed Mrs Wilton.

Abigail opened the door to the ringing of the doorbell to find a uniformed policeman on the doorstep. Behind him stood a police van.

'Inspector Feather has sent me to fetch you,' he said.

'Why? What's happened?' asked Abigail.

'There's been an incident at the Victoria and Albert Museum.'

'What sort of incident?'

'Mrs Wilton went in and set about one of the secretaries, a Miss Huss, and when her husband came out to see what the fuss was about, she set about him as well. All three of them are in custody at Scotland Yard. The inspector wants you with him when he questions them.'

Inspector Feather gave Daniel and Abigail a wry smile as they entered his office. Sergeant Cribbens, puffing away at his pipe, also had a look of amusement on his face.

'Well, it looks like you set the cat among the pigeons right enough,' Feather told them.

'Yes, we heard from the officer who collected us that Mrs Wilton wreaked some kind of havoc at the museum,' said Daniel.

'That woman packs a mean right hook,' said Feather. 'Miss Huss has a black eye and Raphael Wilton a split lip. They're both being attended to by a nurse. No serious damage, just superficial bruising. But there was certainly consternation.'

'Where's Mrs Wilton now?' asked Abigail.

'In an interview room. I'm going to talk to her first before I quiz Wilton and Huss. I sent for you because the chief superintendent's away at the moment. He's at some conference with other senior officers and top civil servants from the Home Office. I thought it would be useful to have you around while I question them. After all, it was you who found out that Wilton and Huss were having an affair.'

'Have they admitted that?'

'No. Nor have they admitted to killing Tweed. Both deny it vehemently. You've met them before so I'd like you just to sit in and watch, and tip me the wink if you think there's anything I should ask.'

Mrs Wilton sat primly to attention on her chair in the interview room.

'Why did you attack Miss Huss and your husband?' asked Feather.

Daniel and Abigail sat at one side of the room, observing. Sergeant Cribbens sat next to Inspector Feather, taking notes.

'Because they were having an affair,' said Mrs Wilton. 'That hussy was having sex with my husband on regular occasions.'

Feather produced the letter Daniel had written and straightened out the creases in the paper from where it had been screwed into a ball.

'Did you know about their affair before you received this anonymous letter?' he asked.

'I suspected it,' said Mrs Wilton.

'Why?'

'Because my husband hasn't shown any amorous interest in me for some times. At one time he was very keen, so I had my suspicions as to what was going on.'

Feather looked at the letter, then asked: 'You went to the Bradbury Hotel?'

'I did, and they confirmed what this letter says. That my husband and that hussy used to book a room once a week, sometimes more, to engage in their sordid relationship.'

'They claim they were working when they were there.'

'Ha!' snorted Mrs Wilton. 'That's what the manager told

me, so I sought out one of the maids and she told me that she'd gone into the room by mistake one afternoon and found Miss Huss and my husband dressing!'

'Well, that seems pretty conclusive,' said Feather as he, Daniel, Abigail and Sergeant Cribbens walked down the stairs to the basement interview rooms, where Wilton and Huss waited, each in a separate room. 'They were definitely having an affair.'

'But did they murder Herbert Tweed?' asked Abigail.

'That's what we hope they'll tell us,' said Feather. 'The same routine as with Mrs Wilton, I'll do the questioning, Sergeant Cribbens will take notes, and you two sit at one side and observe. I may have some trick questions,' he warned them. 'Just to see what turns up.'

Miss Huss was sitting on a wooden chair at a wooden table and she scowled at them as they came into the room. The skin around her left eye was indeed blackened by a purple bruise.

'What are they doing here?' she demanded as she saw Daniel and Abigail.

'Mr and Mrs Wilson are also engaged in the investigation,' said Feather, taking his seat.

'What investigation?' barked Huss. 'That mad woman assaulted me. She should be in here, not me. I'm the victim.'

'Mrs Wilton is being interviewed separately,' said Feather. 'Do you still maintain that you and Mr Wilton were not engaging in a relationship and that your visits to the Bradbury Hotel were purely for business purposes?'

'I do,' said Huss fiercely.

'Although we now have a witness statement from one of the hotel's maids that she inadvertently entered the room while you were there and discovered both you and Mr Wilton in a state of undress and putting on your clothes.'

'She's lying,' spat Huss.

'Was Mr Tweed blackmailing you and Mr Wilton?' asked Feather.

This question obviously struck home, because Huss looked taken by surprise. Then she recovered and said: 'Why would he be blackmailing us?'

'Over your affair,' said Feather. 'If it became public knowledge both you and Mr Wilton would be dismissed from the museum.'

'I've already said, there was no affair.'

'You and Mr Wilton were seen calling at Mr Tweed's house on the afternoon of the day he died,' said Feather. 'No one else called there that day. So you were the only ones who could have killed him and hung him from the bannisters.'

'That wasn't us,' said Huss. 'We weren't there.'

'You were seen.'

'It must have been another couple.'

'We can soon sort this out by taking you both to the Tweeds' house and letting our witness see you. She got a good look at both of you.'

'Impossible,' sniffed Huss.

'Why? Because you had a hat on, as well as a scarf, and your coat collar was turned up when you went in?' asked Feather with a smile. 'But you lowered your scarf when you came out.'

'No I didn't!' she snapped. The horror filled her eyes as she realised what she'd said. 'I meant … I wasn't even there!' she stammered desperately.

* * *

'We're making progress,' said Feather as they walked down the corridor towards the room where Raphael Wilton waited.

'She'll still protest her innocence, no matter what you throw at her,' said Abigail.

'Let's hope that Mr Wilton is more co-operative,' said Feather.

Wilton was sitting at a bare wooden table, just as his wife and Miss Huss had done; but whereas both women had been upright, defiant and aggressive, Wilton looked cowed. He had a split upper lip and scratches down one side of his face. What was worse, they guessed, was that he knew his career was over.

'Your accomplice, Miss Huss, has admitted you both went to Tweed's house that afternoon,' said Feather after they'd taken their places. 'We know from our witness that no one else called there that afternoon. So you were the only ones who could have killed Tweed and hung him from the bannisters.'

Wilton looked at the inspector, and Feather could see that the man's mind was racing desperately to come up with some kind of defence. Finally, Wilton said: 'Yes, we were there, but Tweed was already dead when we arrived.'

'Then how did you get into the house?' asked Feather.

'The front door was unlocked.'

Feather shook his head: 'Our witness said Mr Tweed opened the door to you and your companion and welcomed them in.'

'They're wrong, whoever they are.'

'Was Tweed blackmailing you over your affair with Miss Huss?'

'There was no affair.'

'You went to the Bradbury Hotel solely for work relating to the museum?'

'Yes.'

'Did you work in the nude?'

Wilton looked at Feather, bewildered. 'What on earth do you mean?'

'We have evidence from one of the hotel's maids that she accidentally entered the room and found both you and Miss Huss in states of undress, putting your clothes on.'

Wilton's face closed up into a scowl.

'I have nothing more to say,' he said flatly.

Feather, Daniel, Abigail and Cribbens returned to Miss Huss in the other room.

'Mr Wilton has admitted that you both went to Mr Tweed's house together,' Feather told her.

'He may have gone there, but I didn't,' said Huss defiantly. 'He must have taken some other woman with him.'

'Oh, come on, Miss Huss,' said Feather gently. 'Not long ago you said you hadn't lowered your scarf as you left the house.'

'No I didn't!' protested Huss. 'You got me confused. You're twisting my words.'

'So when Mr Wilton says you were both at the house together, and that you found Mr Tweed dead when you arrived—'

'Yes!' she burst out, almost grateful at this straw being offered. 'That's how it was! Mr Tweed was dead. He'd hanged himself.'

'So why did you claim you weren't there at the house?'

'Because I thought it might look suspicious and I'd be blamed for something I hadn't done.'

'Like, kill Mr Tweed and hang him from the bannisters to make it look like he'd committed suicide?'

'I didn't! I never even touched the body. I was too shocked.'

'What did you do?'

'We left immediately.'

'Our witness says you were in there for about half an hour.'

'Who is your witness?'

'Someone who lives in the street.'

'I bet it's that nosy old biddy who lives opposite. She's always spying, the cow. But she was obviously confused in this case. Old people get confused.' She leant forward and said in a challenging tone to Feather: 'If you put her up as a witness, a good barrister will make mincemeat of her. An old woman, all confused. I bet her eyesight's bad, as well.'

Feather, Daniel, Abigail made their way up to the ground floor and the interview room where Mrs Wilton was still waiting.

'You're free to go, Mrs Wilton,' Feather informed her. 'But you may still face charges for assault.'

'No court will find me guilty,' she snapped as she rose to her feet. 'I only did what any self-respecting woman would do to defend her marriage.'

They watched her leave, and Daniel asked: 'Do you think she wants to stay married to him?'

'No, but she wants the respectability of being married to a senior director at the Victoria and Albert Museum,' said Abigail. 'Those afternoons at the Bradbury are going to cost him dearly.'

'What's going to cost him even more dearly is being found guilty of murder,' said Feather. 'It was definitely the pair of them who killed Tweed. They keep trying to come up with defences, all of which are obviously lies.'

'Inspector!' boomed a voice.

They turned and saw the bulky figure of Chief Superintendent Armstrong striding across the reception area towards them. 'I hear you've arrested the people who killed Herbert Tweed.'

'We believe they killed Tweed, sir, but they're resisting giving us a confession,' said Feather.

Armstrong turned to look at Daniel and Abigail, then turned back to Feather.

'What are they doing here?' he demanded.

'They were instrumental in uncovering what happened, and why the pair killed Tweed,' said Feather.

Armstrong turned to Daniel and Abigail, a scowl on his face as he snapped: 'How?'

Daniel explained how he and Abigail had discovered that Wilton and Huss were having an adulterous affair. 'We suspected that Tweed was blackmailing them over it. Tweed was a crook, as you know. So, to shut him up, they went to his house and killed him.'

Armstrong turned back to Feather. 'How sure are you of this?'

'Very sure,' said Feather. 'We've got to the stage where both Wilton and Huss admit they were at the house, but now both are claiming that Tweed was dead when they got to his house.'

'And have we got evidence to prove they're lying?'

Feather nodded, 'Dr Proctor said that Tweed was knocked unconscious before he died, so he can't have hanged himself. We have a witness who saw Wilton and Huss call at Tweed's house on the afternoon he died. The witness says she saw Tweed open the door to them and invite them in. The witness saw the couple leave half an hour after they went in.'

Armstrong gave a look of grim satisfaction. 'Excellent!' he said. 'If you give me all the details I can take over from here. We'll wrap this up.' He turned to Daniel and Abigail. 'We won't need you here. This is a police investigation.'

'You might,' said Abigail. 'As Inspector Feather said, we were the ones who uncovered what was going on.'

The chief superintendent shook his head. 'Oh no,' he said firmly. 'This is one where the police get the credit. I'm not having you two muscling in and claiming it.'

'There won't be any credit, Chief Superintendent,' said Abigail. 'At least not publicly. Certainly not as far as the press will be concerned. Remember the instructions from Her Majesty: there must be absolutely no publicity if the murders have been committed by a member of the staff at the museum. In this case, two members of the museum staff will be charged with murder, one of them a senior director. If that comes out it will disclose the motive, they were being blackmailed by another senior member of the museum over an adulterous affair they were having.'

'And that's without bringing in the possibility that Herbert Tweed was the one who killed Andrew Page,' added Daniel.

Armstrong stared at them, in shock as the realisation of what they'd just told him sank in. There would be no glory here. No major headlines full of praise for the work of Chief Superintendent Armstrong and his squad of detectives at Scotland Yard. No messages of gratitude from Her Majesty.

'So we've solved a case and no one will ever know about it,' he said, stunned.

'Some people will know about it,' said Abigail. 'Us, for example. And I'm sure you'll have to tell the commissioner. But after that, I think there'll be a veil of secrecy over everything.'

'I expect even the trial will be held in secret,' said Daniel. 'It's certainly the sort of thing Special Branch are in favour of, so Commander Haggard informed us.'

'All right, blast you!' barked Armstrong. 'You can sit in. But you stay quiet. If you've got anything to tell me, you say you need to speak to me and we'll go out of the room and you tell me there. While they're in Scotland Yard, this is still my show. Have you got that?'

'Absolutely, Chief Superintendent,' said Abigail.

CHAPTER THIRTY-SEVEN

This time Armstrong had brought both Wilton and Huss into the same room. It was fairly obvious to both Daniel and Abigail that whatever love and loyalty Wilton and Huss had felt for one another had disappeared in the face of the questioning they were under, especially the more aggressive attitude of the chief superintendent. It wasn't long before Wilton crumbled under the heavy pressure from the chief superintendent and admitted that Tweed was blackmailing them over their affair.

'But we didn't kill him.' he insisted. 'We went to plead with him. His demands were bleeding me dry. There was a bit of an argument, and he fell and banged his head. Suddenly, he was dead. We were worried that people might think we'd done it. Killed him. So we hung him from the bannisters thinking everyone would believe it was suicide.'

'The doctor says he wasn't dead when he was hung from the bannisters, just unconscious. So it was hanging him that killed him,' Armstrong challenged him, his fierce gaze switching from the man to the woman and back again.

'It was an accident,' Wilton implored him. 'We were sure he was dead.'

Abigail wrote a few words on a piece of paper, which she passed to the chief superintendent. He looked at them, regarded Abigail with curiosity, then asked Wilton: 'Did Andrew Page tell you he had suspicions about Hebert Tweed regarding financial issues at the museum?'

Wilton shook his head. 'No,' he said. 'Mr and Mrs Wilson mentioned that, but Mr Page never said anything. I doubt if he was aware of it.'

Abigail passed another question to Armstrong. The chief superintendent looked at the words she'd written, then asked Wilton: 'Do the curators, people like Page, have access to the accounts ledgers?'

'No,' said Wilton. 'The ledgers were the responsibility of Mr Tweed. At the end of each financial year the auditors look at them.'

Armstrong looked at Abigail and asked: 'Have you anything more to ask on this topic, Mrs Wilson?'

'Yes,' said Abigail. 'Did you examine the accounts ledgers yourself?'

'No,' said Wilton. 'I told you before when you asked if I knew that Mr Tweed was defrauding the museum, I had no idea. As long as things ran smoothly there was no need for me to look at them.'

Although both Wilton and Huss stuck to their defence that Tweed had been dead when they hanged him from the bannisters, Armstrong formally charged them both with murder and had them taken away to be remanded in custody.

'It's now all about the trial, and how good their barrister is,' Armstrong declared after the two had been taken away. 'If their mouthpiece can convince the jury of their story, they might get away with manslaughter.' He looked at Abigail, curious, and asked: 'What was all that business about the ledgers, and who knew what?'

Abigail hesitated, then, with an apologetic look at Daniel, she said: 'We've been thinking that it was Tweed who murdered Andrew Page because Page had found out he was defrauding the museum. But, from what Mr Wilton said, that's unlikely.'

'So you're now saying that Tweed didn't kill Page?'

'That's my feeling,' said Abigail.

'So who did?'

'That,' said Abigail, 'is the big question.'

'Well, we've got the people who killed Tweed,' said Armstrong, pleased. 'I think I'll go and pass the news on to the commissioner, safe that this time we've got the right people.'

Armstrong hurried up the stairs, eager to report his success.

'Right, Sergeant,' said Feather to Cribbens. 'We'd better go to the office and write up the statements.' He nodded to Abigail and Daniel. 'The chief superintendent won't say it, but I will. Well done. Without you two we wouldn't have got them.'

Daniel and Abigail shook hands with the inspector and the sergeant, then made their way up to reception and out into the street.

'You were right about them,' Abigail said to Daniel.

'I was,' said Daniel.

'I still don't approve of your method,' she said. Then she softened and added: 'But I have to admit, we wouldn't have got this result without you doing it.' Then, awkwardly, she added: 'And I'm sorry, Daniel. I didn't mean to show you up that way, saying it wasn't Tweed who killed Page. I'd have preferred it if we could have questioned Wilton ourselves on our own, but that obviously wasn't going to happen.'

Daniel gave her a rueful smile. 'Don't worry, my pride can take it. What made you think of asking those questions?'

'I was thinking about Tweed,' said Abigail. 'His character. He was guilty of fraud, and of blackmail, but both are a far cry from actually killing someone by cutting their throat. That suggests a different sort of person.'

Daniel nodded thoughtfully. 'Yes, what you say makes sense. I should have thought of it myself.'

'Blame it on the bang you received on the head,' smiled Abigail. 'You would have come to it eventually.'

'So who do you think did kill Page?'

'Someone ruthless.'

'Kurtz? He'd have a motive if he'd been sent over to disrupt Page's spy ring.'

'But the spy ring in Germany had already been exposed,' pointed out Abigail. 'There was no reason for him to kill Page. If he wanted to find out what was happening at the British end, who Page's contacts were, it would make more sense to keep him alive.'

'So who?'

Abigail looked thoughtful, then said: 'I think Gideon Oakley fits the bill. He's quite cold and ruthless, he hated Page intensely, and he's at the museum and in contact with Page. I think we need to look into his actions on the night that Page was murdered.'

'I think we need to find out more about him first,' suggested Daniel. 'The problem is that Wilton is now in jail, and we don't know who else to ask.'

'Yes we do,' said Abigail. 'I suggest we go and have a chat with the remaining secretaries at the museum. They'll be agog to know what's happened after Mrs Wilton attacked Miss Huss and Mr Wilton. We can tell them, and then, in return, they can tell us all they know about Gideon Oakley.'

As Abigail had forecast, the secretaries were eager to find out what had happened after Miss Huss and Mr and Mrs Wilton had been taken away. They were shocked when they learnt that Miss Huss and Mr Wilton were going to be charged with the murder of Mr Tweed.

'I doubt very much if it will appears in the newspapers,' said Daniel, 'but we wanted you to know.'

'I can't believe it!' exclaimed Miss Hart. 'Why?'

'We suspected there was something going on between them,' said Miss Winchcombe, and Miss Picton nodded her agreement. 'But why would they want to kill Mr Tweed?'

'Because he was blackmailing them,' said Abigail.

The women looked at them, shocked.

'So he was a blackmailer as well as a fraudster stealing money from the museum!' said Miss Picton.

'I'm afraid so,' said Abigail.

'How terrible!' cried Miss Winchcombe. 'We all thought he was so nice!'

'Sometimes appearances can be deceptive,' said Abigail.

'What's going to happen to Mrs Wilton?' asked Miss Hart. 'She came in and attacked Miss Huss and then Mr Wilton.'

'That's up to the police,' said Daniel. 'They might charge her, or they might take extenuating circumstances into consideration. The fact that she'd just discovered Mr Wilton and Miss Huss were having an affair.'

'How did she discover it?' asked Miss Hart.

'We believe she'd been suspicious of her husband for some time and had taken to watching them,' lied Abigail. 'It seems she finally went and asked about them at a hotel they used.'

'How awful!' said Miss Picton. 'Thank you for coming and telling us.'

'We felt it was your right to know,' said Daniel. 'And actually, there's something you might be able to help us with. As you know, we were asked to look into the death of Mr Page, and then that of Mr Tweed. What we're trying to find out is if anyone else had any suspicions about Mr Tweed's activities.'

'No,' said Miss Hart emphatically. 'As Miss Winchcombe has said, we all liked Mr Tweed and still can't believe he was capable of being so dishonest.'

The other women nodded in agreement.

'What we thought might be useful to help us in our enquiries is if we talked to the other curators,' continued Daniel. 'Just to see if they ever had any doubts about Mr Tweed.'

The women looked at one another doubtfully.

'None of them will be in any trouble,' Daniel hastened to assure them. 'It's just gathering facts so we can complete our report to Buckingham Palace. After all, it was Her Majesty who asked us to look into these tragic events, and we're sure you want her to have all the information that's necessary, however irrelevant it might seem.'

The mention of the Queen was the masterstroke that

brought the secretaries into agreement. Abigail wrote down the information as the facts were annotated: the curators' names and addresses and their particular areas of expertise.

'Our aim is to talk to all of them,' explained Daniel. 'But to avoid any embarrassment by our getting things wrong, it would be useful to have some personal information about them. We don't want to upset one of them by asking him how his family are if it turns out he's an orphan and a bachelor.'

The women nodded in understanding at this, and Abigail was able to compile a list of personal details of all the remaining curators, who was married, who was single or engaged, who had children. Of the six original curators, Andrew Page was dead, one – Jeremy Purbright – was in America and had been for two months, while another – Peter Kenton – had been working with contacts in Russia for the same amount of time. Another, Ian Tavistock, had been in Scotland talking to tartan designers and manufacturers for the past two weeks and was still there.

That left two still operating from the museum offices: Gideon Oakley and Frederick Fellowes, although Miss Hart informed them that Mr Fellowes had recently sprained his ankle, so was forced to conduct his business mainly by letter.

By the time they left the museum offices, Daniel and Abigail had the information they needed: Gideon Oakley was neither married nor engaged; an only son, he lived with his elderly widowed mother in Clapham. As far as the secretaries knew he had no romantic entanglements, according to Miss Winchcombe 'He's very single-minded, he lives for his work.' All the women agreed that he was not a very sociable person, that he could be quite short-tempered, and that he could express himself quite forcefully if he found an error in the typing of any of his correspondence or reports. 'Not like Mr Page or Mr Fellowes. They're always so kind, and if they find an error – which they rarely ever do – they usually make a friendly joke about it. Whereas Mr Oakley is apt to go rushing off to Mr Wilton to complain. And in a very loud and angry voice. Or, at least, he used to.'

It was half past four when Daniel and Abigail left the museum. Before they left they checked to see if Gideon Oakley was still at the museum, or if he'd gone home.

'Oh no,' they were told by one of the assistants at the ceramics department. 'Mr Oakley never goes home this early. He's always to be found working late, either here or at one of his contacts.'

'Is he here at the moment?' asked Daniel.

'He is, but he's going through some paperwork in the stockroom,' said the assistant. 'He's going to be tied up for at least the next hour. Do you want me to ask him to come and see you?'

'No,' said Daniel, 'There's no need to disturb him. It's not urgent. We'll call again another day.'

'Right,' said Daniel as they left, 'that gives us time to go and talk to his mother before he gets home.'

CHAPTER THIRTY-EIGHT

To make sure they managed to talk to Mrs Oakley before her son arrived home, they decided to catch a hansom cab to Clapham.

'This is getting very expensive,' grumbled Daniel. 'Especially as we no longer have a client paying the bills.'

'I feel we're getting near the end,' said Abigail. 'This will be the last of our expenses.'

The Oakleys lived in a neat terraced house in a tidy suburban street of equally neat houses. Mrs Oakley was a small frail-looking woman who they guessed was in her seventies. She gave them a friendly welcoming smile when she opened the door to their knock.

'Yes?' she asked.

'Good afternoon, Mrs Oakley,' said Daniel. 'My name's Daniel Wilson and this is my wife, Abigail. We're from the Victoria and Albert Museum.'

'That's where my son works,' said Mrs Oakley, a proud smile lighting up her face.

'We know,' said Abigail. 'We're here because of what happened to Mr Andrew Page who worked there.'

She frowned, puzzled. 'Mr Page?' she repeated. 'I'm afraid I don't know the name.'

'He died recently, in tragic circumstances,' explained Abigail.

'Died?'

'Yes. Didn't Gideon tell you?'

She gave an unhappy sigh. 'I'm afraid Gideon doesn't talk about the people he works with. He tells me about his work. He's passionate about pottery.'

'Yes, we know. We talked to him about it,' said Daniel. 'Do you mind if we come in?'

'Not at all,' she said, stepping aside to let them in. 'It's a pleasure for me. I so rarely have visitors.' She led them towards a sitting room and showed them in. It was obvious it was only used for special occasions. The wood of the dark brown furniture gleamed with polish. The ornaments on the sideboard had been lately dusted, and the cushions on the chairs had been recently plumped. This was a room Mrs Oakley was proud to show off.

'Can I get you some tea?' asked Mrs Oakley.

'No, thank you,' smiled Abigail. 'That's very kind of you to offer, but we have to get back to Kensington, I'm afraid.'

'To the museum?'

'Somewhere near the museum,' smiled Abigail.

'The thing is, Mrs Oakley,' said Daniel, picking up the conversation, 'we're talking to everyone that Mr Page worked with again to see if we can find any reason for his death. When would be a good time to come and talk to your son again?'

'The best place to find him is at the museum,' said Mrs Oakley. 'If you're going to Kensington, I'm sure that's where he'll be.'

'Yes, that's where we talked to him before. But we find that some people find discussing things at their place of work can be awkward, so we're talking to them away from the museum.'

'Well, evenings would be best, I suppose,' said Mrs Oakley. 'Gideon's usually so busy during the day with work.' She looked at Daniel and Abigail with some uncertainty. 'You say you've already spoken to Gideon?'

'Yes,' said Abigail.

'How did he seem to you?'

'Very conscientious,' said Abigail. 'And he has such a knowledge of pottery making.'

'Yes. We came from Stoke-on-Trent, you know. That's where Gideon was born and grew up. His father worked at one of the potteries there and he used to take Gideon to work with him.'

'How wonderful that must have been for Gideon,' said Abigail.

'It was where his love of pottery came from.' She looked saddened when she said: 'Sadly, Gideon's father, Arthur, died. But not before he'd asked one of the directors at the company to write to a director friend of his at the South Kensington Museum, as it then was, to see if Gideon could get a position at the museum. And that's where it all began for him. He got the position and we moved to London.'

'And have you been happy here?' asked Abigail.

'Well *I* have,' said Mrs Oakley. Then a doubtful look passed over her face as she added, 'but I'm not sure about Gideon. I know he loves his work, but I worry that he doesn't have any friends. He's got no one to talk to except me, and then he only talks about work.' She looked at them in appeal. 'You said you saw him at the museum. Did you find out if he had any friends there, people he socialised with? He never talks about anyone, you see. That worries me. What's going to happen to him when I die? Who will he have for company?' She gave a heavy sigh. 'He doesn't look after himself properly as it is. Some of the places he has to visit, the pottery makers, are quite messy. He's come home with clay on his trousers. And only recently he must have been to some metal factory or something, because he came home and there was rust on his clothes.'

'Rust?'

'Well, it was rust-coloured. And it was damp. At first, I thought he must have had an accident, or fallen into something. I couldn't get it out. I had to take it to the laundry.'

'Which laundry was that?' asked Abigail. 'I only ask because sometimes we have a spillage at home and it's really difficult to get the stains out.'

'Peg Warburton,' said Mrs Oakley. 'She has a laundry just around the corner. She can get any stains out of anything.'

'What day was that?' asked Daniel.

Mrs Oakley thought. 'It was a Tuesday. The 23rd May. I remember because Gideon was home late that day. He didn't get home until eight o'clock in the evening. He said he'd been working late, and when I pointed out the mess he was in, he said it had happened at a factory he'd been to that day.'

Peg Warburton was a short, stocky woman in her forties and the overriding smell in her shop was of damp from the piles of clothes.

'The stains on the clothes that Mrs Oakley brought me?' she asked. 'Rust, she told me.' She chuckled. 'Rust, my eye. Blood, it was, on his jacket and the trousers. I get slaughterers coming in with their working clothes, so I know how to get it out. I don't know what Gideon had been up to, maybe he'd slipped over in a butcher's yard or something. But I returned his suit to her as good as new.'

It was half past seven by the time they got back to central London, this time journeying by bus. They made their way to John Feather's house.

'At least at this time we won't be interrupting their supper,' said Daniel.

Vera Feather's face lit up with a welcoming smile when she opened the door to their knock. 'John!' she called. 'It's Daniel and Abigail!'

She ushered them into the living room, where John Feather was sitting reading a newspaper.

'Tea?' she asked.

'Yes please,' said Abigail.

'And cake?' asked Vera.

'Oh, yes please,' said Daniel.

As Vera hurried off to get the cake and tea, Feather looked at them inquisitively.

'Something you've found out?' he asked.

'Very much so,' said Daniel. 'We think we know who killed Andrew Page.'

'You think?' queried Feather warily.

'We're fairly sure. His name's Gideon Oakley and he's one of the curators at the Victoria and Albert. He was a rival for the position of liaising with pottery makers in Germany, but Page got the job.'

'That's not enough of a motive to kill someone,' said Feather.

'It is if you're as obsessed as Oakley is,' said Abigail. 'And, more to the point, on the evening that Page was killed he arrived home with blood on his clothes.'

'You're sure of that?' asked Feather.

'Absolutely,' she said. 'His mother spotted it. He told her it was rust he'd picked up at some factory, but we talked to the laundrywoman who cleaned his clothes and she told us it was definitely blood.'

'Have you talked to this Gideon Oakley yourselves?'

'Yes, but some days ago, when we were first on the case,' said Daniel. 'Then, I'm afraid to say, I got diverted with the idea that Heinrich Kurtz was involved. And then, of course, there was the business of Herbert Tweed.'

'You were right about Tweed, and Wilton and Huss,' said Feather.

'But I was wrong about Kurtz,' admitted Daniel. 'We're now sure it was Oakley who killed Page. However, as civilians, we have no powers to arrest him. That's for the police.'

'It's certainly worth bringing him in,' agreed Feather. 'But I'll need to clear it with the chief superintendent first, after the false alarms over Stephen Ward and Herbert Tweed. I'll talk to him first thing tomorrow.'

'There's the possibility that if Oakley's mother tells him she told us about the blood on his clothes he may do a runner,' said Daniel.

'If he does, that'll be conclusive proof,' said Feather. 'I'm sure we'll be able to lay our hands on him.'

The door opened and Vera entered bearing a tray laden with teapot, milk, cups and saucers, and four small plates with a larger plate on which there were four thick slices of fruit cake. Daniel's eyes lit up at the sight.

'Fruit cake!' he said. 'Now my day is complete!'

CHAPTER THIRTY-NINE

Mrs Oakley was laying the table for supper when Gideon Oakley arrived home.

'I've told you before, Mother, there's no need to always have food ready at this time,' said Oakley. 'You know I often work late.'

'It's cold meats and potato salad,' said his mother. 'It's not going to spoil if you were late. Now wash your hands and I'll serve up.'

Oakley took off is coat and hung it up, then headed for the bathroom to wash his hands. When he came downstairs his mother was just putting the two plates of food on the table.

'There,' she said.

Oakley say down and began to eat. Mrs Oakley sat down with him and tucked in.

'By the way, some people came from the museum today asking about you, Gideon.'

He looked at her, puzzled.

'People? What people?'

'A man and a woman. Mr and Mrs Wilson. They seemed very nice.'

Oakley stiffened, suddenly alert. 'What did they want?' he asked.

'They're asking everyone about a Mr Page,' she said. 'Apparently, he died suddenly. You didn't tell me.'

'I'm not interested in the other people at the museum,' he said sharply. 'I'm only interested in the work. That's all that matters to me, not the inane gossip and social chatter that goes on.'

'They seemed very nice people,' said his mother again. 'Quite caring.'

'What did you tell them?' asked Oakley.

'That I worried about you. Not having friends.'

'I don't need friends. I've got you.'

'But I won't always be around, Gideon. Why don't you invite this Wilson couple round to tea one evening? They seem like the type of people who would be nice company for you.'

'I don't need company.'

'When I've gone who'll look after you? Who'll keep your clothes clean after you've been at some pottery factory and got clay all over you?'

'I can look after myself.'

'You need a wife, Gideon.'

'I don't want a wife.'

'This Mrs Wilson is already married, but she sounds the sort you ought to look out for. She obviously looks after her husband's clothes when he gets them dirty.'

'What do you mean?' asked Oakley suspiciously.

'Well, I told her about the other week when you got that damp rust all over your suit, and she asked which laundry I took them to, because she was always on the lookout for a good laundry.'

Oakley stared at her, shocked, then forced a smile. 'I wish you hadn't, Mother. I don't like people at work knowing about my private business.'

'Where you have your clothes laundered isn't a private business,' said his mother.

'It is to me,' said Oakley.

Gideon Oakley stepped down from the hansom cab. He watched it drive off before setting off across the heathland that was Primrose Hill.

A fog was coming down, not the thick foul-smelling green pea-souper that had descended on the night he'd killed Andrew Page, this was light, thin, hazy grey, but it would afford him cover as he crossed the heath to the Wilsons' house.

He had two items with him, the knife with which he'd killed Page, and a skeleton key. Both had come from the museum. The knife was in its leather sheath in the inside pocket of his overcoat. It was a good knife, made in Germany, with a sharp point and two very sharp edges to the flat blade.

He hadn't intended to kill Page, merely to threaten him, hoping to make him back down from the German post he'd been given. All Page had to do was go to Tweed or Wilton and say: 'On reflection, I think Gideon Oakley is better qualified to add this post to his own.' That's what Oakley had suggested to him when he'd learnt that Page was to be given the German posting. Which should have been his, by rights. Who knew more about German pottery than he, Gideon Oakley? Pottery had been his life. No, more than his life, his passion. Page knew that. But Page had refused.

Oakley had spent the past few months since Page's appointment thinking of that refusal, his anger and resentment at Page building up in him, until it consumed him, finally erupting on the day that he and Page both left the museum at the same time. Page had been working overtime, as the curators often did. Herbert Tweed had been in his office, still working, but everyone else had left for the day.

'Page, I need to talk to you,' Oakley had said.

Page had turned to him, curious.

'What about?' he asked.

'We can't talk here. What I have to say needs to be said in private.' He gestured towards the marquee. 'We can talk in there.'

'It's locked,' said Page. 'See, the bar's in place.'

'We can slip underneath the canvas,' said Oakley.

'Why should we?' asked Page.

'Because what I have to say is important. Not just to me, but for you.'

Page shrugged. 'Very well,' he said.

Page lifted the canvas and slipped beneath it into the marquee, Oakley following.

'Now,' said Page, 'what's so important that we have to sneak in here to talk about it?'

'The German position,' said Oakley.

'Oh, not that again,' said Page wearily. 'Look, Oakley, I accept that you know more about pottery than I do—'

'*German* pottery,' stressed Oakley.

'All pottery. But I know more about industrial procedures.'

'We aren't talking about industrial procedures here,' burst out Oakley angrily. 'We are talking about a craft.'

Page shook his head. 'I'm sorry,' he said firmly. 'Mr Wilton has assigned it to me. That's the end of the matter.'

'Oh no it isn't!' said Oakley, and he pulled the knife from his pocket and aimed it at Page, who stared at it in disbelief.

'For heaven's sake, Oakley, what do you think you're doing?'

'I'm getting back what should have been mine,' Oakley told him through gritted teeth.

'With a knife?' said Page incredulously. Then he laughed, mockingly. 'You're mad, Oakley. I'm not staying here to listen to this.'

He began to walk towards the marquee entrance, but Oakley darted ahead of him, standing between Page and the curtain, knife held out pointing at Page.

'Yes you are,' he said. 'I want you to write a note to Wilton here and now telling him that you are standing down from the German position and recommending me for it.'

'Never!' said Page defiantly, and he strode forward towards Oakley, a grim look of determination on his face, his hands outstretched to grab hold of Oakley and hurl him aside.

Did I really mean to kill him? Oakley wondered now. *No. Just to threaten him. Make him write that note.*

Instead, Page had hurled himself suddenly at Oakley, and the next second the knife blade had sunk into Page's chest, going easily through his coat and his jacket.

Page had gasped and then begun to fall.

Oakley had pulled out the knife and thrown it down on the ground and had torn open the falling Page's coat to see how bad the damage was, if any, hoping that it had just been the shock that had led to Page collapsing, but as he did so blood had spurted out from Page's chest, splashing on Oakley, and he saw the gash in Page's shirt where his heart was.

Page's eyes were still open and he was staring at Oakley, incomprehension on his face.

I can't let him live, thought Oakley desperately. *If I do, he'll tell on me.*

And he slashed at Page's throat with the knife, and suddenly there was more blood gushing out, this splashing on Oakley's trousers as Page tumbled to the ground.

Oakley had been shocked at the amount of blood pattering the gravel around Page's body. Fortunately, the gravel was loose. Oakley scattered the blood-stained gravel with his feet, then carried clean gravel from other areas and scattered it on top of the bloodstained gravel until all traces of the blood had gone from the surface.

When the police came to the museum asking questions, he told them that when he left the museum offices, Andrew Page had still been there, working on something. He'd then gone home. His mother could verify that.

But the police hadn't bothered to check with his mother.

Then those two private detectives, the Wilsons, had arrived, and at first he'd been worried; but they soon turned out to be as ineffectual as the police. He was surprised at this. He'd checked on them, being as meticulous in his research on them as he was about pottery. They had a surprisingly good record on solving crimes, which had initially worried him. But then, when he saw that they appeared more interested in both Tweed and Wilton, he felt safer.

Until now. Their visit to his mother had been no accident, no casual encounter. They had suspicions about him. And his stupid mother had told them about the rust stains – which is what he'd told her they were – on his clothes. Even worse, she'd given them the name of the laundry who cleaned them, and there was no doubt in his mind that Peg Warburton would have told them the stains weren't rust, but blood.

When he'd been researching into the Wilsons he'd found a magazine article about them. It had been about their new home in Primrose Hill with pictures of the different rooms, the designs and decor, so he knew which was their bedroom on the first floor of the house. He'd also learnt from the article that they liked to get to bed early. Mrs Wilson had said this was a habit she'd developed from working as an archaeologist in Egypt, where working hours were set by daylight.

He knew he had to deal with them tonight, before they could start bringing in the police the next day.

He reached the house and took the skeleton key from his pocket. He'd taken it from the display of locks and keys through the ages, and it was claimed that this particular skeleton key could open any lock. He pushed it into the keyhole of the front door and gently manipulated it, then slowly turned it. For a second it stopped, and then – to his relief – he felt it click forward.

Gently he pushed at the door. It swung quietly inward.

He crept into the darkened house and stood for a while adjusting his eyes to the gloom. The curtains on the landing window had not been drawn, so light from a distant street lamp filtered through the thin fog, helping him to make out the stairs to the first floor.

The stairs were carpeted, which made his ascent silent. From the pictures in the magazine he was able to identify the door to the Wilsons' bedroom. He saw that it was slightly ajar, which meant there would be no danger of him making a noise by turning the door handle.

He took the knife from its sheath, then slipped into the bedroom. In the gloom he could make out the double bed in the centre of the room. Two shapes could be seen beneath the blanket. The Wilsons. He was relieved that they slept together, rather than in separate beds, or even in separate rooms. This way he could finish both of them swiftly. After his experience with Page, getting covered in Page's blood, he'd decided to just stab them each once through the blanket so the blood wouldn't splash out on him. After that first stab, he'd stab again and again to make sure they were dead.

He crept forward towards the bed, the knife raised in his hand. He reached the side of the bed and suddenly plunged the knife down, the blade ripping through the blanket and sinking deep into the body beneath. He was just about to lift it up and stab down into the second body, when an excruciating pain surged through his head and everything exploded.

CHAPTER FORTY

Abigail walked into the bedroom from the spare bedroom where she and Daniel had decided to stay in case of such an attack. Daniel stood over the fallen body of Gideon Oakley, patting the police truncheon in his hands.

'My good old faithful billy stick,' he said, looking down at Oakley. Like most former policemen who moved into plain clothes or retired, his truncheon had been his own personal weapon and it had been kept in a dresser drawer since he'd stopped being a uniformed beat copper. Made of lignum vitae, the hardest wood known, it had never been used in anger since he'd joined Abberline's squad of detectives at Scotland Yard, until now.

'Is he dead?' Abigail asked apprehensively.

'I hope not,' said Daniel. He bent down and checked for a pulse.

Abigail switched on the electric light and Daniel took a hand mirror from the dressing table and held it to Oakley's mouth.

'He's still breathing,' he announced as he stood up.

'What shall we do with him?' asked Abigail.

'I'll get some rope and we'll tie him up. Then we get a hansom and take him to Scotland Yard and leave him with a note of explanation for Chief Superintendent Armstrong and John Feather to deal with when they come in.'

Daniel left and returned a few minutes later with two lengths of cord, while Abigail knelt down beside the unconscious man, checking on him. She helped Daniel tie the cord around his ankles, then secured his wrists behind him, before wrapping more cord around his arms and legs.

'Shouldn't we take him to a hospital first?' asked Abigail, concerned. 'Remember when you were hit on the head you could have died. You were unconscious for days.'

There was a groan from Oakley, and then he tried to rise, but found himself trussed up.

'Somebody hit me,' he said blearily.

Daniel showed him the truncheon. 'And I'll hit you again if you cause us any trouble,' he warned. He took a length of cloth from a drawer and tied it around Oakley's mouth to gag him, then turned to Abigail. 'Can you go and find a cab? I'd better stay here in case he becomes troublesome.'

'I think I'd rather take my chances here,' said Abigail. 'After all, he's bound pretty securely. And a woman out in the streets at this hour isn't always safe, even in an area like this, especially with the fog coming down.'

'Good point,' said Daniel. He handed her the truncheon. 'If he causes trouble, smack him with this.'

Abigail took the truncheon and looked at it warily.

'The last time I used one of these I broke someone's arm,' she said doubtfully. 'Remember, Abberline left me his to protect you.'

'He came here to kill us,' Daniel pointed out.

'Yes, that's true,' said Abigail. She pulled a chair near to the fallen Oakley and sat on it, the truncheon held firmly in her hand. Oakley looked up at her, fear in his eyes.

'I think you'll be safe,' said Daniel.

'I know I will be,' said Abigail firmly.

'I was talking to Oakley,' smiled Daniel.

The next morning, Daniel and Abigail arrived at Scotland Yard and asked for Chief Superintendent Armstrong or Inspector Feather.

'They're both expecting you,' said the sergeant at the reception desk. He grinned. 'After the package you left them last night. Inspector Feather said for you to go straight up when you arrived.'

Sergeant Cribbens, Inspector Feather and Chief Superintendent Armstrong were all in Feather's office when Daniel and Abigail entered.

'Ah, there you are!' boomed Armstrong. 'About time! What's all this about this Oakley character killing Andrew Page?'

Daniel and Abigail looked questioningly at Feather, who said: 'I did tell the chief superintendent what you told me.'

'And now I can hear it straight from the horse's mouth,' grunted the chief superintendent. 'Your note said he tried to kill you.'

'Yes,' nodded Abigail. 'He crept into our house with a knife intending to stab us both to death in bed. Fortunately, we thought he might try something like that, so we put a bolster and some pillows in our bed and laid a blanket over them. He stabbed them instead of us.'

'Because?' asked Armstrong.

'Because of what I told you, sir,' said Feather wearily. 'The blood on his clothes the same evening that Page was killed.'

'We suspected his mother would tell him that she'd told us about it,' said Abigail. 'And, being the ruthless sort of person he is, we thought he might try to kill us to stop us telling you.'

'But why would he want to kill Page?' asked the chief superintendent.

Daniel and Abigail told him about the rivalry for the German position, and about Oakley's obvious frustration that he hadn't been given it, and his jealousy that Page had.

'So it was just about a job?'

'To Gideon Oakley, it was more than just a job,' said Daniel. 'Have you spoken to him yet?'

'No. I guessed you two would be coming in, so I thought I'd wait until I'd spoken to you.' He frowned. 'We had to get a doctor in to look at him. He'd received a nasty crack on the head.'

'That was me,' said Daniel. 'Considering he had a knife and had already used it before, I didn't want to take a chance.'

'Yes, I suppose, so,' said Armstrong. He turned to Feather. 'Right, Inspector. Let's go and talk to this Oakley character.' He looked at Daniel and Abigail and scowled. 'I suppose you two want to sit in on it, as well?'

'We did bring him in,' pointed out Abigail. 'And it was us he tried to kill.'

Armstrong let out a heavy sigh. 'All right, but we do the questions, right? You two just sit there and stay silent.'

'Say we have questions?' asked Abigail.

'Only if myself and Inspector Feather haven't asked them already,' snapped Armstrong. 'Is that agreed?'

Abigail looked at Daniel, then nodded. 'Agreed,' she said.

As it turned out, questions to get to the truth from Gideon Oakley were hardly needed. He was desperately eager to talk.

'I didn't intend to kill him,' he told them. 'It was an accident. I pointed the knife at him to try to get him to write a note resigning the German position and recommending me for it. That's all he had to do. Instead, he threw himself at me and impaled himself on the knife.'

'You also cut his throat,' said Armstrong.

'I had no other choice' insisted Oakley. 'I didn't know the knife had gone into his heart, I thought it was just a wound. I had to shut him up or he'd have reported me and I would have lost my job.'

There then followed a long rant about his own expertise in pottery, the value that expertise brought to the museum, and how he'd been unfairly treated by the museum.

'It was you who sent us that anonymous letter warning us off,' said Daniel thoughtfully.

'I'd heard you were good,' said Oakley. 'It was worth a try.'

Afterwards, as Armstrong, Feather, Daniel, Abigail and Cribbens left the interview room, the chief superintendent said: 'Well there's no doubt about this one.' Ruefully, he added: 'Well, we got all the murderers: Wilton and Huss killed Tweed, and Oakley killed Page, but we still can't tell anybody. They're all employees of the museum. Her Majesty won't allow it.' He groaned unhappily. 'It's all so unfair!'

As Daniel and Abigail left Scotland Yard, Daniel expressed the same annoyance.

'One of our biggest cases and no one can know about it,' he grunted. 'So much for helping promote our reputation as the Museum Detectives.'

'You're always saying you hate that label,' Abigail pointed out.

'Well, I do,' said Daniel, 'but I have to admit it's been of benefit to us.' He looked at his watch. 'It's time for our last call to Military Intelligence, to finish off the puzzle.'

'I don't see we need to bother,' said Abigail. 'We know that Kurtz wasn't involved in the murders. He was just a spy.'

'We don't know that for sure,' said Daniel. 'We *suspect* he's a spy. Don't you want to know for sure?'

'Yes, I suppose so,' said Abigail, but without too much enthusiasm.

'Well, I do,' said Daniel.

'Why?'

'I want to know what's going to happen with him. Is he going to be arrested and charged?'

'It's not really our business,' said Abigail.

'You don't have to come to see Blenkinsop,' said Daniel. 'I'm happy to go on my own.'

'I'll come,' said Abigail. 'You might say something that gets us in trouble.'

Edgar Blenkinsop ushered Daniel and Abigail into his office at the Military Directorate.

'I understand congratulations are in order,' he said.

'You have someone at Scotland Yard that keeps you informed?' asked Daniel.

'We have people everywhere,' said Blenkinsop. 'We wouldn't be doing our job properly otherwise. So, what can I do for you?'

'What's going to happen about Kurtz?' asked Daniel.

'Over what?' asked Blenkinsop.

'The fact that he's a spy working for either the Boer or the German government.'

'The feeling is that it wouldn't be advisable to take any action against him. We don't want to escalate the situation,' said Blenkinsop.

'So?'

'So it looks as if he's going to be leaving Britain.'

'And going where? Germany or the Transvaal?'

'Our guess is to Germany,' said Blenkinsop. 'After all, as that letter showed, they're the paymasters here. But I'm pretty sure that Mr Kurtz will surface in the Transvaal in the not-too-distant future.'

'And his sister? Mrs Page?'

'A British citizen by marriage. There's no evidence of any wrongdoing by her.'

'But she must have been helping Kurtz in some way.'

'She gave him house room. He was her brother, after all.'

'And that's it?' asked Daniel, exasperated. 'There's a German spy ring operating in Britain and nothing's being done about it?'

'What do you expect us to do?' demanded Blenkinsop, annoyed. 'Do what the Germans did to ours over there? Execute and torture them?'

'He had a good point,' said Abigail as they headed home.

'Yes, I suppose so,' said Daniel.

As they approached their house, they saw a coach and horses parked outside it.

'It's a royal coach,' said Daniel. 'Look at the royal crest on the door.'

'It can't be the Queen,' said Abigail. 'She's in the Isle of Wight. Perhaps it's the Prince of Wales come to challenge you to a duel for insulting him.'

'Providing it's truncheons at twenty paces,' grunted Daniel.

As they neared the coach the door opened and Sir Anthony Thurrington stepped down.

'Good afternoon,' he greeted them.

'Sir Anthony!' smiled Abigail. 'I hope you haven't been waiting long.'

'A few minutes,' said Thurrington.

'Do come in,' said Abigail, and she led the way down the front path to their door.

'Would you like a tea or coffee?' she asked once they were indoors.

'No Thank you,' said Thurrington. 'I have to get back to the palace. We're due to leave for the Isle of Wight, Her Majesty and all the company.'

'I thought she was already there,' said Abigail.

'No, when she learnt that you were still engaged in investigating the tragic deaths at the museum, she elected to stay and see what happened.'

'How did she learn we were still investigating?' asked Daniel, curious. 'As far as we were aware, she had been told the case was solved.'

Thurrington smiled. 'Her Majesty has contacts in many areas, through which information comes to her. Many people make the mistake of thinking that because she is elderly and physically frail, she is not aware of what is going on. That could not be further from the truth. Remember, this woman has survived eight assassination attempts. She did not survive them by accident or good fortune, she keeps alert to potential problems.'

'But she could have gone to the Isle of Wight and been kept informed there. Why did she decide to stay in London?' asked Abigail.

'There are three things of paramount importance to the Queen: her family, the Empire, and this new museum named after her and her late and much-loved husband, the Prince Consort. These will be her legacy. If any issue arises concerning any of them, she will wait until it is resolved before going away to take some rest.

'She has been informed that Mr Page was murdered by one of his colleagues, a Mr Oakley, and that Mr Tweed was murdered by two of his colleagues, Mr Wilton and a Miss Huss. She has also been told that it was you two who discovered this. She is grateful that the cloud of not-knowing over the museum has been lifted, and she is especially grateful that you acceded to her orders that there should be no publicity about this case.' He reached inside his pocket and produced an envelope, which he handed to Abigail. 'Accordingly, she has instructed me to make an additional payment to the fee you've already been paid.'

Abigail opened the envelope and took out the cheque, which she showed to Daniel. They both looked at Thurrington in surprise.

'This is very generous of Her Majesty, Sir Anthony,' said Abigail.

'*Very* generous,' echoed Daniel, unable to keep the surprise out of his voice.

Thurrington rose to his feet and bowed.

'Now, I must return to Buckingham Palace. The royal train awaits us. Thank you, both.'

They shook his hand, showed him to the door, and watched him walk along the garden path and climb into the coach, which then rattled off.

'Well!' said Abigail, fanning herself with the cheque. 'This has come as a pleasant surprise.'

'A very pleasant surprise,' agreed Daniel. 'She is some woman, the Queen. She's going to be a very hard act for the prince to follow when he becomes king.'

'*If* he gets to be king,' said Abigail. 'With his lifestyle he's as likely to die before she does.' She looked at Daniel. 'What should we do to celebrate?'

'Get to the bank as soon as we can and pay that cheque in,' smiled Daniel. 'Before Her Majesty changes her mind.'

Acknowledgements

It's often struck me that some readers think a novel is the sole work of the author. That's true as far as having just the one name on the cover; but the reality is very different. I spent 40 years as a scriptwriter, writing for British and international television; and – as everyone knows – when creating a script for the screen (big or little), the final product, whether film or television, is the result of a co-operative effort, with producers, directors, cast and crew all having vital input. For me, publishing is the same, but less obviously in the public's perception. In my Museum Mysteries series (of which this is the eighth) and my World War II DCI Coburg series, I depend on the co-operative input of my publishing director, my editors and my agent. They read my drafts and in the gentlest way point out where something doesn't add up, and then make concrete (as well as artistic) suggestions how to correct it and make the story work. An example in this book was the original and slightly confusing timeline of some of the murders – who did what to whom and when. I admitted to feeling bamboozled. Which is when the wonderful team at Allison and Busby very neatly, politely and unobtrusively took me by the hand and led me through the maze and showed me how to get out of the hole I'd dug for myself (and for them). So this is my thanks to them, To Susie Dunlop, to Fliss Bage, and to Jane Conway-Gordon. My thanks and gratitude.

Jim Eldridge was born in central London in November 1944, on the same day as one of the deadliest V2 attacks on the city. He left school at sixteen and worked at a variety of jobs, including stoker at a blast furnace, before becoming a teacher. From 1975 to 1985 he taught in mostly disadvantaged areas of Luton. At the same time, he was writing comedy scripts for radio, and then television. As a scriptwriter he has had countless broadcast on television in the UK and internationally, as well as on the radio. Jim has also written over 100 children's books, before concentrating on historical crime fiction for adults.

Jimeldridge.com